DOGS AND MONSTERS

ALSO BY MARK HADDON

Fiction

The Porpoise

The Pier Falls

The Red House

A Spot of Bother

The Curious Incident of the Dog in the Night-Time

Poetry

The Talking Horse and the Village Under the Sea

DOGS AND MONSTERS

stories

Mark Haddon

DOUBLEDAY
New York

 Published in the United States by Doubleday, a division of Penguin Random House LLC, New York, and distributed in Canada by Random House of Canada, a division of Penguin Random House Canada Limited, Toronto. Originally published in hardcover in Great Britain by Chatto & Windus, an imprint of Vintage, a division of Penguin Random House UK.

www.doubleday.com

Book design by Casey Hampton
Jacket illustration by Oliver Munday
Jacket design by Emily Mahon

Library of Congress Cataloging-in-Publication Data
Names: Haddon, Mark, [date] author.
Title: Dogs and monsters : stories / Mark Haddon.
Description: First edition. | New York : Doubleday, 2024.
Identifiers: LCCN 2023054984 (print) | LCCN 2023054985 (ebook) | ISBN 9780385550864 (hardcover) | ISBN 9780385550871 (ebook)
Subjects: LCGFT: Short stories.
Classification: LCC PR6058.A26 D64 2024 (print) | LCC PR6058.A26 (ebook) | DDC 823/.914—dc23/eng/20231204
LC record available at https://lccn.loc.gov/2023054984
LC ebook record available at https://lccn.loc.gov/2023054985

MANUFACTURED IN THE UNITED STATES OF AMERICA
10 9 8 7 6 5 4 3 2 1
First Edition

To Zack and Alfie

CONTENTS

DOGS AND MONSTERS

THE MOTHER'S STORY

I

My husband had ordered me up to the Long Gallery. He had not spoken to me directly for a week and I did not know whether to expect an apology or a continuation of the angry tirade that had concluded our last meeting, or indeed whether he was about to carry out some of the more lurid threats he had made. It seemed entirely possible that the summons was nothing more than a ruse to get me away from my apartments so that some of his thugs could burst in and cut Paul's throat whilst I was not there to protect him, so I told the wet nurse to take the boy to some obscure corner of the servants' quarters and barricade the two of them behind a locked door which she was to open only at my command.

It was early October, a day of high wind and driving rain that sucked the light from the sky and made a musical instrument of every leaded pane. The chimneys sang and the fires danced in the downdraughts. I had lost a great deal of blood during the birth and been too nauseous to eat rich food since. My skin was pale, my cheeks sunken and my step unsteady so that when they saw me some of the servants froze briefly before pausing and bowing, thinking, perhaps, that I was an apparition and not their flesh-and-blood mistress.

I stopped to gather myself on the staircase leading up to the gallery. The wind in the Great Court was twisting, now this way now that, like some chained, ill-tempered animal so that the high windows were briefly clear enough to show the pewter sky and the wing of the palace opposite, and in the relative quiet I could hear the rusty squeal of the weathervane twisting on the roof above my head, then water was hurled against the glass as if from a great pitcher and the scene vanished.

I climbed the last flight and, in unison, two surly footmen unlatched the heavy double doors to usher me inside. My husband's elkhounds got to their feet and began barking immediately. I could smell that one of them had pissed somewhere in the room. I waited for them to settle, then walked along the line of portraits of my husband's forebears who seemed half-alive in the jigging light from the sconces. He was sitting in one of four chairs facing each other at the far end of the room, like a solitary lutenist waiting for the rest of his consort. Attendants stood either side of the far door like caryatids.

"Why have you called me here?"

"I have invited someone to join us."

"And that person is?"

"You look unwell."

Once upon a time I had taken his refusal ever to answer a direct question as a sign of his quick wit, but I was no longer willing to play a game in which my role—indeed everyone's role—was to remain at a disadvantage, always reaching for a volley that was just out of their grasp. I took a seat and tried not to waste my effort by pondering the nature of whatever drama he had planned. It would be tiring enough in and of itself. Rain smashed against the windows and a log in the fireplace broke and slumped, sending up a great jet of sparks. I heard footsteps on the staircase and my husband casually stood and looked out of the window with his hands crossed behind his back, feigning indifference about the guests he had himself invited.

I thought at first that the engineer and his son had arrived before those intended guests on account of some emergency, a flooding perhaps, given the weather. My husband let them stand at the end of the room for an uncomfortable length of time, then turned and shook his head as if roused from some reverie by their appearance. "Gentlemen, forgive me. Join us. Take a seat." So they were indeed our guests, though quite how I was to be involved in a conversation about hydrology or the construction of bridges I had no idea.

Now that I had the opportunity to see the two men at close quarters as they walked towards us it struck me how weak a family likeness they shared. The father was renowned, my husband had said on numerous occasions without ever stooping to suggest that he shared this opinion, for the brilliance of his mind. There was something of the rodent about him, wiry, furtive, dishevelled. I don't think he'd been in this room before. Certainly, he was taking careful note of its architecture and contents as they walked its length. I wondered idly if he were looking for an escape route should one prove necessary. He was a good head shorter than his son, who could have carried his father under his arm as easily as a rolled tapestry. I doubt the son had ever needed to look for an escape route. I have known several young men of his kind, who mistook the goodwill generated by their handsome looks and radiant physical prowess for fundamental qualities of the world. They burnt brightly and briefly at court before crashing to earth, victims of intrigues and duplicities of which they were utterly unaware and against which they were powerless to fight.

As they were taking their seats the son turned to me and said, "It is good to see you. We were all greatly worried about your health."

The inappropriateness of this direct address was so utterly guileless that my husband was caught off guard and forced to be gracious in return. "You are kind." I liked the boy immediately.

Once we were seated my husband waited for everyone to become still. "Gentlemen . . ." The word sounded less respectful this time around. He lowered his voice and leant forward with his elbows on his knees as if we were in a tavern and about to play a round of cards. "My wife has given birth to a mooncalf."

The words struck me like a slap across the face. The appearance of the engineer and his son had sent my thoughts in another direction entirely and my guard was down. I sat back in my chair and recited, silently, some lines of Sidney to calm my mind.

Come Sleep, O Sleep, the certain knot of peace,
The baiting place of wit, the balm of woe,
The poor man's wealth, the prisoner's release . . .

"It is a repellent chimaera, part human, part ape, part God alone knows what."

"The child is a boy." I could not help myself. My husband turned to look at me. "His name is Paul."

"We give names to dogs." He held my eye. "It means little." He turned to the engineer. "If it lives it brings dishonour upon me and undermines my authority. As would the rumour that I had killed my own son. Sadly, my wife is sentimental and will not allow it to . . . pass away in its sleep." He filled the pause with an airy gesture as if to show how clean his hands would be after some soulless factotum had done the murder on his behalf. "The child must live. And yet the child must not live." He looked into the fire. "I am told, repeatedly, that you are an ingenious man, that buildings, excavations, waterworks, canals are merely specific instances of your general genius. I am told that there is no problem you cannot solve." Rain lashed the glass. "So I would like you to solve this one for me."

I do not believe that this was a genuine proposal. Rather, I believe my husband hated the idea of another man in his orbit being constantly touted as brilliant and was pleased at having found a way of humiliating both him and me at the same time. Only later would I look back and realise that my husband had done something crueller still. The engineer and his son were in a foreign country with neither friends, family nor connections. They were, for all the engineer's vaunted brilliance, employees, and they were being given information which could not be allowed to spread beyond these walls. It was a death sentence.

If the engineer was aware of this at the time he seemed untroubled. He slipped into cogitation the way a swimmer slips into deep water, the ripples dispersing and the surface becoming still. I had the eerie sense that he had left us and gone to another place altogether, searching, hunting, thinking. The son's eyes burnt a hole in the polished wooden planks of the floor. At length the engineer resurfaced and said quietly but firmly to my husband, indicating the attendants, "Tell your men to leave us." Either he was not intimidated by my husband or his absolute engagement with the so-called problem had rendered my husband's intentions irrelevant.

Once the men were gone the engineer raised his hands and paused for a few moments as if he were about to conduct a piece of music. "There is, in the royal stables, an exceedingly beautiful bull, nine hands high, with a soft, golden coat entirely free of blemishes, a gift, I believe, and a very valuable one."

I glanced at the boy and saw that he was as puzzled as I was.

"Go on," said my husband.

"A year ago, your wife conceived an unnatural passion for this animal." He looked directly at me while he was saying this but with no sense that I was a person looking back at him. I wondered if I had heard him correctly. "Unable to keep her feelings secret she came to me and asked me to help her have intercourse with this bull."

My husband got to his feet. "This is vile."

"Deliberately so." The engineer did not raise his voice. "Much depends on it being a story that people will listen to greedily and be desperate to pass on. As for your wife's request, given our respective stations, I felt that I had no choice but to agree to help her."

My husband looked at me. Did he think the story might be true? I do not know which of the two men I despised more at that moment.

"I made a hollow cow with a comfortable interior where your wife might position herself so as to be easily pleasured."

"I have heard enough." My husband walked towards the door, doubtless intending to order his men back in so that they could drag the engineer away prior to his execution.

"Small wonder," said the engineer quietly, "that she would later give birth to a creature that was half-human, half-bull."

My husband stopped midway between the chair and the door and turned.

"The existence of this creature should leave no stain on your character. No blood of your own flows through its veins. It owes its existence only to your wife's appetite. The real victim here is you."

"He is a boy." I could not remain silent. "Why are you telling these detestable lies?"

The engineer ignored me. "You cannot kill your wife's offspring. Nor can you give it a place in your home. Nor, indeed, can you release a monster into the wild."

"He is not a monster."

The engineer remained focused on my husband. "So you will do what one does with all wild and dangerous animals."

"And that is . . . ?"

"You will imprison him."

"Let me bring him here," I said. "Look into his face and you will see that he is just a boy."

"Which is why no one will be allowed to see him," said the engineer. He turned to look at me. "We will build a maze of tunnels underneath the palace. The monster will sit at the centre of this maze."

My husband sat back down and let out a long sigh as if he had seen the flaw in the engineer's preposterous plan. "You cannot build tunnels underneath the palace."

And this is the moment I remember most clearly from that afternoon, partly because it was so eerie and partly because it made no sense till weeks later. The engineer raised an index finger and began, slowly and carefully, to draw a convoluted figure in the air in front of him as if pencilling a preparatory drawing onto a canvas that only he could see. He lowered his hand. "It is already done."

The engineer's son stood up so violently that his chair was sent clattering onto the floor behind him. "This is not right. To do this to a child. Even if this is a jest of some kind. It is obscene. I will not be party to it." The door at the far end of the room opened just before he reached it. One of the footmen stepped over the threshold. The boy did not break stride. He lifted up the man by the scruff of his neck and dropped him to one side, the way you might lazily cast off a coat when coming inside on a winter's day. Then he was gone.

Again the engineer seemed unperturbed. "I will deal with him." Which indeed he did, though I doubt that even he, at this point, knew the violence this would entail.

I believe I was not intended to witness Paul when he came out of my womb but the second midwife failed to move swiftly enough into my line of sight. I'd not seen a baby before, except for those which had been bathed and swaddled in advance, and seeing only blood and slime and what looked for all the world like several portions of wet meat in the hands of the first midwife, my presumption was that something had gone terribly wrong and that I was looking not at a newborn child but at a part of my own body which had torn free. If I had possessed the energy to feel violent emotion of any kind I would have been terrified, but I had been in such pain over so many hours that I was clinging to wakefulness like a shipwrecked sailor grasping a shattered barrel and all I could do was to let go and pass into a great enveloping darkness, not caring whether it was sleep or death, only that it required nothing of me.

When I came round there was no blood or slime or wet meat and the nurse was cradling what I could clearly see was a living child. I briefly entertained the suspicion that they had obtained this baby from elsewhere and were taking advantage of my naivety to convince me that I had given birth to it, but when I reached out and she handed the child to me I felt a great wrenching in my abdomen and knew with an adamantine certainty that he was mine. I pushed the blanket aside so that I could see him properly. He had the softly folded face of a bat and the most exquisite fingers. Far from feeling that a part of me had been removed I felt that, for the first time in my life, I was whole. I lifted him and kissed his tiny mouth and he farted loudly and damply and, after a brief pause to check that I was not going to consider it disrespectful, everyone in the room began to laugh.

I am tempted to write, *I did not realise that there was anything wrong with Paul until* . . . but I still do not know if there *was* anything wrong with him. I believe it is entirely possible that all the wildness and the damage were the results of his being treated like an animal and that the healthiest of children would have fared no better if they were tortured in a similar manner.

It was when my husband did not visit that I began asking questions, and it was the evasiveness of the answers I received which made me anxious. The wet nurse said, after being pressed repeatedly, "He does not look like other babies."

I replied, affecting a knowledge that I did not have, that all babies looked different just as all people looked different.

She stared at her hands. "He looks different in a way that does not bode well. And he has no great strength in his limbs."

"He drinks. He smiles. He cries."

She was silent for a long time before saying, "I believe that we are all God's creatures. I believe that we are equal in His eyes, the rich man and the poor man, the nobleman and the cripple." She glanced at me to ascertain whether she had said something offensive. I nodded at her to continue. "But men do not always act as if this were true. So you will have to fight to protect your son."

I wanted to thank her for speaking openly but I felt so great a sinking of my spirit that I dared not speak.

My husband did not visit. He condemned our son having never seen him, never held him. And this is one of the many hard lessons I have learnt from this whole sorry story. There is nothing more terrifying than the monster that squats behind the door you dare not open.

They took Paul away three nights after our meeting in the Long Gallery. I woke to find one of the palace guards sitting on the side of my bed with a hand over my mouth. He smelt of vegetable stew and urine. I could hear Paul screaming. I tried to fight the man off but he only squeezed my jaw harder. "If you leave this room tonight we will slit the boy's throat. Do you understand?"

I nodded as best I could. I heard Paul's echoing screams grow fainter as he was carried further and further away through the palace.

"Good."

My wet nurse put up a sterner fight and suffered three broken fingers for her pains. I was too angry to weep. I waited till daybreak, then went to see my husband and told him there was only one monster in the palace. He said I should be more grateful that he had allowed the child to live. I asked him where Paul was.

"I have left everything in the hands of the engineer."

"May you both rot in hell."

I would not see my son again for several years.

I found the engineer in the corner of the courtyard behind the kitchens where three labourers were digging a trench. He was leaning on a trestle table set up between a cone of fresh soil and a pyramid of lifted cobbles. One of the men was down in the trench which was already deep enough to hide him completely. I could hear the damp crunch of his spade as it bit into the earth.

"Where is my son?"

"I am unable, of course, to tell you where he is at present, but where he will be is down there." He seemed genuinely pleased to have an audience to whom he could brag of the cleverness of his plan. Not for the last time I thought that his deviousness was allied to, perhaps even dependent upon, a profound stupidity.

"Have you seen him?"

"I do not believe that an answer to that question would help either of us."

"He is not a monster."

"People are seldom interested in the truth. It is so much easier to believe in the macabre, the preposterous. Do you really think that there are inhabitants at the corners of the map who shelter from the heat of the day under one giant foot or whose faces are set in their chests?" He leant a little further towards me as if sharing a secret between good friends. "And hell? A place where souls burn for eternity in vats of fire? It is the invention of a madman. But how eagerly we all cling to the story despite the sleepless nights."

"Why are you doing this?"

He paused for a few seconds and I think it may have been the only time he spoke to me without guile. "So that I and my son can return safely home. I would have thought that was obvious."

"And you care nothing for other people's suffering."

He gestured towards the medallion hanging at my neck. "That was made from silver mined by slaves in the Americas. It will then have been stolen by an English privateer from a Spanish ship whose crew will have been burnt, executed or drowned in the encounter. Look around you." He gestured to the palace. "It is a fight between dogs. The only innocents are at the bottom of the pile."

I do not know when the stories began to circulate. In truth I was so haunted by what might be happening to Paul and what would happen to him in the future that I had given no thought to my own role in the vile story concocted by the engineer. If people were laughing at me behind my back it did not register. I spent a good part of my days restlessly wandering the palace like an animal driven by a mechanical urge to search for its stolen young. One day I found myself passing the laundry when I overheard a conversation between the two serving women. It was the whispering which pulled me up short of the doorway, their desire not to be overheard. At this distance I remember only the phrase, *She wanted to be fucked by a bull,* and the drawn-out, theatrical *No . . .* of the reply.

I could have had them whipped, I could have told them to stop believing in such self-evident nonsense, but the engineer's words were still fresh in my memory. The truth weighed as nothing against the childish excitement I had heard in their voices. And if the story had reached the laundry, it was doubtless everywhere, lodged in the mind of the dignitary to whose drone I was politely listening, being shared among the gaggle of ambassadors who went silent at my approach . . . and I was powerless to stop it.

The engineer and his team worked in the kitchen courtyard for a month. A deep square pit was excavated, a low brick wall laid inside the perimeter, a stout roof built over it and the earth and cobbles of the courtyard re-laid to hide it. The floor of the resulting dungeon was bare stone sloping towards a gravel soakaway. There was a stone water trough and, above it, a dripping spigot. The space was seven or eight yards across and just high enough for a short man to stand upright. A narrow flight of stone steps led steeply down from the cobbles of the courtyard to a padlocked hatch. This was the only way for light to enter the dungeon. The space itself was so dark that you could see nothing through the bars except, on bright days, a few pale stripes of sunlight falling onto the stone floor inside. This was where my son, the monster, would live.

It was the engineer's son who told me these details. He had little choice but to be party to a project that promised to be his and his father's best chance of staying alive and returning home, but he remained profoundly uneasy. He was nervous of revealing his hand to anyone but he had an open manner which made concealment pointless, and was clearly angry with a father who dismissed his son's moral principles as unhelpful indulgences.

Having finished work in the kitchen courtyard they began excavating a plot outside the palace walls beside the stable block, digging into a broad, grassy mound and covering the hole with a pair of padlocked double doors made of oak, from which barrowloads of earth were removed and into which barrowloads of stone and timber were taken over the coming months.

This would be the entrance to the underground maze.

Except that there was no maze. There was never going to be a maze. The doors and the dungeon in the kitchen courtyard would never be connected. "My father says that mazes are puzzles for children. You can find your way in and out of a maze with nothing more than a ball of twine and a clear head." There was, instead, behind the double doors, a long tunnel which bent sharply three times. "After the third turn the darkness is absolute. I've been down there myself with no candle, no lamp. Within a few minutes you begin to feel as if you are floating. It is hard to retain one's balance. A few steps further and there is a sheer drop into a very deep pit. My father is installing spikes at its base."

I confessed that I did not understand. "Why go to such lengths when no one in their right mind is going to venture into such a place?"

The boy was silent for a long time. "There is no maze and yet there is a maze." He made a gesture not unlike those his father sketched onto the air of the Long Gallery during our first meeting. "It is a story of a maze. My father made a few drawings. He mentioned it casually to a few people. Now everyone is talking about it. They cannot let go of the idea. They are bewitched by it."

"I still fail to understand how this benefits anyone."

He took a deep breath. "Prisoners will be sent through those doors. The doors will be locked behind them. Everyone will assume that they have been eaten alive by your son."

I could barely speak. "He is a baby."

"And he will grow into a creature who is half-bull, half-man who sits at the centre of a fantastical underground maze and eats human flesh, and the story will spread far and wide and people will be terrified and they will love being terrified and your husband will be in possession of a weapon which has cost him no more than two holes in the ground."

I entered a darkness like the one he had just described. I was losing my balance.

"I think my father is an unkind and amoral man who is at ease with causing great suffering so long as it furthers his work or saves his skin. But I think he understands the human soul better than any of us."

I carried on looking for Paul with no success and decreasing vigour as my strength declined and my mind became less and less well. I guessed that he was being kept on some isolated farm hundreds of miles from the palace by people who had no clue as to his true identity, but I could not rest, like a grieving bitch whose puppies have been taken away in a bag and drowned and who can do nothing but prowl and keen. I would see a maid with a bundle of linen in her arms and my heart would race and I would have to place my hand flat against a wall and close my eyes and compose myself so that I did not run after her and tear the imagined boy from her arms. If I woke in the night and heard the peacocks crying out I knew, with absolute conviction and for far too long a time, that it was my stolen child calling me.

I avoided my husband whenever possible. I regularly absented myself from state occasions on the grounds of an illness that was both strategic and very real, and my husband rarely complained, mostly, I suspect, because I was no longer a decorative addition to any gathering. Nevertheless he came regularly to my chamber and forced himself upon me in the hope that I would bear him a son of which he did not need to dispose. I asked him the first time, as he wiped and dressed himself, whether he was not afraid that I would bear him a second Paul, and he replied, calmly, that the mooncalf was not his child. It was the product of a bestial union and my perverse nature. I was genuinely unsure whether he said it to cause me pain or whether he had begun to believe the story.

II

Years passed. I began to think that it might be better if I never saw my son again, that he stood a greater chance of happiness if he remained as the nameless child of that peasant family and were not drawn back into the machinations my husband and the engineer had jointly set in train. But my wishes and the wishes of my son played no part in their plans.

I was not told that he had been brought back to the palace. I only knew, by dint of the whispered conversations which stopped as soon as I entered a room, that something concerning me was afoot. When I heard it said that *They've put the monster in the maze*, my heart was filled with a swirling, poisonous stew of relief, anxiety and fear, and it took me several days to summon the courage to go down to the kitchen courtyard and confirm my suspicions.

I will never forget that first visit. It was a mockingly beautiful spring day. I took a route through the herb garden. The air was warm, the sky was a deep, untrammelled blue and there were clouds of bees around the lavender bushes. The chitter of birdsong bounced around the palace walls. I should have found some solace in these things but I was aware only of the profound disjunction between the world around me and that lightless pit towards which I was walking.

I heard the faint echo of his screams before I reached the courtyard. I stopped in the archway to gather myself, thinking that I should try not do anything foolish or indecorous, but I could not control myself. I ran over the cobbles and down the steps and gripped the iron bars of the grille set into that little hatch and stared into the dark. I wish I could say that I tried to offer some words of comfort to my son, but I could only stare into the darkness from which his screams were coming and cry out his name, over and over, not even knowing whether it was a word he would recognise, until I had no voice left and could do nothing but weep.

After a time whose length I could not measure I dried my eyes with my sleeve and looked around and the kitchen staff who had been watching me scattered like mice. I cared little for having abased myself. I told my son that I loved him and that I was sorry, then I sat back against the stone wall of the sloping steps and the rotund pastry cook, whom I recognised, came out bearing a pair of figs and a crust of bread in a little tin bowl.

"For your son."

I threw the bread and figs into the cell. The bread hit the stone floor and rolled away into the dark but one of the figs lay in the striped patch of light near the hatch. I watched it for a long time and the vision of the tiny hand which appeared momentarily to retrieve it felt like a nail being driven between my ribs.

I came to the courtyard every day. I sang songs, I told stories. I went to the estate workshops and acquired a little knife and some chunks of white pine and whittled a figure of a man and a woman and a menagerie of creatures which I conceived of as the passengers on Noah's Ark and I posted them through the grille. I was thinking, perhaps, of how it is possible to survive a disaster so absolute it destroys the entire world.

My husband was told about my routine and sent a chamberlain to inform me that my behaviour was unseemly. I said that if I ran naked through the palace covered in my own excrement it would be more seemly than what my husband had done to his son, and that he should use these exact words when delivering my answer.

Paul wept a great deal and screamed often and was sometimes silent and unresponsive. I learnt that he could say the word "Mama" and was, for a few minutes, profoundly moved until I realised that he was referring not to me but to a woman I had never met. I consoled myself that he had the capacity for speech at least.

For a couple of weeks he wore a rudimentary woollen jerkin and trousers but he soon managed to lose these. From early on his body was spotted with lesions though I was unable to ascertain whether these were sores or rat bites.

My presumption about the engineer and his son was both correct and incorrect. They had not received a death sentence, not directly at least, nor were they in possession of information which had to be kept secret. As the engineer explained, he could stand on a stage in every market square in the land and inform a crowd of what he and his son had done but it would count for nothing set against the story of the monster in the maze. I read this explanation in a letter he sent to my husband, who had refused a meeting in person with the engineer, doubtless fearing that he might, again, be outplayed. The letter came from the fifth-storey apartment in the easternmost tower where the engineer and his son were being held. It was a comfortable kind of gaol in which they were fed well and could receive visitors so that my husband was able to claim that they were merely being held on retainer at his beck and call for future projects, though none of those future projects materialised.

I visited them on one occasion. I am unsure about my motives, knowing only that they were several and contradictory. I wanted both to remind the father what he had done to Paul and to apologise to the son for what had been done to him. I remember thinking that their living conditions were not only immeasurably better than Paul's but better than the living conditions of the palace servants. In spite of this the son seemed diminished by being confined to such a small space, like a horse that has not been ridden or a too-long-kennelled dog, whereas his father seemed possessed of the same spooky doubleness I had witnessed in the Long Gallery. His body might be present but his mind was ranging elsewhere. I also recall several peculiar details which have been underscored in the book of memory by subsequent events. There were breadcrumbs on the sill of the open window and two dead pigeons lying beside the grate, for cooking and eating I presumed at the time. More mysteriously, the engineer was weaving a basket, presumably in order to add it to the stack of baskets in the corner of the room, none of which seemed very well constructed. Meaning to mock him I said, "Are you building some fantastical vehicle for your escape?"

He looked at me with the same blank expression he had turned on me at our first meeting and spoke with the same toneless voice. "I am."

"Then I wish you luck."

His son interrupted. "And how is . . . ?" He paused and glanced at his father though I could not tell whether his intent was apology or provocation. "Paul. How is Paul?"

"How do you think he is?" I was angry with his father mostly, but the son was a softer target. "He is a tiny child in a dungeon you helped build."

"I'm sorry. I did not intend . . . I mean only that I wished that none of this had happened."

"And why did you come to see us?" asked the engineer.

The question took me by surprise. I was accustomed to wandering the palace without being asked about my itinerary. I had come, I think, in the vain hope that I would find the two of them in some distress and the vainer hope that this distress would prove some small compensation for Paul's suffering. "You are surprisingly comfortable here."

The son was on the verge of speaking but he was silenced by an inscrutable glance from his father who turned to me and gently lifted the bouquet of wicker wands and the penknife and said, "It is a great calmative to keep one's hands busy."

I was about to cross the threshold when the son stood and asked me to wait before pressing a small book into my hands. I could see from the gilt lettering on the spine that it was a collection of *Essais* by Michel de Montaigne in the translation by John Florio, though what was most remarkable about it was that someone, the engineer's son himself presumably, had stitched—with more skill than his father had been constructing his baskets—a number of fine leather straps onto the cover and tied them so that opening the book would involve the undoing of four convoluted and elegant knots.

"I hope that it may bring you some small solace."

I nearly said that no gift from him or his father could bring me solace of any kind but I could hear what sounded like genuine remorse in his voice. I felt tears welling in my chest and I was fearful lest I allow them to be seen. So I took the book, turned away silently and departed. It was the last time I would see either of them alive.

I visited Paul twice a day. Our interaction was so restricted and his command of language so weak that I was unable to tell whether he derived comfort of any kind from my voice for the padlocked hatch prevented our touching and Paul himself remained in the shadows except to grab food or other offerings which lay near the hatch. For my own part I knew only that, painful as the visits were, if I didn't make them then I would never forgive myself.

As well as "Mama," he knew the words "cold" and "hurting," a fact which gave me little consolation. It would have been easy to convince myself that he said other things, whole sentences sometimes, but we all hear what we want to hear in meaningless babble, just as we see faces in clouds. If he played with Noah and his wooden passengers I saw no evidence. Indeed a poorly carved lion from which the back legs had been broken off lay in that pale patch of striped light for an entire week without being moved. I do know that he spent a great deal of time sitting and rocking backwards and forwards to provide himself with some rudimentary comfort, much like a bear trapped in a too-small cage in a travelling fair. Sometimes I heard him doing this and saying, "Bad . . . bad . . . bad . . . bad . . . ," though I never knew whether he was commenting on himself, on the situation, on me or on some imaginary entity in whatever dreams filled the perpetual gloom of his imprisonment.

He was five years old when the first prisoners were sent into the so-called maze. The event was the cause of much gossip in advance and the cart bringing them to their final destination had to cut a path through a crowd of eager onlookers in order to reach the double doors set into the mound by the stables. It was, I gather, a tremendous disappointment. These spectators were used to barbarous entertainments of a kind that I myself had seen on several occasions in person, and more times than I wanted in my memory: boys fighting their way to the front of the crowd in the hope that they will be splashed with blood; a blade thumping so heavily into an ash block that you could feel it in your feet and chest; the pitiful sight of someone who does not weigh enough or has not dropped far enough for their neck to be broken and is now climbing the very air in a mad tarantella to the cheers of the crowd. These people were being treated, instead, to the anticlimactic sight of a handful of dishevelled men being ushered into a dark corridor and having the door shut behind them.

The spectators returned several days later, however, when word began to spread about the noises being heard underground. The faint screams were proof that the monster had finally found his victims and was either eating them alive, leaving them half-eaten, or chasing them through the windings of the maze. This was a new kind of entertainment, all the more delicious for taking place largely in the minds of those who heard the screams or ghoulish tales from someone who had themselves heard the screams. After several weeks it was possible, according to the pastry cook, to smell the decaying bodies if one stood near the double doors or one of several vents set into the base of the palace walls whose function, I guess, was to broadcast this clue to the grisly events going on underground.

I was quickening with my second child at the time and suffering not only the sickness that comes often with pregnancy but a secondary sickness of the spirit. I was convinced that I would not love the child since I was no more than a brood mare upon whom the father had forced himself. Yet I feared, simultaneously, that I would give birth to another Paul and that I would be the child's only defender.

The confusion in my head mirrored the madness I saw around me. I could understand that people with tedious lives, a poor education and a taste for the macabre might lap up stories of a monster hidden beneath the palace. What I failed to comprehend was the way people who should have known beyond doubt that the story was ridiculous became equally credulous. Hitherto the kitchen staff had been sympathetic to my plight. They knew Paul was a human baby and their words and actions showed that they believed he and I were victims of a great wrong. Yet when the stories started to circulate about prisoners being eaten alive, they began to change. No screaming could be heard in the kitchen courtyard. There was no smell of rotting bodies. Paul cried like a child and no one else, living or dead, was glimpsed through the grille in the hatch at the base of the steps. Nevertheless, some of the staff refused to take food to Paul.

"For what possible reason?"

"For fear that he will grab them and drag them into his cell and eat them." The pastry cook shook her head wearily, as if the stupidity of young girls was sufficient explanation.

"He eats carrots and fruit and bread soaked in milk."

She shrugged. "I sometimes think people get a great deal of unaccountable pleasure from being absolute fools."

I believe their foolishness was motivated by something sharper and more pressing. Those with any conscience were uncomfortable with the knowledge that a child was imprisoned only yards away from where they worked, and they leapt at the opportunity to think of this child as a terrifying creature whose incarceration was justified, and the relief this lie promised was sufficient to persuade them to throw reason to the wind.

They found the body of the engineer's son little more than fifty yards from the window of the apartment where they were being held. His neck was broken and his chest was punctured by a wooden gatepost onto which he had fallen. I heard the story from my old wet nurse who was equal parts gratified and outraged. Apparently the boy was wearing a pair of wings constructed from wicker wands, candlewax and pigeon feathers.

"His father'll be over France by now."

The truth, I suspect, was nastier and less fantastical. I believe the engineer realised that he could escape by sacrificing his son. It would also conveniently relieve him of the discomfort of returning home with a young man who would tell his mother and his siblings that their father had sacrificed someone else's child. I think he lied to his son consistently over many months knowing that he was planning his death. I think his son was persuaded to try the wings first. He may not have liked his father, not least because of the way the engineer saw other people as mere counters in a game, but he never lost the belief that his father was cleverer than everyone else. He simply forgot that *everyone else* included himself and that he was, ultimately, one more counter. Five storeys. Perhaps the wings slowed his descent a little. His death was almost certain. I have held doves. They weigh next to nothing. I have snapped partridge bones in my fingers. That is why they can fly. But the imagined possibility of flight is a powerful drug that can make us blind to many ordinary and disappointing facts.

My guess is that the engineer burnt his own wings and waited till his son's body had been found. After that he may have done little more than shave his head and beard and walk down the stairs past the distracted guards. I suspect that the widespread belief that you are a hundred miles away soaring like a hawk acts as a very effective cloak of invisibility.

I said nothing. I might have felt some satisfaction at the idea that the engineer had slipped out of my husband's grasp had it not been purchased with the death of his son for whom, in spite of everything, I felt a certain fondness. It was this fondness which prompted me, some days after his death, to take down from a shelf the volume of Montaigne he had pressed upon me at our final meeting. It took me some time to untie the tight and complex knots whose function, I presume, was to prevent me opening the book in the presence of his father, for when I finally opened the covers I discovered that a section had been hollowed out with a knife and contained the key to a padlock. I waited until past midnight so that I stood the best chance of avoiding interruption by any of the palace servants, then took a small oil lamp and went to the kitchen courtyard.

"Paul, it's me. I'm coming in. Don't be frightened."

The padlock was stiff, having not been used since the hatch was first closed upon him, the hinges of the hatch, too, so that I had to thump the weight of my shoulder against it several times before it lurched free of its damp frame and swung inwards, allowing me to climb through the narrow opening. My glimpses of Paul had hitherto been so fleeting and so partial that I had not thought about how he would move, and in my agitated state I briefly believed I was watching, not my son, but a great spider, scuttling away from me on all fours to press itself against the far wall. He was panting and whimpering and clearly terrified, protecting his eyes from the light of my lamp with his hands. I quietly swung the hatch shut behind me and sat against the wall under the hatch, with my little lamp in front of me so that I was clearly illuminated. Then I sang "Ah, Poor Bird" and "Spring, the Sweet Spring" until I could see him growing a little calmer.

The air was thick with the smell of urine and faeces and unidentifiable things were skittering in and out of cracks in the wall. The floor upon which I was sitting was wet and covered with small bones and fruit pits. Paul himself was so filthy that it was hard to make him out clearly in the juddering light against the dirty brickwork. He was naked and his hair was long and thick and matted. He was squatting with his arms wrapped around his knees in order to take up as little space as possible and reminded me of nothing so much as a chained ape who had arrived in the company of a band of players the previous summer, its sullen, defeated air, its long, sad arms.

"Do not be afraid. I am not going to hurt you."

On my way to the courtyard I had allowed myself to entertain a fantasy in which I took Paul out of his underground prison, the two of us slipping away from the palace and building some kind of simple life together in which I was finally able to be his mother, the only bar to the realisation of my fantasy being the risk of discovery. I saw now that I had been naive and that whilst this dungeon might seem a terrible place to others, it was all he knew. If the simple presence of his own mother was terrifying, how much more terrifying would be the rest of the busy, glaring world?

I apologised for having frightened him and said that I would come again the following night with something good for him to eat and drink. I picked up the lamp, climbed back out through the narrow opening, locked the hatch behind me and had to kneel and weep in a corner of the cold garden, the palace windows black above me, Orion stern and pitiless overhead.

I returned the next night bringing a pear, a sweet biscuit and a cup of milk. The pear and the biscuit tempted him halfway across the floor in order to retrieve them and scuttle away again, but if he had ever used a cup he had forgotten how and when he grabbed it he spilt the milk onto the floor. The following night I brought a heavy bowl and held it at arm's length while he dipped his fingers in it, licked them, then lapped at the milk like a cat. He looked up at me after doing this so that I was able to see his face for the first time since he had been taken from me. Beneath the dirt and the scratches he no longer had those same softly folded features he had as a baby. His face had opened and flattened. He did not look like other boys. I wondered if this was what angels might look like if we were granted the ability to see them directly, as men were sometimes allowed to look upon the face of the divine in ancient times.

After a week of visits he no longer whimpered in my presence or pressed himself against the far wall. Slowly, he began to take food from my hand. I wanted badly to bring down a bucket of warm water and a cloth and clean his dirty face and body and trim and wash his hair and cut his long, broken nails but I knew that it would take a great deal more work to earn that kind of trust.

I started to teach him simple words—parts of the body, numbers, "take," "drop," "hold," "eat," "drink" . . . but I became aware immediately how inextricably tied language was to the world we use to describe and navigate it. How can one talk about fields or towns, about dogs or the stars, if one is unable to see these things? For a brief period I brought along books containing pictures—a bestiary of wild animals, a swimming manual, a collection of illustrated Bible stories for children—but he seemed unable to understand that these arrangements of lines on a flat page were simulacra of solid objects in a world he remembered perhaps only as a distant dream if at all.

He grew ill at one point, a hacking cough that persisted for several weeks, after which I asked one of the palace physicians to pay him a visit. The odious, moustachioed man laughed and said he did not want to be torn limb from limb and eaten alive. I said that I did not know whether he should be more ashamed of his stupidity or his lack of charity. He gathered himself, became serious and said that perhaps it would be "better for all concerned if this illness progressed and brought an end to this whole, sorry business."

"Better for Paul himself?" I asked. "Or better for everyone else?"

"You have given him a name." He raised his eyebrows in mocking disbelief. "Well, I can see how that has complicated matters."

The most hurtful thing about the exchange was its kernel of truth. I genuinely did not know whether Paul's death would be, for him, a relief. If pressed I could not have pointed to anything in what passed for his life that incontrovertibly gave him joy, even my own visits. I can say with certainty only that he grew accustomed to me. He was angry sometimes, though it was not always obvious why. Sometimes I found him in such an agitated state that I curtailed my visit immediately, partly so as not to cause him any more distress, partly so that we were not discovered should he decide to cry out with particular violence.

I tried very hard indeed not to think about his future.

III

The last few months of my pregnancy were uneventful. The morning sickness vanished, I experienced no weakness of my joints, no back pain, no difficulty sleeping. In my upside-down world I interpreted this as presaging either a terrible birth or a birth of something terrible, but my labour was shorter and less painful than it had been with Paul, and when my daughter was born most of the women in attendance were quick-witted enough not to express their delight at her being a reassuringly ordinary human child. As soon as I saw her my secondary, spiritual sickness vanished, too. It did not matter how she had come into the world. She was her own person entirely and only the most ungenerous spirit would blame her for what had or had not come before. She was also plump, loud and hungry. I said that I would feed her myself and, after a few stern words, the chief nurse relented.

My husband appeared at my bedside the following day and thanked me for giving him a daughter, and his sentiment seemed so utterly genuine and I was so exhausted that I did not think him hypocritical or cruel, but was simply grateful that he was treating me as a woman and not an abomination.

I had told Paul in advance that I was pregnant with his sister and there would come a time in the next month or so that I would be unable to visit him for several weeks, but I did so mostly to alleviate my own feelings of guilt rather than in any expectation that he would understand. In the event I managed to slip my leash and pay him a nocturnal visit only ten days after giving birth. He lashed out at me when I entered the vault, leaving three scratches from his broken, dirty nails down the side of my neck.

"I'm so sorry. I would have come to see you if I could." I took my fingers from my neck and saw, in the lamplight, that they were covered in blood. I was not unhappy. It was the first time we had touched one another since he had been stolen from me and there was a perverse comfort in this. I knew, too, that he missed me if I did not visit.

A few weeks later we reached some kind of rapprochement and in return for some gingerbread and a basin of weak beer he allowed me a brief embrace. I was shocked to feel how thin he was. He did not know how to hold another person so it was like hugging an animated tailor's mannequin but I am embarrassed to confess that it gave me more joy than holding his sister in my arms, perhaps because it happened not in the natural course of events but in the face of everything which had been pitted against us.

If one were to follow it back to its very roots, perhaps this is where the rift between my daughter and I began, like a long crack in a plastered wall that is hardly visible at one end, but at the other is wide enough to threaten the collapse of a whole house, though there is no dearth of additional reasons for the distance that grew between us over the coming years. First and foremost she was her father's daughter. It would be wrong to say that his relief at her safe birth and her unexceptional physiognomy dissolved his prejudices concerning women in general. It would be more accurate to say that he treated her as an honorary man, a status aided by her physical strength, her taste for rough-and-tumble games and a wilful nature he indulged at every opportunity. Certainly, it was clear from early on that she was to be considered his de facto heir. In other circumstances he might have seen her only when she was paraded to demonstrate some recently acquired skill, a French song learnt by heart, for example, an embroidered sampler or a silverpoint drawing of a rabbit. But he was almost motherly in his attentions, sometimes simply sitting with her on his lap and looking at her in a state of pleasurable vacancy. Later he would take her hawking and riding. He had a tiny bow made so that he could teach her archery and was unreasonably amused when a courtier had to have one of her very first arrows pulled from his thigh. The man walked with a limp from then on and was always referred to by my husband as Bull's Eye. On one occasion she asked to play a lute belonging to one of the court musicians. When the poor man was told to hand over the delicate instrument she became angry that it would not perform for her in the way that it performed for him and she smashed it on the floor. In my husband's defence he did not find this funny, but neither did he reprimand her or pay for a new lute.

I did not tell her the story of her brother. If none of the adults in the palace, supposedly blessed with reason and judgement, were capable of understanding, then why would she? I took even greater care that she did not know of my night-time visits. I did not want her to be possessed of a weapon she might be tempted to use against me. In contrast, she was told repeatedly by her father, by nurses, by tutors, about the monster who lived at the centre of a maze beneath the palace, specifically that she would be fed to him if she did not behave.

So many prisoners met this supposed fate that, every few months, a group of palace guards armed with muskets and torches escorted a band of workmen into the tunnels. With cloths wrapped around their faces to protect them from the noxious vapours, they used hooks and poles to remove the bodies which had collected at the bottom of the pit. These were dragged out into the daylight and laid on the flagstones outside the doors of the maze, partly so that families could claim their dead (though few of the bodies could be identified with any certainty after the rats had had their fill), partly as a deterrent and partly as a putrid emblem of my husband's power, precisely as the engineer foretold.

In the dark and secret stomach of this great whale of lies were Paul and I, spending several hours together most days, growing gradually more and more accustomed to one another. I taught him new words, I taught him to sing (the noise was not unlike the noise I imagine a dog might make if it were musical, but it gave him joy). I brought him some coloured chalks and drew figures of men and women and animals and birds on the brickwork but he had enough language by this time to tell me that they "moved around" and "hurt" him when I wasn't there, so I brought a cloth on a subsequent visit and wetted it under the spigot and let Paul remove the figures. He seemed to get more joy from this magical act than from my creation of the figures in the first place.

I brought in a pair of stout, well-whetted scissors and cut both his hair and his nails. The cut nails I dropped into the soakaway where I regularly swept other refuse at the beginning of my visits. The locks of hair I washed and saved in a small walnut box decorated with inlaid ormolu which sat beside my bed.

Paul continued to move around on all fours, for what was the point of standing, let alone walking? But I was adamant that there would come a time when he would need to do both so I taught him to dance, for I could think of no other reason to get him on his feet. He was clumsy but I believe he found the repeated movements soothing, and some of my best memories of those years are of nights when we held one another and I sang and we moved back and forth in the light of my little lamp in time with our looming shadows.

Come Sleep, and with thy sweet deceiving,
Lock me in delight a while,
Let some pleasing dream beguile
All my fancies, that from thence
I may feel an influence,
All my powers of care bereaving . . .

My daughter asked, on numerous occasions, as she got older, to be taken to see the monster. I would not stoop to saying that it was too dangerous, the reply she got from everyone else, so we fell, every time, into an interminable wrestling match of words. I said that he was not a monster because monsters did not exist. She said that he ate people so he had to be a monster. I said that if you fell over and knocked your head in a pig pen they would finish you off quicker than a bucket of acorns and pigs were very much not monsters.

"Why, then, do they not put pigs at the centre of the maze?"

"That is a very good question."

"That was not an answer."

"You would make a fine lawyer."

"I would, but you still have not answered my question."

I said that the so-called monster was a human being and I was not going to let her gawp at him as if he were an animal in a circus. She asked why not. I asked whether she would like it if I brought people to gawp at her. She said that she was a princess and that being marvelled at was part of her job. I said that if she were living in a dungeon she might feel differently. She stamped her foot, quite literally, and said that she wanted to see the monster and that I was making her sad and angry. I replied that it was good to feel sad and angry sometimes and not always get your own way and that if her every whim were to be indulged she would grow up to be a very objectionable young woman.

It was one of her tutors, I believe, who finally gave in to her demands. She told me excitedly about the visit the day after it happened, exulting in her ability to get round my prohibitions. The monster was, she said, the worst thing she had ever smelt.

"So you were disappointed and did not get to see him after all."

She gave me a smug smile and paused before answering. "I did indeed see him because one of the women from the kitchen brought us some meat on a skewer."

It had become, I later found out, a sport, to dangle some titbit between the bars and tempt Paul to snatch it away, and the fact that it was a dirty, frightened little boy who sometimes darted into the faint light of the hatch to grab some food somehow never erased the conviction that those offering the food had come face to face with a creature who would have torn them to ribbons were it not for those bars. Some particularly bold young men—and the serving staff told me this only under duress—would goad one another to reach through the bars with the food in their hand and grab Paul's own hand when he tried to take it.

To prevent this happening I ordered one of the workmen from the estate office to put extra bars on the hatch to the dungeon and told the kitchen staff that if any of them were found to have given food to people wishing to feed my son they would be out of the palace by the end of the day and would not return.

"He came really close and took the meat from the skewer," said my daughter. "He was covered in dirt and he growled at me, but I wasn't frightened."

I had the overpowering urge to slap her hard across the face. I closed my eyes and, without considering the consequences, said quietly, "He is your brother." She seemed genuinely puzzled as to the rules of this new game. "Your father could not bear the fact that his child was . . . imperfect. So your father told a terrible lie and locked your brother underground." I wanted to say, *He dances*. I wanted to say, *I hold him in my arms*. I wanted to say, *I love him*. But I knew that I had already gone too far. I was punishing the wrong person and I was putting Paul in danger.

"He is not my brother," she shouted. "The monster is not my brother. You will be punished if you say things like that."

The following day I was summoned to see my husband who asked me why I was filling my daughter's head with such poisonous nonsense. She was standing beside him when he said this, wearing a faint smile which made it look as if he were reading words she had herself dictated. A small group of courtiers was observing the encounter.

I said, "There will be a day of reckoning—"

My husband cut me off. "I am wondering whether the creature is fast coming to the end of its useful life."

I took hold of myself. I said, clearly and slowly so that everyone in the room would remember the exact words of my apology, looking first at my husband and then at my daughter, "I apologise for filling my daughter's head with poisonous nonsense."

My husband sat back and nodded to himself, pleased at having received my obeisance. Without so much as a glance at her father, my daughter performed an almost identical gesture. I bowed in a manner that looked, I hope, repentant, then I turned and left the room and did not see my daughter for several months.

But a day of reckoning was indeed coming, and when it arrived it would destroy both of them utterly.

My husband might have entertained the idea of dispatching Paul like a dangerous animal but he was too firmly wedded to the power which emanated from the maze and its monster to carry out his threats. So Paul was left alone, and grew and became stronger, and whilst he could be affectionate and loving he was sometimes overtaken by violent rages which he could not, or would not, control, so that I was, on occasions, frightened for my own safety. He had enough language now for us always to converse briefly through the grille before I took the decision to open the hatch. Sometimes an entire week would pass until a storm had blown itself out and I felt safe in his presence again.

He was in the habit of saying, sometimes in anger, sometimes in sadness, "I hate you," and all I could do was to apologise profusely and say that I loved him. Who else could he blame for the rats and the dark, the sores and the sickness? Beyond the faces of those who fed and mocked him from the far side of the bars the rest of the world was mere abstraction.

His sister's moods were, like her brother's, volatile and unpredictable. Her whims were repeatedly indulged and my prediction was correct. She was indeed growing up to be an objectionable young woman.

Did she think of him as her brother? She had, by now, heard all the stories and, in angry moments, would use them against me.

"Do you really believe that I had intercourse with a bull?"

"It's what everyone says."

"People say a great deal of nonsensical things. You're an intelligent young woman. What do *you* think?"

"I dislike being interrogated."

"And I dislike being slandered."

"If I had a child like that I would not want anything to do with it."

"*Him*. Not *it*. He is a person."

"I refuse to be lectured like this."

"Your father does something similar."

"I have no idea what you are talking about."

"He is incapable of answering questions. He feels it is beneath him."

"I think you are very bitter."

"I would have good reason."

"I am bored of this conversation."

She was bored of many things. She did not understand that the pleasure which comes from nothing more than satisfied wants palls quickly, and that what we most value is often achieved by hard work. Small wonder, then, that she was an easy target for a wealthy and well-connected young man. Nor, I think, is there much mystery in how they met. Everyone in the palace had heard about this handsome young prisoner and the terrible fate which awaited him. She wanted to see him and what she wanted she usually found a way of getting.

There is no one left who can tell the truth but I imagine something like this. She was showing off. She told him that there was no maze, just a tunnel and a dirty, deformed young man locked up underground. The stench he had smelt on his way to the prison was generated by the bodies of men and women who had fallen into the pit, or died from lack of food and water, or who had turned on their fellows in the belief that they were the monster. He could see that she was trying to impress him and realised that this was a weakness he could exploit. He offered her an escape from this petty provincial milieu where her true value was not appreciated, and she fell for it. Doubtless using her usual combination of flattery and threat, she ordered a bull's head in a sack from the palace kitchen and told one of the warders to give her a key. This all happened in the middle of the day. The point was not to slip away unnoticed in the small hours, but to generate such chaos that they could leave in full view of everyone and nothing could be done about it.

There was always a pair of guards at the doors of the maze, but they were elderly and their function was largely ceremonial, for who would break into such a place knowing what they might encounter or release? If my daughter commanded the guards to stand aside it would have taken only moments for her promised saviour to slide a crowbar behind each hasp and staple and crack the locks away from the wood. He threw the doors open, stepped inside and pandemonium broke out. The crowd which always hung about the entrance to the maze dispersed howling, some running as fast and as far as possible, others to find a safe place from which they could watch people being eaten alive when the monster emerged. But the monster did not emerge. On the contrary, one by one, people who had been waiting in the dark for days, certain that they were going to be eaten alive, began to stagger out into the daylight, some into the arms of astonished friends and relatives.

The stories which spread everywhere within hours of the events themselves all mentioned that the intrepid foreign adventurer was carrying an axe in his right hand when he entered the maze. What none mentioned was what he was dragging in his left. My guess is that it was a sack from which, once he was deep in the tunnel, he took out the bull's head. I do know that after a tense wait he emerged, smeared with blood, and rolled the severed head aloft onto the dust in front of the mound.

Anarchy ensued. If the palace guards were among the watching crowd, hoping to recapture the foreign prince, they stood no chance. There were no rules any more. The power of the royal house and its functionaries had depended largely on the fear generated by this mythical creature, and there was no longer any reason to be frightened. I heard it said that some of the guards themselves dropped their weapons, took off their armour and joined in with the carnival.

I do not know how my daughter and the man she naively hoped would be her future husband got away. In the circumstances they could simply have taken a carriage from the adjacent stables and ridden to any number of nearby ports without the horses needing to break into a sweat.

Quite by chance I was with my husband when he heard the news. I had never previously seen him lost for words. He seemed paralysed by the news and asked for it to be repeated several times. His daughter had been taken from him, but something else of equal importance had been shattered.

"Find her," he shouted at the hapless chamberlain who had delivered the report. "Find her and bring her back. Go."

I should have worried more about my daughter, but I had no inkling of the terrible fate that lay ahead of her, and I had other things on my mind, for I knew that if I acted swiftly, with the palace in uproar and my husband distracted, I could organise a disappearance of my own.

I dressed plainly and packed a bag with my least ostentatious and most serviceable clothes. In the base of the bag and in various places about my person I hid pieces of jewellery. I told my old wet nurse to find the pastry cook and for them both to meet me in the kitchen courtyard. I arrived to find Paul in a foul mood. I told the pastry cook to bring whatever she could find of his favourite food—honeycomb, beef dripping, cream with sugar and vanilla seeds—along with a basket of bread and meat for ourselves. I told the wet nurse to find some boots, a pair of men's stockings and a cloak with a deep hood.

Paul did not want to leave his dungeon. He had no knowledge of the outside world. It was like asking someone to walk into flames or jump into a raging torrent, and who but martyrs can do such things with confidence?

"Paul, you have to trust me. Remember, I have never deliberately hurt you. I know that this will be the most difficult thing I have ever asked you to do. But you will thank me for it." I was getting this wrong. I had to see this from his point of view. I held his face and made him look at me. "We are going to take you to a new home. It will be warm and dry. There will be no rats. There will be light when you want light and dark when you want dark. When you are there no one will be allowed to hurt you."

We were interrupted by the pastry cook bearing a chunk of honeycomb in a triangle of waxed paper and a clay bottle of beer. He looked at her, then at me, then at her again. Apart from the silhouetted heads and hands which had fed and mocked him through the grille, she was only the second person he had seen since his entombment. I was thankful for her radiant good cheer. I think even Paul could tell that she meant no harm.

"Here." She handed him the honeycomb and the beer, which pleased him so much that he took the subsequent appearance of the wet nurse in his stride.

I told her to go to the stables and order a carriage and a fresh horse and began the intricate task of dressing my son. I slipped the stockings and boots on while he was sitting, then stood him up. "I know it makes you uncomfortable but it will keep you safe outside." The palace was in uproar but a soiled and naked man who could not walk properly would draw attention in any crowd, however preoccupied. "Paul, please." He refused to let go of the honeycomb and the beer and a good deal of both ended up on the cloak.

"Now we must go. We have very little time."

"Don't want to go," he said, backing away from me. "Good in the dark. Scared of outside."

"Paul, listen to me . . ."

"We may be too late," said the pastry cook.

We turned as one and saw the hatch kicked open.

"Where is he?" said the man, clambering through the little hole in the wall. I could see only his silhouette. He was, I think, one of the palace footmen and was carrying what looked like a long poker. There were two other men behind him. I heard the clank of their makeshift weapons as they clambered into the cell.

"I have no idea," said the pastry cook, who was thinking more quickly than I was. "The place was empty when we got here."

"Well, where in God's name is he?" The footman sounded angry and disappointed.

They were looking for the headless body of a monster to parade as a trophy. Paul began to growl like a cornered dog, terrified by the invasion of these strange and noisy creatures into his domain. I was terrified, in turn, that if he kept making these kinds of noises they might think him another monster and a justifiable target for their disappointed anger. "Go," I said quietly, pushing him towards the hatch. "Quickly. Go."

The wet nurse emerged from the midst of a crowd of servants, soldiers and courtiers gathered at the top of the steps. "I have a carriage."

She pulled Paul from above, I pushed him from below. He was covering his face to protect his eyes from the light and whimpering. When we reached the level of the cobblestones the crowd parted and stepped aside. He stumbled and fell several times and we had to hoist him back onto his feet on both occasions. In his ill-fitting boots and his hooded cloak he looked like a creature children might imagine rising in churchyards on foggy nights but he was one of the monster's intended victims, a lucky escapee shattered by his experience. What else could he be? The monster was dead.

"Be brave. You cannot go back now. Take my hand."

So we began our zigzag progress through the palace, Paul staggering like a drunken sailor trying to make his way down a pitching deck. The sun dazzled him and the palace was alive with yells and shouts so that he kept dodging and ducking and throwing an arm above his head, thinking many of them were emitted by creatures swooping to attack him. Turning now this way, now that, he growled and snapped at both real and imaginary people passing by. Perhaps he was overwhelmed by space itself, for how does one comprehend four storeys of windows, an acre of lawn, a vista of forested hills between buildings if one has never seen anything more than eight paces away?

In spite of his bizarre appearance and my status, no one stopped us on our journey to the stables. The world was ringing with fear and wonder. We were uninteresting details.

We reached the stables to find that the carriage my old wet nurse had commandeered had been commandeered in turn by the palace guards, and we were forced to take an open wagon more suited to farm use, with high sides and a rudimentary tarpaulin stretched over four wicker hoops. The horse yoked to the wagon looked more like a plough horse, but the ensemble would hold no one's attention on a country road and for this I was grateful. I was relieved to discover that my favourite roan had not been purloined in the general mayhem and saddled him. What I recall most vividly from those few minutes in the stable, however, is Paul's reaction to the horses. He went up to the animal shackled to the traces in front of our wagon and placed his hands flat against her flecked, cream flanks, then leant in close and pressed the side of his face to her and remained there for some moments. I asked him about this later but, as was often the case, he did not have the words to explain. At the time I had the unnerving conviction that he believed he was meeting an old friend. Perhaps he had seen horses when he was a baby and they lived on in his dreams, slow, patient giants watching over him during his imprisonment.

I touched his shoulder. "Paul, we have to leave."

The wet nurse guided him up into the wagon, I mounted the roan and we moved into the sunlight.

Unlike everyone else, the two young soldiers manning the gate recognised me and were puzzled by my appearance as part of this small and motley crew, one of them rubbing his eyes with both knuckles as if compelled to act out his disbelief. Having no other option, they opened the gates for us, I asked for directions to Norwich, assuming the story would rapidly find its way back to my husband, waited for them to close the gate behind us, then set off in the opposite direction.

IV

We saw roadside shrines and hay being gathered in. We passed through a ford and were held up behind a small lake of sheep being moved between fields. We saw a barn being built and a herd of deer flying across a field with such unearthly grace that they seemed not to touch the ground at all. I had witnessed similar things from the warm interior of a well-upholstered carriage and never realised that the effect of a picture relies as much on the frame as the content, for there was a terror and a brightness to these sights which seemed entirely new. We saw a house on fire on a hilltop, something I had never witnessed before and it seemed like an omen.

Paul spent the first part of the journey lying on his side in the back of the wagon, the cloak over his head, until, without warning, he got to his feet, lost his balance and fell onto the roadway. He lay motionless for a good while and I was anxious that he might have struck his head, doing himself a serious injury. Then he got to his feet, shook off his boots and kicked them to the verge, lifted his cloak, squatted and shat profusely in the middle of the road. This done, he stood up and looked around. Perhaps this vast new world was easier to examine now that he was not surrounded by shouting people and soaring buildings but was simplified to earth and sky. He stepped through a gap in a hedge and walked barefoot into the centre of a small, muddy field.

The wet nurse asked if she should venture into the field and bring him back.

"Let him be for a moment."

He turned slowly, taking in the ring of the green horizon. He bent and picked up a handful of mud, squeezed it and tasted it. He threw his head back and made a noise like the howl of a dog which might have been happiness, pain, wonder or some other emotion none of us could feel having not led his strange life. He then walked calmly back to the road, climbed into the wagon and we continued our journey.

We were, in our various ways, profoundly unqualified for finding our way across the country, a young man who had spent most of his life in a single underground room, two servants who had never travelled further than the nearest town on market days, and a pampered woman who could describe the wanderings of Odysseus but who had made her journeys in the real world by stepping into a carriage at one end and stepping out at the other. I had been given no time to make plans. I had an idea that we would try and find our way towards the house of a childhood friend who had grown into a prickly, unpredictable woman who detested my husband—the reason we had not seen one another for more than a decade—but I had only the name of the village where their manor house was situated, no map and a great disinclination to ask for directions and leave anyone with a memory of having encountered us and been told our destination.

We pulled off the road into a wooded clearing near a small stream where the horses could drink. It was September but the day's warmth seemed to vanish with the light and we were relieved when the pastry cook said she would build a fire. When her attempt failed, the wet nurse began to cry and I was unexpectedly cheered to find that my pampering had not made me the weakest of our party. I gave the bag of bran to Paul and showed him how to feed the horses and was touched by seeing the care with which he did this. We huddled in the back of the wagon and ate half of our meat and bread. The cloud cover had thickened towards the day's close and we could see neither moon nor stars so that once the last of the sun had gone we were covered by a darkness so absolute that we could not see one another's faces. Paul was, predictably, untroubled, even by the noises emanating from the surrounding woodland. The pastry cook reassured me that a series of particularly unsettling shrieks was the noise of foxes mating. But the wet nurse had started to weep again, so I sang some of the songs I had previously sung to comfort Paul in his distress and when I had run through my small repertoire the pastry cook chimed in with some bawdier lays of her own.

We slept fitfully, lying beside one another for warmth on the hard boards of the wagon, and in the small hours I woke to find that the cloud had cleared and I could see, beyond the black tracery of the trees, a three-quarter moon and a dusting of blue-white stars. What I could not see was Paul. Panicked, I disentangled myself from my sleeping companions and climbed out of the wagon, terrified that he was lost or, worse, that he had made his escape, thinking himself more at home among wild animals than with his own kind. Drawn by the sound of snoring, I found him asleep between two horses, on his back like a child, arms thrown wide, undefended. It was, I believe, the first moment that I had seen him genuinely at peace.

The following day we rode through drizzle falling without stint from a low and featureless grey sky. I sent the wet nurse into an inn to ask for directions, then rode ahead so that neither I nor Paul would be seen waiting. She returned with the news that my friend's manor lay some two days ahead if we took no wrong turnings.

Throughout the afternoon Paul became increasingly distressed for reasons none of us could fathom. He sat in the back of the wagon rocking back and forth, saying, "Won't . . . won't . . ." and "Eat you alive." When he began striking himself in the face, I tried to calm him by putting my arms around him but he threw me off violently. I waited for the storm to abate a little, then gave him some bran with which to feed the horses and this calmed him somewhat.

That night I gave in to the wet nurse's pleas and we lodged at an inn so poorly appointed that I woke in the small hours, my stomach complaining bitterly about the hard bread and lumpy pottage I'd been given, listening to rats among the roof beams and thinking wistfully of the clearing in the wood. The following morning I gave the wet nurse money to find her own way home on condition that she misidentified the inn and the village where we had parted company.

Predictably we took several wrong turnings and were forced to spend another night by the roadside, though the pastry cook had acquired some tinder and a candle at the Maypole and was as excited as a small boy when she found two lumps of flint and, at the cost of some bruised and cut knuckles, succeeded in starting a small fire, a phenomenon which fascinated Paul until he burnt himself trying to grasp a handful of it, after which he sat some distance away, as if the flames were an ill-tempered, untrustworthy animal.

Poor roads, one of which came to an abrupt end at a rocky escarpment like a closed entry to fairyland, and the complexities of turning a wagon round in a narrow lane, meant that we arrived at my friend's estate after midnight and I thought, consequently, that we would have to decide between vaulting a locked gate and spending a third night in the wagon, so I was surprised to find the gates open and to see small lights burning on the ground floor of the house at the far end of the drive. I should have been more anxious but I was exhausted and emboldened by our adventures and the palace we'd left three days before felt as distant as the Americas. When the door was opened by one of my husband's secretaries, a stout, fussy man who waddled like a badger, I knew that the wet nurse had a better memory and a weaker will than I had hoped.

He made a stiff little bow that failed to be either stern or subservient. Then my friend pushed him to one side, examined me with some bewilderment before saying, "Dear God, you look like a farmer's wife." She stepped a little closer, lifted her nose and said, "You smell like one, too. Come inside."

She was, I think, one of the few people who never believed the infamous story concocted to justify Paul's imprisonment. She thought most people were idiots and proclaimed that if the majority believed something it was therefore bound to be wrong. Certainly she betrayed no surprise when I ushered the barefooted Paul into the house in his filthy, tattered cloak and stockings. When Paul snarled at the two soldiers standing behind the secretary, however, one yelped and jumped backwards, clanking the rim of his helmet against a cast-iron lamp bracket.

"Catherine?" my friend shouted to some absent servant. "Heat some water."

Paul was suspicious of the filled hip-bath in front of the kitchen range. He drank a little of the water but was not keen to engage with it any further. Only when I took off my own shoes and stockings and stood in the water could he be persuaded to imitate me and stand in the other end of the bath. I turned him around and took off his cloak. He had the body of a grown man, not dissimilar to that of my husband, for all that my husband had disowned him. I sponged his back and shoulders with soap and a rough flannel. It would have seemed wrong were he not so innocent, like a hound being washed down after a muddy November hunt.

I stepped out of the bath and gave him the flannel which he proceeded to suck. "Sit down then. If you are not going to wash yourself perhaps we can soak some of the dirt off."

He slumped into the bath and I jumped backward to avoid the great skirt of soapy water that took flight and slapped onto the stone floor. He seemed shocked for a moment, then burst out laughing. Hooting like an ape he slapped the water with the flat of his hand, sending more of it all over the kitchen floor.

My friend appeared at the door. "I heard the noises and was worried for your safety."

"He is happy."

"My dear, are you crying?"

I had not noticed. "I believe I am."

She turned through a half-circle so that she was not looking at a naked young man in the bath and addressed her words to a dresser full of crockery. "They want to take you back."

"Would you have us here? Not in the house. That would be an imposition upon you and your brother and it would not suit Paul. In some small part of the property, perhaps. Until we can find a place of our own. We do not want luxury."

"Your husband's secretary seems very determined."

"Paul was tortured. I can think of no simpler way of putting it. By his own father. We allow pigs to associate with their own kind. We allow pigs to see the light of day."

"My brother says he does not want to lose this house by angering your husband. I think he is a coward and a fool. But his fear is not unreasonable."

"Tell the secretary I will talk to him in the morning. In the meantime I would be grateful if you could find me a towel and some clean clothes for my Paul." I touched her arm. "And thank you for your kindness."

I was sitting on the floor beside the dining table vainly trying to feed Paul porridge without soiling his borrowed clothes. The foolish and cowardly brother had arranged meetings with tenant farmers in the hope that this vexing situation would be resolved in his absence. My friend was pacing. She had put the secretary in very spartan lodgings and given him no breakfast. When he arrived, accompanied by his tiny retinue, he was in a foul mood.

"We need to leave now. If you do not do so voluntarily then we have been advised to treat you as a prisoner."

"Neither I nor my son are going anywhere."

"I do not like doing this . . ."

"What you like or do not like is of no interest to me."

The secretary closed his eyes, breathed in and let out a long sigh as if his patience had just been exhausted by a truculent child, then he nodded to the soldier on his left who stepped forward to seize me. Paul growled as he drew close and when the soldier placed his gloved hand around my upper arm Paul sank his teeth into the man's wrist, twisting his head and pushing the man's arm away with both hands as if trying to rip a gobbet of meat from a tough joint. I'd never seen someone bite another person with unrestrained, violent intent. I saw the wound later and I am not surprised that the soldier screamed. His partner ran towards us, drawing a short sword from the scabbard at his belt. I had nothing to hand but a bowl of lukewarm porridge and my own body. I threw the porridge and put my body between him and my son.

I am unsure precisely what happened next. I was in a good deal of pain and there was blood in my eyes. I remember trying to disentangle myself and kneeling on broken earthenware. At some point my friend's servants arrived. They were big men who had been treated with condescension by the secretary the night before and were consequently not disposed to be gentle.

Paul and I had shared a wound, me on my arm, him on his shoulder, which would have been a good deal more serious if either of us had borne the brunt alone. The soldier he had bitten was leaning with his back against the stone hearth, too tired to scream any more but breathing hard and bleeding heavily. Paul was still growling at him. The second soldier lay on his back like an upturned beetle, wiping porridge from his hair, more surprised than anything else. Somehow, my friend, like a presiding goddess, was in possession of the soldiers' two short swords. Judging by his demeanour, my husband's secretary had watched all this from a distance with a mixture of distaste and relief, having not made a single move to intervene.

I was helped to a chair at the table and sections of old bedsheet were brought downstairs and torn into strips so that Paul and I could have our wounds dressed, though Paul seemed intent mostly on licking the deep gash on his shoulder, a more effective treatment, I suspect, given how much more quickly his wound healed over the following weeks. The injured soldier was given a conspicuously smaller and less fresh piece of torn sheet. "To keep your blood off my floor," said my friend.

I gave the secretary an ultimatum. "Tell my husband that if he allows me and Paul to lead quiet, undisturbed lives he will hear nothing from us and be glad of it." He opened his mouth. "This is not a conversation." He closed his mouth. "The alternative is for him to live with a very angry wife and a son who has inconveniently risen from the grave. It will make all our lives easier if my husband thinks that this is his own inspired idea. I am sure you can work out a way of making this happen. To have survived as long as you have in your position you will have done something similar on many occasions."

We moved into an almshouse on the property, my friend's brother's insistence that we find somewhere else to live diminishing a little every day that we heard nothing from my husband. Indeed, some months later he received a letter from my husband thanking him for having taken on the task of being my guardian, keeping a careful watch over me and limiting my pernicious influence. The letter made no mention of his son.

I read, I rode, I sat with my friend, and whilst never becoming independent of her kitchen I learnt how to cook a number of dishes for myself. We had no servants since Paul trusted no one but me, so I let the pastry cook join my friend's household. I would like to say that I embraced this simple life and became a better person for it. The best I can say is that I grew accustomed to waking to a cold house and restarting the fire of the previous night, to spending the greater part of my time in three rooms, to squinting in candlelight and to sweeping my own floors. Whenever I succumbed to self-pity

I reminded myself how easily cruelty took hold among those who lived in large, warm, well-lit houses kept clean by people to whom the owners gave hardly a passing thought.

Paul spent the greater part of his time outside the house, much like a pet cat or a dog. He was impervious to cold and wholly unpersuaded by the merits of hygiene. He slept in a bed at first, only because it gave him some comfort to mimic me in this alien place, but as he grew used to the house and the estate he started sleeping on the floor and, during warmer weather, in the stables, or in hollows he made for himself in the undergrowth among the woods at the back of the property.

Slowly and reluctantly I gave up on the idea of educating him, realising that I was attempting only to satisfy some need of my own in which he had little interest. He never learnt to read or write. He acquired more words but he rarely used them. If he understood pictures, and I suspect that he did not, they never held any interest for him.

He never spoke about his imprisonment. Perhaps the breach between his old and new life was so abrupt that he could not connect the two. Perhaps he did not possess the language. Perhaps it was too painful a subject to entertain.

Most days he was quiet and gentle, but there were periods when he was in thrall to an anger that could not be softened or reasoned with, an anger directed largely at himself. I would sometimes find bloody gashes where he had bitten his own arm like a rabbit trying to free itself from a trap. My friend had issued stern instructions to her staff and their dependents that Paul was to be treated with dignity, but stern instructions are challenges to wayward children and there were those who called him names or goaded him. Unfortunately, a small boy whose arm he broke in one of these encounters was the son of a local squire. Luckily, my friend said, he was a bumptious and self-important child who had learnt to be bumptious and self-important from his bumptious and self-important father, and the interaction would be an educational one.

Perhaps it was no surprise that he preferred the company of animals. It was an indiscriminate love. Between rats and horses, between snakes and crows, he made no distinctions and had no preferences, so that I was always braced when returning to the house, never knowing what horrors might await me. A toad in a chamber pot of dirty water on the kitchen table sticks in my mind, and until my dying day I will not put on a pair of boots without turning them upside down and shaking them vigorously to remove whatever animal might be hiding inside (I believe it was a mouse which bit me). He ate insects as if they were sweetmeats.

He never learnt to ride but would often sit in the stables for long periods. He would collect seeds and sit with impeccable stillness until birds came and perched on his outstretched hand to eat them. He would squat in the long grass in front of the trees outside the house and it was evident, from the movements of his head and eyes, that he was reading the woods with the same intensity and the same rapt enjoyment another young man might apply to a book. I looked out of the window one day and saw a deer walk up to him and if I had not known better I would have sworn that the two of them were having a conversation.

With people he showed none of the same ease, even with me. I grieved, at first, that I could not hold him in my arms to make up for all those years during which I could only speak to him through a metal grille. Any embrace initiated by me was brief and clumsy and made him uncomfortable. But there was a compensation. We were one another's fiercest protectors and I knew that he would never leave me as other children leave their parents, to marry, to work, to travel. He might sleep among the trees on a summer night, he might rage and hurt himself, he might seem sometimes to inhabit a world as strange and distant as the moon, but he always came back to me. I was his harbour and his rock, as he was mine.

But what of my daughter? What of the man who claimed to have killed my son and carried her away? What of my husband? What of the engineer?

My daughter was left to die on a remote and uninhabited island. The offers of marriage, of freedom, of escape into a wider world were no more than bait, which she might have suspected had she not grown up surrounded by people whose job was to please her at every turn. They put her ashore mid-journey, she was fed a sleeping draught and woke late to an empty bed, the windy smack of canvas, the sodden ash of last night's fires and her husband's ship shrinking steadily on the beaten blue. She walked the ragged circle of coast which now marked the limit of her world and found that she was alone. Whether she died of cold, starvation or heartbreak, whether she took her own life in desperation or grew weak and was killed and eaten by the animals of the island is not recorded.

The young man who had abandoned her was so pleased to be returning home after his cunning escape that he forgot to run up the white sails that would announce his success and docked to find that his father had thrown himself from a cliff, thinking his son had been eaten alive by the famous monster.

The exchange of information between households was so infrequent and paltry that we did not know for several months that my husband had left the country to travel on the Continent. It took even longer for us to hear that he had died while overseas. It was said that he had gone in search of the engineer, eventually tracking him down in Sicily where he was in the employ of a wealthy man by the name of Cocalus. Clearly the meeting was not a happy one for my husband was murdered in his bath by Cocalus' daughter, who poured boiling water over him. Though I have heard versions in which it was Cocalus who poured the boiling water over him. Or even the engineer.

Of the engineer himself I have heard nothing. It matters little. These are only stories, and I do not trust stories. Much as I despised him, the engineer was right. The truth is dull fare and we are dangerously enamoured of the extraordinary. These days if I read or hear some glittering tale and find my attention being held fast, I ask myself, *What suffering might these fabulous events conceal? Where am I being encouraged not to look? Who benefits if I am distracted and do not witness the mundane round of ordinary cruelty?*

More often than not, I close the covers or walk away and stand, perhaps, as I'm standing now, in the wood and brick doorway of the almshouse and remind myself that we can trust only that which we can touch with our own hands and see with our own eyes. It is shortly after dawn in spring and I am old and Paul is a grown man yet remains a child. He is crouching in the wet grass in a ragged nightshirt waiting to play with the fox cubs who were born several weeks ago in the dirty, compost-warmed gap behind the glasshouse. I step back inside the hallway and pull the door half-across so that I am harder to see and smell. And here they come, all four of them, tumbling and big-pawed, thrilled by the world, springing into the air to pounce on earwigs and butterflies and their own tails. Paul extends his hand and they lick it. From the mouth of the makeshift lair, their mother watches, attentive but wholly unafraid.

THE BUNKER

Nadine was returning from a day shift at the hospital when it happened for the first time. A fug of sweat and cigarettes and damp coats on the top deck of a number 23, then a windy walk high over the river on that fine white rainbow of cast iron, stopping at the central point as she always did, to lean over the railings and pretend for a few moments that she was airborne like the ravens that played out there in the updraught. A few blessed moments with no people making demands of her before she returned home to the flat, Edith handed Bennie over and she was at someone's beck and call again. A hundred feet below, a small boat puttered upstream on the dirty, moss-green tide. She glanced at her watch and felt a stab of guilt. Time to go.

Past the laundrette, the bookies and the Trawlerman, then dipping into the Co-operative for a *Telegraph* and the pint of milk her mother-in-law would almost certainly have forgotten to buy.

She crossed the cool, tiled hall of the Mansions and stepped into the lift. A ring of light appeared around her fingertip as she pressed the button for the fifth floor. The doors closed, the slack in the cable was taken up and she rose through the building.

Halfway between the second and third floors she tasted something bitter at the back of her throat. Her legs became unsteady and she had to grip the metal rail to hold herself upright. The brushed steel of the lift's wall, the emergency sign, her own hands, none of them seemed real. There was a loud, sparking crackle and the world shrank to a single bright point, like a television screen being turned off. She floated briefly in absolute darkness, then light and noise flooded back and she was standing, not in the lift, but at the side of a busy road looking at a row of dirty red-brick houses in the rain. The street was full of people, running, shouting, crying. She recognised none of the buildings. She had never been here before. One woman simply stood and stared into the distance, dropped bags of shopping at her feet, a tin of Ambrosia creamed rice rolling into the gutter through spilt flour turning milky on the wet pavement.

A white and sky-blue panda car screeched to a halt at the kerb beside her and a policeman got out. "Nadine Pullman?"

She was too shocked to reply, shocked that she was visible, shocked that someone knew her name, that she was not just looking at this scene but a part of it.

"Get in." She didn't move. "I'm serving you with a B47 notice, now sodding well get into the car or I swear by Almighty God . . ."

She got into the car. The policeman jumped back into the driving seat and gunned the engine. A woman in an olive gaberdine grabbed the wing mirror and screamed for help. They roared away from the kerb and she tumbled backwards, holding the ripped-off mirror in her hands.

The car tilted and squealed round the corners. A zigzagging Bedford truck came close to hitting them.

"What's happening?" It was her voice but it wasn't her voice.

"What the bloody hell do you think is happening?"

They crested a hill and skidded into a small lane. "Out!" He left the key in the ignition. Three men were running up a concrete staircase built into a high grass bank. One of them was wearing a butcher's apron. She could hear sirens. "Move!" She tripped and lost a shoe. The policeman grabbed her arm and dragged her up the steps, scraping her ankles and ripping her stockings. He pulled her through a thick double door into a crowded entryway, then let her drop. A man and a woman ran up the steps behind them, waving cream certificates with red seals. A bald man in spectacles barked, "Last two!" and as they crossed the threshold he swung the heavy door shut and it rang like a gong. He locked it with quarter-turns of the levers at its four corners.

There was another sparking crackle, everything shrank to a similar bright point, and after a few moments of darkness Nadine found herself lying on the floor of the lift. How long had she been away? Seconds? Minutes? The door was open and Mr. Kentridge from flat 17 was staring down at her. "Are you unwell, Mrs. Pullman?"

She got slowly to her feet, explaining that it was her time of the month and that this sometimes made her sick and light-headed. "I need to go and sit down."

He held up his hands, not wanting to continue a conversation on this subject. She walked to the door of the flat, steadying herself against the wall, then turned to make sure that he had entered the lift and descended.

Martin's mother was asleep on the yellow sofa, eyes closed, head resting against the antimacassar. Bennie was dozing in her lap, thumb in his mouth. She wanted a cup of tea but didn't trust her shaking hands with the kettle, the matches and the gas. Instead she opened the window and lit a Kensitas. The sun was starting to go down and lights were coming on, the dark buildings turning slowly into advent calendars.

The panic in the streets, the green metal door, the airlock. There was no doubt about it. Mr. Kentridge had suspected nothing, that was some consolation. She massaged her forehead as if the problem were merely a headache. From miles away she heard the sad song of a ferry clearing the harbour. That unforgettable vision of her uncle's final minutes, so clear she forgot sometimes that she had not witnessed them with her own eyes, the neighbours dragging him out of the cottage and into the little strip of woodland beside the railway. She had seen him a couple of days before the end, raving about sinks and fire orders and black holes. Her aunt's desperate desire to save him warring with the knowledge that the fight was already lost. "There's nothing more that we can do, Nadine. Please. We need to get away from here." Hoping that the doctors would reach him first. Though who knew which fate was worse.

"Mummy . . . ?" Bennie was waking.

They said that if you'd been there once then you were lost. But who would be foolish enough to broadcast their good luck if they had visited the other world and come back merely scorched?

"Mummy . . . ?"

She cooked a lamb and carrot stew. She remembered and forgot and remembered, every occasion a jug of iced water down her spine. Edith complained about her hip. She heard herself being sympathetic and was surprised at the skill with which she dissembled. Bennie was teething. She rubbed clove oil on his gums. What would happen to him? Not just the absence of a mother but the taint of having had this mother in particular.

Martin returned just after seven. Nadine hoped he would sense her distress but he was preoccupied with some difficulty at the workshop involving a three-piece suite and an unpaid bill. After supper Martin played snap and piggybacks with Bennie, then put him to bed. The adults then listened to Joan Sutherland on the radio.

She lay in bed unable to sleep, Martin dead to the world beside her. So gentle for such a big man. She'd seen him lift a car so that the wheel could be changed. They'd met at a coffee concert in the Wellesley Room, Martin absurd in his undersized suit. Haydn's

"Sunrise" before the interval, Beethoven's "Grosse Fuge" after. Two brilliant violins poorly served. He could protect her. She had thought it before they'd even spoken.

She had two fathers. One was sober, one was drunk. The first became the second when the sun went down. The beatings weren't the worst. It was the waiting in between which ate away at her. She brought Martin home for tea and Martin held her father's eye for the most uncomfortable ten seconds of her life and her father never touched her again. But now? This wasn't a drunken father. This wasn't a flat tyre and a missing jack.

Above her in the gloom the plaster cornices turned slowly monstrous.

Three uneventful days encouraged the hope that she'd had a very narrow escape, the burden of her terrible secret growing slowly lighter as she changed dressings and emptied bedpans. The man who had fallen from the scaffolding two months earlier took his first steps and they threw a party.

On the fourth day she was sitting on one of the benches outside the staff canteen, next to the blackthorn hedge which half-hid the boiler plant. She was eating the mustard and potted meat sandwich she had made that morning and wrapped in greaseproof paper so that she could carry it in her handbag. Again, the bitter taste, the sparking crackle, the darkness and, suddenly, she was holding an exercise book bearing a black crown and the words *AWDREY LOG: Supplied for the Public Service HMSO Code 28-616*. She could smell sweat and human excrement. Mounted on the wall to her right was a grid of tiny wooden boxes, the kind a school librarian might use for storing index cards. One was labelled *DEAD*, another *CONFIRMED*.

Three men in pigeon-grey military jackets were leaning over a broad table. Behind them was a wall of Perspex on which a big map of the country had been gridded and subdivided. She was in a room smaller than half a tennis court. It had no windows. One of the men looked up. His stubble and his red eyes suggested that he had neither slept nor shaved for several days. "Well . . . ?"

"Two new blasts. Blast one: fifty miles, bearing a hundred and fifty-two degrees." The words were coming out of her mouth but she had no idea what they meant. "Six to eight megatons. RAF Scampton."

"Dear God," said the man. "And the second blast . . . ?"

"The second . . ." Her mind was blank.

"For Christ's sake, we do not have all day."

His colleague turned to him, a gangly man with a wizard's beard who was clearly not used to wearing a uniform. "I fear that we have all the time in the world."

"Miss Pullman." The red-eyed man turned back to Nadine.

"A little kindness would not go amiss," said the bearded man.

"Miss Pullman—" the red-eyed man ignored his colleague—"there is limited air. There is limited water. You have a job to do and that is the only reason you are here. Illness is not an option. Mental collapse is not an option."

The sparking crackle sounded again and after a short period of darkness she was lying on her back staring up at a blue sky, the blackthorn bush and two worried people gazing down at her. Dr. Cairns offered a hand to ease her to her feet. Sister Collins guided her to the bench. Cold sweat and a deep churn in her guts. "Nurse Catterick, fetch Nurse Pullman a glass of cold water."

It was only a matter of time now. Her friends and colleagues wouldn't turn her in, but gossip spread and it only took one person who valued their safety above your life. Dr. Peterson had been taken away in a black van, Nurse Nimitz had been taken away, the handsome Trinidadian man with sickle cell had been taken away . . .

. . .

She went home early, bright autumn sun falling on a world to which she no longer belonged. There was a fair in Queen's Gardens, a chained baby elephant in a nest of straw, painted horses turning, a jaunty pipe organ and the smell of burnt sugar.

She had no idea what to expect from this point on. They had wiped her uncle from the family record, as if ignorance were a form of protection, and what she heard elsewhere was a tangle of gossip, half-truth and scaremongering. Some said that it was contagious insanity, others that these were echoes of past events, others that they were premonitions of events still to come. The end of the world, some whispered.

There were no articles in the papers. It was not discussed on the radio or the television. Her lack of interest seemed shameful in retrospect. Not once had she put herself in these shoes. So much suffering and her only thought had been relief that it was happening to someone else.

She had Bennie on her knee when it happened for a third time. "This is the way the ladies ride. Clip-clop, clip-clop . . ." Edith had retreated to her room with *The Grand Sophy* and a mug of cocoa which might or might not have contained a shot of Bowmore, and Bennie was hungry for some of the riotousness that Edith's age and hip were making increasingly impossible. "This is the way the gentlemen ride . . ."

It was quicker this time, more like a doorway than a journey. No bitter taste, just a rapid crackle, Bennie falling backwards out of her grasp, and she was waking from a shallow sleep in a cramped dormitory of eight bunks. Half-submarine, half-boarding school. Her skin was sticky, her hair lank. A woman in uniform was waiting to take her place under the dirty sheet and khaki blanket. The words *Royal Observer Corps* curved over a red aeroplane on her shoulder.

Nadine looked down and saw that she had been sleeping in an identical grey uniform. Fifteen other women were climbing out of bed. Fifteen different women were waiting to take their places.

Someone was singing "Walking Back to Happiness."

"For God's sake, Rita. Can it, will you."

"Girls, girls . . ."

The women crossed the corridor and entered the room she recognised from the last time. The strip lights, the Perspex wall maps. She was the tail of the crocodile. The red-eyed man stepped in front of her and closed the door so that they were alone in the corridor. The chug of machinery somewhere and the faint odour of diesel fumes. She could see now that there was a triangle of waxy flesh on his chin where no stubble grew. He had been burnt as a child, perhaps.

"I need to know one thing and one thing only."

"What's that?"

"Can you do your job?"

She closed her eyes and looked into her mind and saw fragments of something which had broken or fallen apart . . . a boiler suit made of white cotton . . . the EM wave and the optical wave . . . the sound of someone weeping at the end of a phone line . . .

"Miss Pullman . . . ?"

She felt a rising panic and a painful yearning to be somewhere safe with no responsibilities. Her knees gave way and she slid down the wall until she was sitting on the scratchy grey carpet, sobbing.

"I think that's a fairly conclusive 'no.'"

Martin sat in the rocking chair beside the bed. She had been away for longer this time.

"Where's Bennie . . . ?"

"He bumped his head. My mother has taken him to the fair.

Toffee apple and candyfloss. He will be royally sick by the time he gets home."

"I should have told you earlier."

He cupped her cheek in his hands and shook his head. Was he saying goodbye? Were the doctors drumming their fingers in the living room, giving the two of them a final few moments' grace? Under the fear was a relief she had not expected.

"We're going to see an exorcist."

Were it not for the steady confidence of his gaze she might have questioned his sanity. She knew about exorcists only through fourth-hand stories. She had always assumed that they were figments of desperate imaginations.

"There are things I have never told you." He got to his feet. "Things you were safer not knowing." He handed her the black duffel coat he had laid over the arm of the chair. "Put this on. We have a long, cold walk ahead of us."

They slipped into an alleyway off Weaver's Lane, then cut across the graveyard of St. Saviour's. Martin was a big man who attracted attention but the few people who passed them in the darkened streets seemed not to notice them. Only a dog was disturbed by their presence, growling at the end of its chain, hackles up and head down. It was the strangeness of the evening, perhaps, or her growing detachment from her own life, but she felt as if she were traversing a city which was almost but not quite identical to the one in which she lived.

He said, "I told you sometimes that I would be working late. It was not always true." He said, "I've never talked about my sister. We lost her. I promised I would never lose anyone again." He said, "I've done this for nineteen other people. I hoped I'd never have to do it for you."

They were heading downhill towards the docks. Fish and marine oil on the wind. The lights of the *Raleigh* still blazed, its patrons blurry behind dripping, foggy glass. They walked through a mazy canyon of warehouses. A big rat trotted casually past like a tiny insurance clerk late for the office. A misty smudge of moon lit their way. They turned a corner and the moon was swallowed by a double-funnelled steamer in red and cream, roped to the quayside and portholed on three decks from stem to stern.

Martin led her to the foot of a cast-iron fire escape which rose steeply to a door between two dirty, lit windows which might have been the eyes of a harbourmaster's office were it not for the lack of signage. They mounted the ringing steps.

The exorcist was a plump, forgettable woman whose ivy-green cardigan was fastened by walnut-brown toggles. She greeted Martin with the wordless nod one gave to a colleague. "So this is Nadine."

There was a Rolodex. There was a vase of dying irises. There was a framed reproduction of Bruegel's *Fall of Icarus*, the glass cracked at the corner. A bagatelle board leaning against a wall would have seemed bizarre on any other day. Nadine took the empty armchair.

"I'm afraid we have no time for pleasantries." The woman was steelier than she appeared. "You have to trust me completely and you must do exactly as I say. There is no alternative." Nadine glanced round and Martin nodded his assent. "The next time you cross over I will be waiting for you on the other side. We will not mention this meeting. We will not talk of Martin or your son. We will not talk of this world. Do you understand?" The woman leant forwards and Nadine saw a charm bracelet slip from the cuff of her cardigan, a silver chain from which hung a little silver crow, a little silver moon and a little silver hammer.

"I understand."

"I will try hard to find you a way home. I cannot tell you in advance what it will be. I can only tell you that I have not failed yet." Somewhere nearby the bell of a mariner's chapel tolled twice. "I must go. I have difficult work to do." The exorcist stood slowly. She seemed to be in some pain. "When you next see me I will be changed."

She took a macramé shoulder bag and a dark blue cagoule from the back of the chair. "Get some rest." Then she was gone.

Martin sat on the arm of the chair and held her. She had many questions, but to ask any of them would open the door of the aircraft mid-flight. Better not to see how far she had to fall. She wanted more than anything to be with Bennie.

"Remember that first long walk we took?" Martin sandwiched her tiny hand between his great paws. "Near Minehead?" A thundercloud had risen over Selworthy Beacon and the sunshine was replaced suddenly by a slate sky and hail like conkers. They ran hand in hand for a pillbox where they startled the sleeping, ownerless spaniel who would later accompany them for the remainder of the walk. "Let's take it again . . ."

She leant her head against the dependable mass of him. "OK."

"So . . . I picked you up from your parents' house. It was half-past nine in the morning. You were wearing the orange skirt with the yellow circles . . ."

An hour, two hours . . . She slept and woke and did not recognise her surroundings and was briefly terrified until she saw Martin, only to succumb to a different fear when she remembered why she was here with the dying irises and the bagatelle board. She slept again and woke and drank a glass of tepid water from the pitcher on the desk, and was standing at the window watching faint smudges of pumpkin-coloured light pick out the cranes and the hulks at anchor when she left the world for the final time.

No taste, no noise, no darkness. Instantly she was sitting at a Formica-topped table in a canteen. On the far side of the table was the gangly, bearded man. Behind him sat a uniformed woman Nadine did not recognise. She had a lazy eye and black, black hair. There was a serving hatch and the rank perfume of boiled vegetables. She looked around for the exorcist but there was no one else in the room. The Formica had unglued itself from the chipboard at the table's corner.

"I apologise for Major Pine's graceless behaviour. He is correct, but there are many different ways of being correct." She could hear now that the man's accent was a soft, lowland Scots. "In better times you would have been cared for." He sighed. "But in better times our lives would not depend on a man like Major Pine."

His female colleague sat back and said nothing, as if she were supervising the man's training.

He cleared his throat and read from the sheaf of stapled papers. "You signed documents during your training to the effect that if, on active service with ROC Group Number Twenty, you became incapacitated either physically or mentally . . ." He dropped the paper. ". . . and some more turgid bureaucratic nonsense I won't bore you with." He rubbed his eyes. "They want you to sign a piece of paper. Can you believe that? Because the last man in the world will be some prig from Whitehall trudging across the scorched wasteland checking paperwork." The woman seemed neither surprised nor affronted by the diatribe. He pushed a pamphlet across the table. "Predictably, they provide a helpful guide to the situation."

Expulsion: A Guide to Short Term Survival. She flipped through the pages. *Root vegetables from allotments and gardens may provide another source of relatively uncontaminated food* . . . There was a diagram showing how to kill a poorly drawn dog, though whether for protection or consumption it was not immediately clear. She was transfixed by the backs of the hands that were and weren't hers, the dirt under the nails, the faint blue of returning blood. They were so real. She had never heard anyone speak about how utterly convincing it all was.

"You know as much as anyone." The man shrugged. "Leeds has gone. Manchester has gone. The destruction is widespread from Holy Loch south. In other circumstances I would pray for God to go with you, but my faith in the old chap has been somewhat undermined of late." He stood up and pushed his chair back under the table, the legs screeching on the lino. "I wish you a strong wind off the North Sea and a cache of tinned beans." He gestured towards the door. "Let's get this ghastly business over with."

The woman followed them into the corridor. Where was the exorcist? Nadine was increasingly certain that something had gone wrong. The man stood aside so that Nadine could take the stairs first. She felt sick. None of this was real. She had to remember that.

The man waited for a few seconds, then said, "I would much rather that this passed off without any unpleasantness."

She climbed to the concrete landing where she had entered the building that first time. A big cream hatch stood open revealing an airlock not much larger than a toilet cubicle, rubber seals, pressure gauges and a red warning light in a sturdy wire cage. The far wall was a sealed, identical hatch. And beyond that?

"It will be cold outside." The black-haired woman held out a dark duffel coat, identical to the one Nadine had worn for the long walk earlier that evening, but older and dirtier with a skirl of torn lining dangling below the hem. Worlds slid over one another, like a cathedral reflected in a café window, like the beach and the christening on the same photograph.

And then she saw them, in the shadow of the woman's military cuff, a crow, a moon, a hammer. "Thank you."

The man stared hard at the wall over Nadine's shoulder, unwilling to meet her eye. She stepped into the airlock. She was not going to turn round. She was not going to treat him like a real person. She focused instead on a long cream-coloured drip where a painter had overloaded his brush. Were these the echoes of some vanished world? Was this the future? It seemed inconceivable that her own mind could conjure a universe so rich in detail.

The man said, "I wish you luck," the hinges squeaked and, with a soft kiss, seal met seal. There were four muffled clangs as the locks were turned on the landing, then nothing, only the sound of her breathing in the steel chamber.

She closed her eyes and pictured herself unconscious in the armchair in that little room, Martin at the window waiting for her to be returned to him. Outside, dockers yelled and busy tugboats worked at the jigsaw puzzle of the big freighters. Bananas and coal and coffee. Bennie would surely be awake now, wanting to know where she was.

Nadine opened her eyes. There was a dirty grille at waist height. There was an abandoned pair of black wellington boots. There was a waste bin bearing the label *Contaminated Overalls Only*. In what way was a duffel coat meant to help? Had she deceived herself? Had she seen what she wanted to see in the glitter of some other jewellery?

The red light came on and began to turn. Then the alarm went off, stupidly loud in such a small space. She covered her ears. Five, six seconds? The alarm stopped and the red light went out. She took her hands from her ears and heard the dull hiss of air pressures equalising. The big door unlocked itself and let in a thin slice of grey light and a sweet, charred smell which raised the hairs on the back of her neck. She put the duffel coat on for the small comfort it offered and carefully opened the door.

The panda car was burnt out, the paint black and blistered. Orange rust was already eating away at the unprotected metal, the tyres were gone, the glass was gone. There were no windows in any of the buildings. Many walls had fallen. Roofs were shipwrecks of black timbers. A thick, unwashed fog hid the far side of the park across the road. Every patch of grass was dead. She walked down the steps. Two silhouettes on a nearby wall looked like the shadows of children if children could leave shadows behind. The airlock bumped softly shut behind her. She listened. It was the kind of silence she had only ever heard on a still day in the mountains.

A burnt dog lay beside the burnt car.

There was movement in the corner of her eye. She turned and saw a tramp standing at the lane's dead end, holding the hand of a girl of seven or eight. Their faces were soiled. He wore three dirty coats and carried a crowbar. There was an open wound on the girl's cheek.

"Oi! Lady!"

The woman had been right. The air was bitterly cold. She slipped her hands into the pockets of the duffel coat. There was something hard and heavy in the right-hand side. She lifted out a tarnished, snub-nosed pistol. The words *Webley & Scott Ltd, London & Birmingham* were stamped into the side of a fat, square stock. The trigger guard was a primitive hoop and the hammer looked like a sardine key. A gentle squeeze of the trigger showed that the machinery was oiled and ready.

"You were in that bloody bunker, weren't you!" The man was limping towards her, dragging the girl behind him. "You did this!" He swung the crowbar around, indicating the fallen walls, the dead grass. "You people did this!"

Suddenly she understood. "You have to trust me completely." Nothing had gone wrong. The exorcist had found her a way home.

"Are you listening to me, lady?"

She put the barrel of the gun into her mouth and bit the metal hard to hold it steady.

MY
OLD
SCHOOL

1976

After all these years I can still remember seeing him for the first time. We were several weeks into the summer term of my second year. Lunch had just come to an end and we were heading back to our studies before getting changed for afternoon games. He was standing in the foyer wearing a uniform newly purchased from Godber's on the High Street—plum-coloured jacket, white shirt, plum and gold striped tie, grey worsted trousers with ironed creases down the front, polished black shoes. I remember catching a glimpse of what I guessed was his parents' bottle-green Rover 3500 pulling away down the gravel drive. His name—Graham Meyer—was written in clumsy khaki capitals with enamel modelling paint on the cheap, wooden trunk at his feet.

He was big for twelve years old, tall, bulky, a physique that could have been a godsend if he were willing to use it to protect himself, but it was clear from the way he hunched his shoulders and squirmed uneasily inside an ill-fitting jacket that he was uncomfortable in his body and wanted to take up less space, to vanish into the background. He did not look like someone who would start a fight, or indeed win one that someone else had started. I knew, too, that his arriving in the middle of the term was a sign of some significant upset in the rest of his life, and that his parents either knew nothing about how schools like this worked or cared very little for his welfare, otherwise they would have delivered him to Fairfax or a prefect instead of leaving him to fend for himself and driving away.

A part of me recognised a kindred spirit, and if the encounter had happened outside school during one of the holidays I would probably have gone and talked to him, but the rules were different here. I could see instantly that he was going to be bullied and I did not want to be nearby when it happened. I suffered enough on my own account and if someone new was going to be the target for a portion of that nastiness I was only too happy to let it happen and keep out the way. So I avoided his glance, shouted, "Wait for me!" to no one in particular and jogged through the foyer leaving him to fend for himself.

I remember my own arrival at the school five months earlier. If anything I was more at sea than Meyer. Three of my grandparents worked in factories, the fourth—my mother's father—was a cinema organist and pianist-for-hire who drank himself into an early grave. My father left school at sixteen with no qualifications to become a semi-professional footballer. He could also draw and paint beautifully (his watercolour of a brown bear at London Zoo hangs above my desk) and after National Service in the Royal Engineers he took advantage of easier entry to higher education for demobbed men and qualified as a structural engineer. His numeracy and spelling were poor (he was, I think, dyslexic though he would have scorned the label) but he was ambitious and bloody-minded and after a few years he set up his own practice and became well off in a way that no one in either his or my mother's family had ever been. He gave his parents the money to buy their council house and we moved to a village outside town where we had a thatched roof and three acres of garden.

In spite of this he yearned for something more. He mocked people with degrees who read big novels and spoke foreign languages, but showed, in their presence, a queasy deference which made him seem like a small boy and left me feeling embarrassed on his behalf. He'd climbed a long way up the ladder but remained at some ill-defined mid-point that didn't quite feel like a destination.

It was he who had wanted to go to boarding school, he who had wanted an entrée to a world from which he felt excluded. And he would have fitted in perfectly. True, there were Greek lessons and boys with double-barrelled names but it was not otherwise greatly different from National Service—tepid showers, open dormitories, rugby on muddy pitches in driving November rain, the relentless banter. If you joined the cadets you could even fire a gun. He liked a fight (he still had a shelf of boxing trophies from school) and he could turn his hand to pretty much any sport, and whilst it was the academically gifted boys at school who got prizes on speech day, the most popular boys were those who "showed character" by doing just enough work and kicking over the traces.

I was more like my mother than him, unathletic, anxious and often unhappy. I was most comfortable in my bedroom reading encyclopaedias, building models and doing experiments, and I can still remember the pleasures of painting an Airfix Hurricane or seeing bright blue crystals growing on the end of a piece of cotton suspended inside a jam jar of saturated copper sulphate solution. I had friends but I didn't greatly enjoy the rough-and-tumble of life outside the classroom.

Boarding school was presented by my parents as a valuable opportunity. I also knew that it would cost them a great deal of money. Refusal was unthinkable. Besides, it was a world of which I knew next to nothing. I was eleven years old and trusted my parents and believed that if you were polite and well-behaved and did what you were told by adults in positions of authority then everything worked out for the best.

I had visited Frobisher House once with my father during the spring holidays and we were given a tour by the housemaster, Geoffrey Fairfax, who said, at one point, "Don't worry, we'll give him a sound thrashing if he steps out of line," and laughed and tousled my hair, and what I remember most about the interaction was the sudden warmth I felt for this man who included me in this complicated joke and who touched me with an affection my father never showed. We sat in his study where logs crackled in the hearth and the fishermen and peasants and beautiful women in the blue Chinese tiles of the fire surround were part of a story I couldn't work out, and I felt like the child in the fairy tale who must leave home and place themselves in the hands of the wise teacher who can foster the special powers which have gone to waste in the village.

When I returned in September after a final term at the local state junior school it felt like a very different place. I was two hundred miles from home with a thirteen-week term ahead of me among boys I'd never met before who seemed to have arrived knowing exactly how the institution worked because they had all come from prep schools that worked in a similar way.

I've visited prisons several times in my adult life and the sounds and smells take me right back to that first term—the yells and shouts, the acoustic of a building without carpets or furniture, the reek of sweat and flatulence and cheap deodorant, and something less palpable, a prickly tangle of pecking orders and unwritten rules and invisible lines that must not be crossed.

Junior boys were given no personal space. I was to share a study with someone whose name I no longer remember because his protruding eyes and glum expression earned him the name "Frog" by which he was then known for his entire school career. The room was about eight by ten feet with a small window looking onto a scrubby central quadrangle of gravel and poorly tended shrubs.

The plaster was so chipped and pitted that in one place, just beside my equally battered desk, it looked as if a previous occupant had tried to dig his way out but given up when he reached the brickwork. Upstairs, the junior boys' beds ran down either side of the main dormitory, separated from one another by head-high wooden partitions. Each partition had a curtain you could pull across but the price of the privacy you gained was not knowing who might be on the other side of the curtain about to whip it aside. Scariest of all, for me, were the toilets in both the dormitory and the changing room downstairs, which had doors that reached neither the floor nor the ceiling so that it was easy for someone to grip the top of the door and look over it or set light to a ball of scrunched-up newspaper and roll it into the stall when you were sitting on the toilet (the latter happened to me only once, thank goodness) so that I soiled myself several times during those first few terms because I was unable to hold on until the bathroom was empty.

During our first year we did our nightly homework session in the boys' dining room. At some point during the ninety minutes Fairfax would emerge from the door to the private side of the house smoking his pipe and walk slowly around the room, stopping here and there to examine this or that boy's work. I find it hard to understand in retrospect quite why I found this so profoundly unnerving except that I found every aspect of that place unnerving. A fear ran constantly under my every waking moment like a deep, discordant basso continuo, a fear either that someone might do something to me or that I might be punished for some offence I had unknowingly committed. Even now, over forty years later, I sometimes hear a door open with the pained, squeaky click of that white door in the far corner of the Frobisher dining room and my heart immediately beats faster, the hairs stand up on the back of my neck and I feel that sinking plunge of fear.

My fear was not unjustified, nor is the comparison to a prison as far-fetched as it might seem. There was a game called "Spartacus" which involved throwing a garden fork the length of the main corridor in an effort to make it bounce and spark off the floor tiles, then stick into the study door at the far end, a game which was officially banned after a first year came out of his study at the wrong moment and was taken to the City Hospital in Nottingham with a bloody gash and a broken kneecap. On one occasion a pair of boys in the year above staged a duel in the dormitory in which they turned deodorant aerosols into home-made flamethrowers. The result was spectacular, one of the boys was badly burnt, the smell lingered for many weeks afterwards and Fairfax beat not only both combatants (the latter after he was discharged from hospital) but two other boys who had failed to protect their partition curtains from being destroyed.

Fairfax was notoriously lax about whom he beat. A boy in the year above was queueing to get a buttery slip signed after lunch one day and was beaten six times after Fairfax mistook him for someone else. When the surprised and tearful boy complained that he'd done nothing wrong, Fairfax replied, "You've got six on credit, then." Some years later, Fairfax was about to beat the same boy for a misdemeanour which he had indeed committed when the boy said, "I've got six on credit, sir." With barely a pause, Fairfax said, "You're lucky. I was planning to give you twelve." It was a story I heard Fairfax himself tell on several occasions to general amusement.

In my third year Becker, a boy in Hudson, a house on the edge of town, started a fire in the laundry room and the sleeping boys in the adjacent junior dormitory woke and escaped only minutes before the roof collapsed. Becker was prosecuted and sent to borstal and was remembered mostly as the idiot whose actions caused the innumerable night-time fire alarms and drills that punctuated the rest of my time at the school, and only many years later did I wonder what had made you so unhappy that you wanted to murder twenty sleeping children.

On top of the fear and the lack of privacy I discovered that I was only an average student. At my previous school I had come top in most subjects and as a result whilst I found it difficult forming friendships with other children, pleasing teachers had been easy. Now I was halfway down the class in many subjects and struggling in others, and these rankings were recorded on report cards we had to get filled in by our teachers and present to our housemasters every fortnight.

I wasn't suicidal as such but I do remember the sensation of being trapped inside a life I couldn't bear and there being no way out. Other boys, in my year and in the year above, sensed my anxiety and couldn't resist playing on it, clapping their hands loudly behind my head or leaping out from round a corner to shout "Boo!" in my face for the pleasure of seeing me jump. On Sundays during Reading Hour when we all had to sit quietly in our studies, one of the prefects liked nothing better than knocking loudly on my door, opening it, saying, "He's in here, sir," then laughing as the colour drained from my face.

Towards the end of my second term my grandfather—the cinema organist—died unexpectedly. My parents asked the housemaster to tell me the news and I was ordered to present myself in his study as we were going to bed. Petrified, I put my dressing gown and slippers on, convinced that I was going to be punished and scouring my memory for what the offence might be. When he told me that Grandpa Llewellyn had passed away peacefully in his sleep (I would learn later that he had throat cancer and had died when a major blood vessel in his throat ruptured, effectively drowning him in his own blood) I felt a giddy mix of relief at not being punished, sadness at Grandpa's death and confusion as to why my parents had asked Fairfax to give me the news.

"Such is life," he said, banging out his pipe on the fire surround. "It's all part of growing up. You have to be a man about these things."

I knew that I was going to cry and I knew that I needed to find a place where I was unlikely to be discovered. I said, "I have to go now, sir." I made my way to the toilets in the changing room, didn't turn on the lights, sat in the furthest stall, locked the door and let the tears come. Then I heard footsteps. I knew it was a prefect because they were wearing Blakeys, little metal plates intended to prolong the life of leather heels and toes which also made satisfying clicks and scrapes on tile and stone and which were to be worn—this was one of the many unwritten rules—only by prefects. I heard a window open, the scratch of a lighter and, after a few moments, smelt cigarette smoke. I sat as still as I could. Five, ten minutes? The window was closed and latched, the footsteps headed back past the sinks, then stopped. After a few seconds of silence the lights were turned on. I heard the scrape of a metal heel revolving and steps coming towards the stall.

"Well, well, well. What have we got here?" Timpkin put his head over the door.

I was petrified. Timpkin was known as a sadist who had poured boiling water over the hands of a boy he caught stealing from another boy's room.

Was it the fact that I knew he'd been smoking? Was it because he could see that I'd been crying? Perhaps he was just tired. He slapped the door loudly enough to make me jump and said, "Get the fuck upstairs and go to bed, all right?"

"Yes. Thank you. Yes, I will."

I don't think I'd ever felt as grateful to someone in my life.

My gratitude did not last long. By the following morning everyone in the house knew that I'd been found crying in the toilets. Boys would make weeping noises as I passed them in the corridor or rub their balled fists against their closed eyes and miaow like cats. Perhaps if I'd told them about my grandfather they might have been shamed into backing off but I didn't want to hand over yet more private information in case that became another weapon. After a few days the story mutated. The new version which was spread gleefully around the entire school was that I had been weeping because I was trying—and failing—to masturbate. I immediately became known as Baby Cry-Wank, or Little Baby Cry-Wank, or Ickle Baby Cry-Wank. For a whole term I don't think I heard anyone use my actual name other than masters and a few boys in my own year when we were alone. Even in class other boys would refer to me as BCW, as in, "BCW has his hand up, sir." When quizzed by the master, they would always say, "No idea why he calls himself that, sir," and I would be unable to explain. I was still being called the name when Meyer arrived in the house but it was being used with such regularity that it was starting to lose much of its sting. Thirty years later I bumped into one of the boys from my year in a crowded pub in Canonbury and he said, "BCW, mate!" with a broad smile containing no malice.

Someone must have taken pity on Meyer and informed the housemaster of his arrival because we got back from games to find that he had been installed in the study of a boy called Barnes. He was the only boy in the year not to have to share a study thus far but none of us begrudged him because in our eyes he was more than a little sinister. He had entered puberty early in a way that seemed unnatural rather than enviable. He had muscles and a moustache at twelve, his face was peppered with acne, there was a vinegary tang to his body odour and something simian about his rolling gait. It was a running joke that he would be convicted of some terrible sex crime in later life and, unlike many of the stories boys told to mock one another, there seemed to be some shard of truth in it. One evening

Barnes came into the games room doing up his flies and an older boy whose name I forget, said, "Oi-oi. Barnes has been fucking one of the bodies he keeps in the boiler room." The two reasons I remember it are, firstly, because the comment was followed not by laughter but by an awkward silence acknowledging that a line had been crossed, and, secondly, because Barnes shrugged and said, "You're just jealous."

Barnes reacted to losing half his study space by ignoring his new room-mate. I never talked to Meyer about it so I can't be certain but my impression was that in the remaining term and a half of that year he didn't speak to Meyer once, treating him instead like a large piece of unwanted furniture he had no choice but to live with and step around.

Meyer was possessed of two shortcomings which were to prove his undoing. He was desperate to be liked and he didn't know how to make this happen. He would regularly misjudge a mood, often failing to hear the unspoken message in a gesture, a tone of voice. He would walk up to a group of boys in the year above and try to join in with their conversation. He would slap other boys on the shoulder and say, "Well done," like an approving uncle. It didn't help that he was physically clumsy. I remember him accidentally sweeping a plate onto the floor at lunch and everyone cheering. He was so pleased at getting what he thought was the acclamation of the entire house that he deliberately dropped a second plate, after which you could hear a pin drop because Fairfax was sitting only one table away and this was clearly the act of a crazy person. Perhaps Fairfax thought something similar because Meyer wasn't beaten, only sent on punishment runs every morning for a fortnight.

It was six or seven weeks after his arrival that Meyer went missing. We'd finished our homework and returned to our studies when we were all called back for a house meeting. We sat in our lunch places and swapped ideas about what might have happened to cause such an extraordinary turn of events. Then the white door in the far corner of the room opened with its pained, squeaky click and Fairfax entered, pipe in hand.

Fairfax was a performer, always confident that he could get a laugh out of his captive audience or cow them into silence but something rang false about his tone on this occasion. Even I could see that he was trying to put a positive spin on something that could turn out to be very serious indeed.

"We seem to have mislaid a boy," he said. "Neither hide nor hair of young Mr. Meyer has been seen since lunchtime. So I am going to need your assistance to track him down before we have to inform the police and start dragging the river which will be very embarrassing indeed."

He divided us into groups and told us where to search, the younger boys in the house and its grounds, the older boys in the town. Nigel Castell, a boy in our year who never tired of telling us about his father's glorious exploits as a colonel in the First Battalion of the Royal Anglian regiment, took it upon himself to organise our particular group and the situation was too serious for us to waste time arguing with him.

Castell announced that he and I would search the private side garden—a wide, neat lawn, a ridged and furrowed vegetable patch and a stretch of scrubby no man's land with a compost heap and a shed sloping down to Cooper's Lane. It was late and the light was turning and I remember being scared that I would stumble on Meyer's body. A boy from home had told us about his father finding a man who had hanged himself in Bettles Copse and I was haunted by the picture he painted of the bloated tongue sticking out of the swollen, purple face and, worst of all, the fact that the dead man had an erection.

To our relief we found nothing and Castell was heading back

to the house when I decided, on the spur of the moment, to turn round. I was remembering, I think, a beech tree in the local park that I used to climb when I was unhappy and be comforted by the idea that I was floating above the world, looking down on everything while remaining unseen. And there he was, in the big oak above the shed, looking less like a boy who had climbed a tree than someone who had been dropped into one. He lifted his hand and waved at me, the way children on bridges wave at cars passing underneath. He was holding an envelope in his other hand. I don't know why I didn't just head back up the garden and tell Fairfax that I'd found him and let other people talk him down. Perhaps it was those childhood memories. I'd not climbed the tree before. Climbing trees was something I associated with being much younger and I always made an effort to seem as grown-up as possible at school. It took me only a few minutes, however, using the roof of the shed as a staging post, to reach him. I found a safe perch on a stout branch nearby.

"I guess everyone's looking for me."

"Fairfax is going a bit mental about it. Worrying that you might be dead and everything."

"I've been up here for a long time."

"The letter."

"Yeah."

"Is that the reason you're hiding?"

"I'm not hiding. I'm more sort of . . ." He stopped and became serious. "Do your parents love each other?"

It was the kind of question that would normally get you punched but it caught me so off guard that I answered it honestly. "No, I don't think they do."

"But they're still together, right?"

"Yeah. They're still together. My father goes to church so he's not meant to get divorced and my mother wouldn't want people to know her as a divorcee because being a divorcee's . . ." "Vulgar" was the word I was looking for but I'd never had this kind of conversation before and it was like speaking a foreign language. "So they're kind of stuck together."

Meyer let out a long, slow breath.

"Are yours getting divorced?"

He nodded, more to himself than to me.

"That's life, isn't it." I sounded like Fairfax—*You have to be a man about these things*—and I was embarrassed by this but didn't know what else to say. "Might even be for the best. For everyone."

"Thanks for, you know, being a good man about this."

"No problem." In truth I was starting to regret the whole conversation and was worried that Meyer would now consider me his friend.

"She's moving to London. And I won't be able to see her."

"You can go to London."

"As in, like, I won't be allowed to see her. As in my father won't let me."

"Because . . ."

There was a long silence before he said, "She was having . . ." He paused to choose the right word. ". . . an affair with another man."

"Right." I was embarrassed by my own humdrum life and the idea of a parent having an affair had an enviable air of sophistication about it.

"You won't tell anyone about this, will you?"

"Of course not." It was one thing for a prefect to tell everyone about a junior boy crying in the toilets. Sharing secrets about someone in your own year ran the risk of you being branded a squealer and coming off worse.

"He took photographs of her."

"Yeah?"

"You know, like, nude photographs. My sister found two of them. In a drawer. She showed them to our father. That's why he won't let us see her. He says if she goes to court he'll use the photographs as evidence."

"Wow."

"That's why I'm here. My father works overseas. I went to a day school before but there's no one at home now. And he's selling the house so he can move somewhere cheaper."

My head spun. The story seemed to come from an X-rated film. There was a composure and a worldliness about the way Meyer told me these things that I couldn't help but compare to my tears after hearing of my grandfather's death.

We sat for a long time looking through the branches, across the garden, the school chapel turning slowly into a silhouette as the sun set behind it. The first bats were starting to emerge, scooping insects from the air in great slicing dives.

"We'd better get back inside. You know, before Fairfax calls in the tracker dogs."

"Do you hate it?" asked Meyer.

"Hate what?"

"This place. The school. Because I really, really hate it."

It seems an obvious question in retrospect but no one talked about hating the school. They hated individual masters, they hated cricket or geography, they hated homework or having to get weekly report cards filled in by teachers, they hated other boys. But none of that hatred was directed at the institution that contained and sustained all these things. Even those it singularly failed to protect seemed blind to its shortcomings. Perhaps everyone felt some version of the indebtedness I felt when my parents suggested I apply for a place at the school. This was a privilege for which people had made sacrifices and to scorn it would be graceless.

I was still working out how to answer when Meyer lifted the letter. "He said, 'Don't expect to see your mother again.' Like, those actual words." His voice cracked a little and he closed his eyes while he calmed himself. "I hate both of them. I hate this place. I don't think I have a home any more. I just want . . . I don't know what I want."

I was out of my depth. I had never had a conversation of this kind with anyone. Real darkness was starting to come down, house lights appearing one by one in the silhouette of roofs on the far side of Cooper Lane. A string of golden street lamps climbed the hill to the sports ground. There was a cherry-coloured star at the summit of the radio mast in the distance.

"OK. I'm going in. Are you coming with me? We can go and see Fairfax together if you want."

Meyer turned and looked straight at me for the first time. "You won't tell anyone about this, right? The letter and everything?"

I stood on the shed roof and looked back up at him. "Hey. What kind of person do you think I am?"

"Just, you know, some of the boys can be really unkind." He lost his footing, slipped and caught himself. He had clearly not spent his childhood climbing trees.

"You all right, or do you need a hand?"

"I'll be fine." He stepped onto the roof beside me.

"We can probably jump from here."

As promised, I went with Meyer to Fairfax's study and I saw a look of relief on the housemaster's face as we stepped into the room before he composed himself, furrowed his brows and said, gruffly, "So, what's the story?"

Meyer was going to speak but I cut him off. "Meyer had some really bad news, sir. He just needed to be on his own."

I went to bed that night gratified that I'd done a good thing, not just that I'd found Meyer and helped placate Fairfax (he sent us both off to bed at the same time saying, "Don't give everyone a bloody scare like that again") but because I had been kind to someone I didn't particularly like and, in return, they had opened up to me and trusted me with something valuable. It felt like a new skill, something I didn't realise I could do. I enjoyed the image of myself rising above the pettiness of boys who flicked each other with wet towels and dribbled into smaller boys' dinners when they weren't watching. Not that Meyer and I could be friends as such, but we shared an understanding and for all that we were looked down upon we were in some ways better than those who mocked us.

Meyer missed breakfast the following morning and came in last to lunch. As was often the case, the only remaining space was beside me. Understandably everyone wanted to know where he'd been when we were all out hunting for him the previous evening.

Meyer shrugged. "I had some bad news. I wanted to be on my own."

It was the tone I'd heard when we were sitting next to one another in the tree and it clearly had a similar effect on everyone round the table because there were no sarcastic comebacks from anyone.

Then he put his hand on my shoulder and said, "This here is a good chap," the way my father might if he were talking with friends in the pub. "He found me and brought me back."

I moved my shoulder out from under his hand but it was too late. Further down the table Pattinson was doing a mime in which he parted a pair of imaginary buttocks and licked the arsehole between them with long, lascivious strokes. Everyone was laughing and slapping the table and thenceforth, for many, many weeks, Meyer and I were referred to as "lovebirds" or "bum-chums."

I challenged Meyer when we were getting dressed for rugby.

"What did you have to say that for?"

"What?"

"That I was a good chap."

He seemed genuinely puzzled. "It was a compliment."

"It made them think we were friends."

"Aren't we friends?"

"No. We're not friends."

"Why not?"

"Because . . . because you always say the wrong thing."

"But you *were* good. You were kind to me."

"You say shit like that."

"It's true."

"It's not true. I wasn't being kind. Fairfax sent us to look for you."

"I told you about my parents and you said yours didn't love one another."

I shoved Meyer hard so that he fell back against his sports locker with a loud *clank* and slid onto the bench beneath.

"Lovers' tiff!" shouted someone from the doorway and for once, I was glad of the interruption which cut the conversation short.

That should have been the end of it. A couple of days and everyone else would have found a new joke or a new victim. But Meyer wanted to demonstrate to all and sundry that there was nothing between us and he did this in ways that were awkward and ostentatious and kept providing fuel for the lovers' tiff joke which ran and ran until the whole thing came to a head a couple weeks later when we were in the washrooms getting ready for bed. A prefect, Rowntree, was on duty and we were queueing up to use the eight basins. The boy beside me finished brushing his teeth and walked away. Meyer was next in the queue. At which point he insisted on performing a little pantomime, stepping aside and offering the vacant basin to the next boy in the queue to make it absolutely clear that he didn't want to clean his teeth beside me. Everyone noticed and a quiet chant of "Lovers' tiff, lovers' tiff . . ." began until Rowntree barked, "What on earth is going on?" and a boy called Hill, who would later become a professional actor, said, without a moment's pause and in a broad, camp, Yorkshire accent, "Well, you see, Carol, these two young, handsome lads were deeply, deeply in love, but something has torn them asunder." I don't know if it was an impersonation of someone on TV, or a character from a film, or whether it was a spontaneous invention but it was so well done that the humourless Rowntree was stunned briefly into silence and even I thought it was quite funny.

Everyone erupted in laughter and Rowntree clapped his hands loudly. "Enough!" He was one of those people who had an obsessive terror of anything vaguely homosexual, who looked for it like a spaniel hunting truffles and felt it was their duty to stamp out any hint of the contagion before it spread. He looked directly at me. "Is there any truth in this?"

"In what?"

"In this story."

"This story that what?"

"Don't be a bloody ass, boy. This story that you and Meyer have been indulging in . . . foolishness."

Some boy in the background was quietly singing, ". . . sitting in a tree, K. I. S. S. I. N. G."

"Be quiet," snapped Rowntree, and turned back to me. "I asked you a question."

I was terrified. I was unused to being in trouble, having spent my life avoiding activities where I might end up having to defend myself, physically or verbally. Rowntree walked over and leant close to my face. "Are you deaf?" He was wearing Brut 33 aftershave and I could see the blackheads on his nose. I heard a faint "Oooh . . ." from a couple of boys behind me, the same noise someone always made when a fight was brewing. I should have just politely said, "No," and let Rowntree get bored or distracted—it would have taken only seconds—but I couldn't bear being the focus of his anger, I couldn't bear being the focus of anyone's anger. And maybe if Meyer had been in my line of sight I might not have said it, but I wanted someone else to be under the spotlight, I wanted to placate Rowntree, I wanted to prove that I didn't care for Meyer.

I said, "He ran away because his father wrote him a letter. His mother was having an affair. The man took nude photos of her. His sister found them."

The room erupted, in the way a football stadium erupts when a goal is scored. Boys were cheering and whooping. I don't know how Meyer reacted, or Rowntree. I know only that I had become suddenly, blessedly invisible. I took my toothbrush and my flannel and my washbag and slipped away to my bed.

The following morning Meyer came downstairs to find a centrefold from a porn mag glued to his and Barnes's study door with PVA which had dried overnight so that he had to scrape it off with a butter knife. Above the picture were written the words *MEYER'S MOTHER* with a thick black felt tip. Using a biro someone had written on the picture itself *Mucho fuckable*.

Meyer was crying while he tried to remove the picture. Barnes, predictably, was completely unfazed. Inevitably, other boys gathered to gawp. At some point Meyer snapped. He turned and grabbed hold of one of the boys who was jeering at him emboldened by the seeming safety of the crowd, a boy whose name I now forget though I can see him clearly. He was two years older than Meyer, taller but lanky, with pale skin and an incipient moustache. Whether Meyer was stronger and tougher than any of us gave him credit for or whether his rage and shame had briefly turned him into a different person I don't know, but he threw the older boy to the floor and started punching him in the face. The fight was greeted with those same jubilant cheers for the first few seconds until everyone realised that Meyer was going to do serious damage, at which point a group of older boys leapt on him and pulled him away. I remember someone in my year who'd seen the fight saying, excitedly, that Meyer was "frothing like a mad dog, I mean literally frothing from his mouth."

The housemaster was informed and Matron was called in to patch up the injured boy who had a black eye and badly split, swollen lips, top and bottom. Meyer himself was beaten six times by Fairfax on the grounds that he had been too lenient after his disappearance and now needed to make amends to ensure that Meyer learnt to behave like a decent human being. We know this because the housemaster told us during one of his occasional lectures in which he expounded on significant decisions he had made, sometimes quoting Cicero, as if he, too, were a great jurist passing down his wisdom. Interrupting this particular lecture, which happened some months later, one of the more forward boys said, "What about the picture on his door, sir?"—less because he was outraged on Meyer's behalf than because you could earn points, both from other boys and sometimes from Fairfax himself, with a robust challenge and a good argument.

"I know nothing of any picture," said Fairfax. "I deal in principles."

The following morning a new naked centrefold was glued to Meyer and Barnes's door. Again Meyer scraped it off with a knife. The performance happened every morning for the following two weeks. It stopped, I guess, only because porn mags were valuable contraband, most of them brought into the house by Warner, an older boy from Leeds who returned to the school at the beginning of every term with a hundred or so copies of *Mayfair, Penthouse* and *Readers' Wives* packed beneath the shirts and trousers in his trunk. (He had a top-of-the-range Bang & Olufsen turntable, purchased with the profits from his business, and even now, long after the demise of the top shelf in the newsagents, I can't see a high-end turntable without thinking of teenage boys furtively masturbating.)

I managed to avoid Meyer for several days, hoping it would all just blow over. I'd never before had to sit with the knowledge that I'd deliberately hurt someone and it was excruciating. I longed for him to start a fight. For the first time I understood that a fight might actually be a good way of resolving a disagreement. I would have happily accepted that black eye and a cut lip simply to get rid of this relentless, twisting discomfort in my stomach. Then we found ourselves sitting together at evening prayers waiting for Mendes, the house tutor, to come through from the private side. Meyer turned and stared at me for a long time. I refused to turn and look back at him. Eventually he said, "You're a coward." He paused. "I'm disappointed, but I understand why you did it."

I looked him full in the face and hissed, as quietly as I could, "I'm not a fucking coward."

He tilted his head to one side and creased his forehead and said, "But you *are*," not so much a disagreement as genuine surprise that I could doubt something so obviously true. "It's OK, though, because I forgive you."

I might have hit him but the door opened with its squeaky click, Mendes came in, we got to our feet and Macintosh, the senior music scholar, started hammering out the first line of "Eternal Father, Strong to Save" on the house piano.

Most of the time Meyer managed to rise above the taunts but he would often do so by adopting that same grating, faux-adult persona which only encouraged his aggressors. Underneath it all sat the tantalising knowledge that if they worked out how to needle him in just the right way he might erupt in another thrilling show of unrestrained violence. So whilst the mystery bill poster gave up decorating Meyer's study door (which bore a ghostly rectangle and the indented words *Mucho fuckable* for the rest of my school career), boys would regularly ask Meyer what colour his Mum's pubes were, or he would overhear someone in a nearby toilet cubicle pretending to be wanking over the now mythical photographs. "Oh, oh, oh . . . Mrs. Meyer . . . Yes, suck it harder, yes, yes!"

I look back now and realise that Meyer was becoming seriously unwell, but this was the 1970s and I don't remember anyone discussing the possibility that children might be depressed. It was rare enough to hear about adult depression. Even now I can see my mother doing an affected little shiver and rolling her eyes at the idea, as if it were a thing you might find people from London indulging in. There were normal people and there were mad people. The latter had nervous breakdowns and went into psychiatric hospitals, a subject that was avoided with the same queasy distaste as what those mythical men in raincoats did with children after they'd lured them into their cars with free sweets.

If you were watching from a distance you might have thought that the bullying was dying down but I learnt something that year which I've never forgotten. Punch someone repeatedly in the same place and the bruising means you can cause the same pain with a fraction of the original effort. Boys would pass Meyer and simply make the noise of a camera shutter or narrow their eyes and let out a tiny groan meaning *I've just ejaculated all over a picture of your mother,* and you could see it hit home. He refused to tell anyone her name so she was christened Gladys. I remember opening at least three hymn books at the beginning of house prayers and finding a naked woman biroed on the flyleaf with huge breasts and vast amounts of pubic hair (this for some reason, was deemed to be part of the joke) and the word *Gladys* written underneath. There were doubtless many more because word finally reached the housemaster who asked everyone, sternly, at the end of one house lunch, "Who is Gladys?" at which laughter erupted and several boys shouted "Yes!" and punched the air as if this public announcement were the aim of the whole campaign.

The following term Meyer cut his wrist with a bread knife. I didn't see this event either but I did see one of the boys who wrestled the knife from him and he was covered in blood—hands, shirt, face, hair—as was the bathroom beside the junior dormitory where he'd done the deed. A bloody handprint on the rim of a basin also sticks in my mind. It seems extraordinary now that this did not ring a loud enough alarm bell, that there were no repercussions for the bullies and that Meyer himself was not offered some kind of support. I don't think he even saw a doctor. Matron bandaged him up and he was given a talking-to by Fairfax. What the housemaster said I have no idea. Meyer was obviously not going to tell us and Fairfax never talked about the encounter. I'm guessing he told Meyer that many people went through a rocky patch during their teenage years, that things would get better and that he should man up and make his father proud. Marcus Aurelius may have been quoted.

Otherwise, little changed. He was given a few days' grace while the bandage was still visible under his shirt cuff, then the jokes started again. There were fewer tormentors this time around. We could all see that this was moving into darker, unmapped territory and some boys no longer wanted to be involved, but others took it as a challenge and the jokes about his mother were now interleaved with jokes about knives, self-harm and suicide. Most were obvious and puerile but the one that sticks in my mind is that whenever he sat down to a meal in the house someone always switched the cutlery around so that he had two forks instead of a knife and a fork. I'm still unsure why such a small thing was so hurtful, though I could see that it was. Was it the fact that it happened three times a day every day for months on end? Because it was mockery masquerading as care? Did the very mundane nature of the joke suggest that there was no escape?

The days were long gone when he made any effort to join in, to curry favour, to be liked. He knew it would only open him up to more abuse. His violent outbursts had stopped, too, replaced by what looked like a sullen acceptance of his lot. From a distance he looked as if he were carrying a big, invisible rucksack.

He played rugby for a while and it might, in other circumstances, have been his salvation. He was not coordinated but he was strong and heavy and tall, and if you fed him the ball he was hard to stop. I was on the touchline for an inter-house juniors game when he tackled a fly half from Davenant and instead of driving him to the ground, hit him in the gut with his shoulder, hoisted him high into the air, dumped him, then landed on top of him, breaking four ribs. It was thrilling, like something out of a nature documentary. The boy was taken away on a stretcher and spent the night in hospital in Nottingham. Equally remarkable was the reaction of the rest of the team who crowded around Meyer in approbation as if they were all best friends. By suppertime everyone knew the story and Meyer was shrugging off requests to tell it from his point of view. When Fairfax congratulated the team after house prayers he said, "It would be indelicate of me to celebrate an event in which a boy belonging to another house ended up in hospital but delicacy can, I think, be overrated."

Meyer refused to play again. Instead he took up cross-country running. He was no runner and I suspect part of the appeal was that once you were out of sight of the master in charge you could slow down and have a solitary walk in the countryside three afternoons a week.

By this time I'd found my own escape in the camera club, having inherited a Nikon F2 Photomic SLR from my father when he traded up. Stop baths and fixer, clothes pegs and squeegees. I spent long hours in the darkroom behind the art block, developing tasteful black-and-white pictures of winter trees and old men on benches and sheep at the fortnightly farmers' market in town.

I kept my distance from Meyer. I was afraid that something terrible was going to happen and I wanted to be as far away as possible when it did. In the event I was in the same room and I saw it happen right in front of me.

This would have been mid-February, during the second term of our third year. I remember that it was a Friday. (The menus were so repetitive that even now I associate Fridays with thin pork slices and tepid gravy, and a pudding of pastry baked with a layer of jam on it which we knew as *millimetre pie*.) We noticed that Meyer was not with us but this was not unusual. We'd grown used to his erratic behaviour and his company never made a meal more enjoyable so we were happy to leave him be, wherever he was. We were heading back to our studies afterwards when we heard a commotion on the stairs at the end of the corridor so I followed a handful of boys upstairs to the junior dormitory.

Meyer was standing on a chair in the middle of the room. He'd fashioned a noose from his thick, baby-blue dressing-gown cord, tied one end around the beam above his head and put the noose itself round his neck. The noose was tight and there was very little slack in the cord. It was early afternoon but he was wearing his pyjamas and he was weeping despite his blank expression.

There seemed to be an invisible barrier around him, holding all of us back. I couldn't bring myself to step into the circle. Perhaps it was shame. Perhaps I didn't want to be seen as Meyer's good Samaritan.

He didn't move, just gazed over everyone's heads into some imaginary distance. There was silence for a brief period, then someone said, under their breath, "Do it . . . Do it . . . Do it . . ."

I can't have been the only person who was horrified by this but the taunter was not going to be put off by the lack of response and when a second boy joined in—"Do it . . . Do it . . ."—I felt the centre of gravity shift in the crowd. A third boy joined in and the chant became louder, there was no embarrassment and the excitement was palpable. "Do it . . . Do it . . . Do it . . . Do it . . ."

Still Meyer didn't move. I desperately wanted him to remove the noose and to get down off the chair before anything horrible happened.

"Do it . . . Do it . . ."

"What the bloody hell is going on up here?" It was Rowntree again. The chanting was so loud and I was so engrossed in what was happening that I hadn't heard the sound of his shoes on the bare wooden boards. He pushed his way through the circle of boys into the centre and came to a halt, clearly taken aback by the sight of Meyer standing on the chair. The chanting died away.

"Get down from there, boy. Get down now."

Meyer seemed as oblivious to Rowntree's command as he'd been to the group of boys yelling at him to kill himself. Still that blank stare straight ahead.

"Can you hear what I'm saying? Stop being a bloody arse and get off that chair."

He'd stepped inside the circle. He was committed. There was now a new entertainment for everyone, with two people involved and no way of knowing what was going to happen.

"Meyer? I'm warning you."

Rowntree couldn't climb up on the chair, he couldn't cut the dressing-gown cord, he couldn't lift Meyer down, but he had to do something.

"Meyer? I am seriously going to lose my rag if you don't listen to me and stop this nonsense immediately."

I still have a very clear memory of looking at Meyer's face—the tears, his complete detachment from everything going on around him—and thinking that his failure to react in any way to Rowntree shouting at him was a surer sign of his troubled mental state than the fact that he was about to hang himself, such was the fear prefects were usually able to generate.

"Meyer? Jesus wept . . ."

Standing at the back of the little crowd, Hill cupped his hands over his mouth and said, in the hushed voice of a sports commentator, "Rowntree is facing a tricky opponent here. You can feel the tension in the stadium." And this, I think, was the moment when something in Rowntree snapped.

He wanted to find out who was mocking him and punish them but he couldn't turn his attention away from Meyer. He yelled, "Meyer!" as if he were calling him back from the far side of the sports ground even though there was not more than a couple of feet between them. Then he kicked the chair away, hard.

Perhaps he was thinking that the dressing-gown cord would snap under Meyer's weight. Perhaps he wasn't thinking. Perhaps he didn't care.

Meyer fell for maybe two feet and came to a ghastly, yanking halt mid-air, his surprised yelp choked off as the cord snapped tight. It can't have been longer than a second at most, but everyone seemed to freeze and watch him, spellbound, his feet pedalling madly, one hand on the cord above his head desperately trying to take some of the weight.

Rowntree bent down, gripped Meyer round the knees, hoisted him and yelled, "Someone get the chair. The fucking chair, for Christ's sake."

The chair was picked up and brought into the circle and it was obvious to pretty much everyone that one of the legs was badly bent, but Rowntree wasn't looking at the chair and the boy holding it didn't have the guts to point out the problem.

"Just put it back in the same place."

The boy put the chair back and Rowntree lowered Meyer onto it. The chair took his weight for a few moments, Rowntree let go of Meyer's legs and breathed out an audible sigh of relief, then there was a loud crack, the bent leg snapped and Meyer fell for a second time. Rowntree dipped down, grabbed him and hoisted him once more and Hill cupped his hand over his mouth and said, "Very tricky passage of play here for Rowntree and he's not handling it well."

"Get another bloody chair!" shouted Rowntree but his face was pressed between Meyer's legs and his voice was muffled so that no one reacted and he had to lean backwards and shout for a second time, "Get another chair!"

Meyer's face was purple, his eyes were closed and his head was lolling to one side. The noose was still tight around his neck. A second chair appeared and was slid into place. Rowntree lowered Meyer's feet onto it, relaxed his grip, stepped back and breathed heavily. "Just . . . don't . . . move . . . all right?" Meyer was heavy and holding him up had clearly been hard work. He was also, clearly, not fully conscious at this point and started falling to one side so that Rowntree was forced to grab hold of him again.

At some point in the middle of this I remember looking away and seeing one of the boys in my year (Jencks? Jenner?) lying face down on the wooden floor beside a bed as if he were asleep. The following morning he appeared at breakfast with a raw, red scrape down the side of his face. He must have passed out at some point during the proceedings and hit the ground face first, though we never did get to find out more because he refused, point-blank, to talk about it.

A third chair arrived. Someone was thinking logically at last. Under instruction from Rowntree, a small group of other boys ringed Meyer and held him in place while Rowntree climbed onto the new chair so that he could release the noose from around Meyer's neck. The cord must have jammed itself tight when Meyer fell for the first time because Rowntree was finding it hard getting sufficient grip on the stretched towelling, swearing quietly to himself as he worked away at it. "Shit . . . shit . . . shit . . . shit . . ." The fact that his hands were visibly shaking must have made it doubly difficult.

Finally the cord came loose and he was able to lift it over Meyer's head. Either Meyer's half-conscious mind now knew that he could relax or the cord itself had been holding him upright, because his legs buckled, he fell into the arms of the boys trying to hold him, Rowntree lost his balance, the two chairs toppled and everyone hit the floor like a pyramid of collapsed gymnasts at the circus.

Meyer was being put into the recovery position (first aid was one of the only useful skills we learnt as cadets) when Fairfax appeared in the doorway and I knew that he was panicking even before he opened his mouth to ask what was going on, because he was wearing only one slipper. We were ushered quickly away and told to get ready for games.

We heard an ambulance siren as we sat in the changing room and a few of us got a glimpse of Meyer being stretchered into the back of the vehicle. Other than that we heard nothing more until a different prefect knocked on my door midway through the evening and I was told to go to the housemaster's study where I found myself in the company of all the other boys who had been in the dormitory earlier in the day, Rowntree included.

Fairfax let the silence run so that we would hear only the lopsided ticking of his grandfather clock and the distant croak of rooks in the big trees outside. "The good news is that Meyer is alive." He picked at the little green tassels which fringed the arm of his chair. "The bad news is that he has suffered, as far as I have been made aware, serious injuries as a result of his misadventure." Two boys passed the window on their way back from orchestra practice, one carrying a violin case, the other a flute in a black box, their shoes crunching on the gravel. "How they will affect him only time will tell. Certainly he will be needing a great deal of medical attention and will not be returning to the school." He paused and it seemed to me that he made slow and deliberate eye contact with every single boy in the room before continuing. "This was a terrible tragedy, a tragedy for Meyer, and a tragedy for his family. We'll never know what led up to Meyer taking this decision—such is the nature of these things—but we can all be grateful that Rowntree happened to be there at exactly the right moment, otherwise it could have been even worse." He paused for a second time and waited.

I put my hand up. I felt ashamed of the way I'd frozen in the dormitory. Perhaps I could now make amends by telling the truth.

"What is it?" asked Fairfax.

"He kicked the chair away, sir. Rowntree kicked the chair away."

Fairfax kept his eyes on me and turned his head very slightly to one side, the way you might if you think you've misheard something important. The silence deepened and stretched. The clock, the rooks. I had the sense that the air had become peculiarly clear, the way it does on snowy winters' mornings, so that if I listened really carefully I would be able to hear the lowing of cattle and the clang of metal gates on farms across the county, the roar of cars and lorries on the M1, individual birds in individual trees from coast to coast.

Fairfax stared at me. I knew what I had to say to make the silence end. *I could have been mistaken, sir.* I was not going to say it. To say it was a lie. But not saying it was like holding a heavy weight. Like Rowntree holding Meyer. I could only do it for so long. And no one was going to step in to help me.

I gave in. "I could have been mistaken, sir."

He maintained the stare for a few seconds longer, then nodded slowly and seriously. “Indeed.”

I was terrified that Rowntree would take some kind of revenge on me and that his failure to meet my eye when we passed in the corridor was merely him choosing his moment and ramping up my terror in advance. It took several weeks for me to realise that nothing was going to happen. Indeed, none of the boys in Fairfax’s study that evening mentioned my intervention and on the couple of occasions when I tried to bring it up I was pointedly ignored. Everyone accepted Fairfax’s version of events. Disturbingly, when I was asked about the evening by boys in my class from other houses even I found myself falling in line as if I was under the influence of a stage hypnotist.

For a period I was genuinely worried that I was going to lose my mind. There was no longer any solid foundation to the world. It was all just stories. At night especially, when I couldn’t get to sleep, I felt a kind of wheeling existential dizziness which threatened to capsize me completely. It was then that I began writing down my own version of the events as carefully and accurately as I could in a small green exercise book with a sugar-paper cover and graph-paper pages. I hid the book at the bottom of my own trunk under the checked rug my mother always insisted on packing in case I needed an extra cover on my bed but which I was always too embarrassed to use. Sometimes I needed only to touch the book in order to be reassured of its existence. I thought about it daily and after a while that thought was itself enough to gently bring the separate parts of my world together again and make them whole.

A sombre atmosphere settled over the house for several few weeks after Meyer’s departure. The oddest thing, looking back, is that while other boys wanted to know the grisly details of the hanging (including whether Meyer had *a stiffy*), I don’t remember anyone wondering what happened to him after he was taken away, what injuries he'd sustained, whether he was permanently disabled, whether he was alive or dead. Fairfax never mentioned the subject again, as if when you left the school you simply ceased to exist and questions about where you were or what you were doing were meaningless.

He wasn't forgotten, however. Only a few weeks later one of the boys in the first year who'd been naive enough to bring a teddy bear to school came upstairs to find that it had been discovered in his bedside cupboard and hanged by the neck from *Meyer's rafter* using the boy's own dressing-gown cord. A story began to circulate that Meyer had died and that the junior dormitory was haunted by his ghost. From then on the tale would be told at some length to every group of new boys at the start of their first term. An hour or so later when they were all asleep an older boy would climb the wooden partitions beside the bed of one of the most credulous boys and fall onto him with a dressing-gown cord around his neck, flour on his face, his eyes closed and his tongue sticking out as if he were the body of the dormitory's former occupant.

As for the real Graham Meyer, it would be over thirty years before I found out what happened to him.

2010

I had little contact with the school after I left. The handful of friendships I'd made, such as they were, did not survive the distances we had to travel to see one another now that we were no longer brought back together at the beginning of every term. I didn't mind greatly. It was a relief to put the place behind me. I went to university and made new friends and was glad to have a life with more freedom and real privacy. The magazine of the old boys' association arrived every year thanks to a string of diligent forwarders and I always flicked through the news items before recycling it. The choir was recording a CD of carols, someone had raised £27,000 for the RAF benevolent fund by cycling to Istanbul, another alumnus was now chancellor of Leicester University. Occasionally I would recognise a former pupil in the news. Martin Hill was a regular cast member in a long-running medical drama. Carl Rowntree was a backbench Tory MP for a rural constituency in the West Country with a raft of antediluvian opinions on the subjects of immigrants, single mothers and fox hunting. Alistair Bird, with whom I'd shared some science lessons, had gone to prison for killing his wife, a case that had made the front pages because of the way he had tried to disguise the murder as an accident in which she had been run over by their own car after failing to put the brake on.

On this occasion, however, I saw that a reunion was being held in central London on a night when I had nothing else planned, and perhaps that was all it came down to in the end, that the opportunity presented itself during a period in my life when empty weekends hung heavy and I was glad of a distraction.

My marriage had recently come to an end. The thunderbolt had arrived out of what I naively thought was a clear blue sky. We had two children, Anita and Paolo. True, I worked long hours, but we had a beautiful house in a clean, safe, leafy neighbourhood, the children went to good schools and we took two holidays every year, one to somewhere hot in the summer for Martina (Crete, Croatia, Morocco . . .) and one in the spring to somewhere cooler with mountains for me (Switzerland, Norway . . .).

During the conversation in which she announced her departure I said that I thought we had a really good life together and she replied, "I want more," and the impression she gave was not of someone who was greedy but of someone who was desperately sad. I said that I didn't understand. She replied, "I'm having an affair. Are you not going to get angry?" and I had no idea how to reply.

It made sense for Anita and Paolo to live with their mother because of the aforementioned long hours so I offered to move into an apartment not too far away. Only afterwards did I wonder if this was another fight I had conceded too easily. Anita and Paolo came round for meals but never used the spare bedroom. "Count your blessings," said Martina, referring, I think, to the mess they made, but she was right in a wider sense, too. I had my health, I had work, I had a place to live, I saw my children most weeks. A good friend had died of a heart attack so catastrophic that being within a hundred yards of St. Thomas' A & E counted for nothing. Another friend's wife had taken their three children to Australia, and whilst the law was on his side any fight would be costly and the resulting bitterness counterproductive.

My parents had been less lucky. A couple of years previously my father had disappeared for five inexplicable and agonising days. A walker eventually found his body in a deep, grassy ditch beside a quiet road some seven miles from the village where they lived. The subsequent post-mortem suggested that he had died on the first day of his disappearance. A policeman explained that a car must have struck him at considerable speed, breaking his knees and leaving flakes of metallic blue paint in the head wound he probably sustained when he struck the bonnet, details I sorely wish I'd never heard and which haunted me for a long time. What my father was doing walking along that particular road was, and remained, a mystery. The car was never traced.

Friends and members of the wider family claimed that it was my father's disappearance which instigated my mother's rapid decline, but I spent those five days with her and I saw that something was already very wrong. Either my parents had kept it from me and everyone else, or their repetitive daily routine had provided sufficient scaffolding to hold her disintegrating mind together. She couldn't bear to be alone for more than a few minutes and would repeatedly call for help, though whenever I came to find her, the question she wanted answering was always trivial. What time was it? What were we having for lunch? The knowledge that her husband had vanished seemed to come and go, and even when she was aware of it she didn't seem to be able to understand the seriousness of the situation. Sometimes she would be frightened but more often she would ask me where he'd gone in a mildly puzzled tone of voice as if he might have popped out to the shops.

There were moments of clarity when she knew that she had a form of dementia. It was something she had always dreaded—"Shoot me if I start losing my mind," she had said often and unhelpfully—so it came as a surprise to find that in those moments of clarity she was remarkably sanguine. I remember her saying, "Everything seems OK, but then I try to do something that should be easy, like locking the house at night, and I can't remember where we keep the back door key. Yet most of the time I feel fine. It's strange, isn't it."

If it wasn't the cause of her decline, my father's death was certainly an accelerant. She was incapable of living safely on her own and a regime of daily visits from care workers lasted only six months during which she complained bitterly and repeatedly about all of them because they cleaned badly or failed to heat her soup sufficiently or they "smelt wrong." I met the one who did indeed "smell wrong" (a combination of soft cheese and mothballs that stayed with me for the rest of the afternoon) but she seemed cheerful and proficient. So I was relieved when my mother accidentally set light to her kitchen and I had to arrange respite care which turned into rolling respite which then became permanent.

Most Sundays I would drive to Norfolk and back and I hope it doesn't sound too cold to say that I looked forward to the chance to listen to audiobooks in the car on the way there and back more than I looked forward to the hour of circular conversations, milky tea and digestive biscuits in between.

All of which is a very roundabout way of saying that a peculiar kind of loneliness attached itself to Saturday evenings and a meal with a group of middle-aged men who'd gone to the same school offered at the very least some kind of distraction. The fact that a speech was promised from Carl Rowntree MP only added a certain ghoulish fascination.

The dinner took place at a club on Whitehall Court near Embankment station, one road back from the river. The ground and first floor were cartoon Victoriana, all beeswaxed wooden panelling, studded red leather and staff in pinstriped waistcoats. After our introductory drinks and mingling, however, we were herded upstairs to a third-floor function room which would not have been out of place in a provincial office block except for windows with the most extraordinary views across the Thames so that from where I was sitting I could see half of the Millennium Wheel turning slowly and the wing lights of jets as they made the last few miles of their descent into Heathrow to the west of the city.

I recognised a few people from school. Some of them had lost so much hair and put on so much weight that I made the connection only after reading their lapel badges. No Martin Hill, no Robert Barnes. I thought I'd made a terrible faux pas when I asked whether the latter had indeed been jailed for some grotesque sexual crime and was met by a brief, shocked silence, finally broken by someone from my house who laughed and said that Robert had clearly buried the bodies in sufficiently isolated woodland and had been a barrister for some time.

Rowntree himself was seated at the top table with the committee of the old boys' association and a couple of masters I recognised from my time at the school, Cooper-Wright who taught history and Dunning who taught chemistry. I felt simultaneously reassured and saddened to see that they were now quite clearly old men and that they were both much smaller than I remembered.

I had a laborious conversation with a man seated to my left who did something managerial for Shell which I didn't really understand at the time and couldn't remember afterwards, then turned to my right and found myself talking to a surgeon who specialised in complex cancers of the head and neck who was fascinating, though his description of a *particularly tricksy* fungating carcinoma was too much even for my strong stomach and I had to put the remains of my duck to one side.

When we had finished our dessert the chairman of the old boys' association got up to introduce the guest speaker. Many of the diners were drunk by this stage and he had to subdue a good deal of jeering before he could make himself heard. When Rowntree stood up, however, there was complete silence.

"A request has been made that I not be too political this evening."

"Shame!" came a cry from someone I couldn't see.

"So I am going to be very serious indeed." It was compelling, the way he altered the mood of the room as if he were simply turning a dial. "As you all doubtless know, Geoffrey Fairfax passed away last year. He was both my housemaster and the man who, for his sins, was tasked with teaching me Latin and Greek. I saw him on several occasions during his final illness and you'll not be surprised to hear that he remained articulate, opinionated and doggedly independent till the very end, despite being in a great deal of pain."

I felt wrong-footed to discover that Rowntree and Fairfax had become . . . was "friends" the right word?

"On the last of those occasions we were sitting in the garden of the hospice where he eventually passed away. It was snowing lightly but we were outside because nothing was going to stop him smoking his beloved pipe. I was shivering. He was wrapped in a blanket and was probably warmed by a good deal of morphine. I was able to tell him how big a part he had played in my life both as a teacher and as a role model. I was not the only one who felt that way. Indeed, he had been inundated with similar messages over the previous weeks. Those of you who were in any of his forms or in his house know how keen he was on quoting his favourite classical authors. On this occasion it was Catullus . . . '*Multas per gentes et multa per aequora vectus advenio has miseras, frater, ad inferias* . . . I have travelled among many people and across many oceans to come to these sad funeral rites, brother, so that I might deliver my final mourning gifts and speak in vain to your silent ashes . . .' I won't tax your patience by reciting the whole thing. Suffice to say I was deeply moved. This was him saying goodbye to me. This was him saying goodbye to the world, a world which is grateful for his presence and poorer for his absence . . . The final line of the poem runs, '*Atque in perpetuum, frater, ave atque vale* . . . And for ever, brother, hail and farewell.' "

We raised our glasses.

"Geoffrey Fairfax. *Ave atque vale*."

"*Ave atque vale!*"

I had braced myself for a speech from the boorish bigot I knew from TV and newspaper articles, perhaps even more boorish and bigoted now that he was on home ground.

"We've said some other sad goodbyes over the past twelve months. In July we lost Maxim Goldberg, choirmaster, exasperated hurler of batons, collector of rare stamps . . ."

The speech was perfectly crafted—five elegies for members of staff who had passed away in the previous year, arranged so that as the list progressed the stories attached to these men became funnier and more ribald. He told a story about another housemaster, Oscar Bakewell, who had died of a heart attack while out cycling at the age of ninety-six. One evening many years ago a boy in his house who had just performed poorly in one of the exams Bakewell himself had set snuck into Bakewell's private study in an attempt to find his paper and make some improving additions. Hearing Bakewell return early, however, he slipped round the housemaster's desk and stood as still as he could behind the curtains. Bakewell took off his coat, pulled out his chair, settled down and worked solidly at his desk for the next three hours. The boy was, of course, petrified and in increasing pain as time went on, hardly able to breathe for fear of making the curtains move. Shortly after midnight, the housemaster put down his pen, stretched and said, "Well, I don't know about you, but I'm off to bed." It had the ring of a story that had been told about many housemasters at many schools over the years but Rowntree told it well and everyone laughed.

He ended by talking about Jez Raven, a French teacher famous for his lunchtime drinking sessions and unfocused performance during early afternoon lessons. Short-sighted, short-tempered and foul-mouthed, he was also tasked with refereeing football games where he was known for blowing his whistle mainly when the action was happening too far away for him to see clearly, on the assumption that some boy was bound always to have committed an infraction of one kind or another. ". . . and who will ever forget the semi-final of the house cup between Portland and Wentworth which he threatened to stop because there was too much swearing by both sides? 'I've had one bugger, three shits and a fuck so far in this game. Any more and I'm sending you all off.'" Rowntree raised his glass. "To Jeremy Raven, wherever you may now be. I hope they have a decent bar with a wide selection of fine Scotch whiskies."

As the cheers died down he turned the dial one final time. "In a world full of division and anger it's good to know that some things still bind us together, that we can sit in this room and share these stories, that we can travel to the far corners of the world yet remain bound by our mutual history, that we can depend on one another, that we are brothers." He raised his glass and toasted the school and we all toasted with him.

He sat down, the chairman of the old boys' association thanked him, coffee and port were served, the seating plan disintegrated and a raucous, carnival atmosphere overtook the room. Further down my own table a song started up to the tune of the "Colonel Bogey March." "Paisley has only got one ball, Scunner has two but very small, Dinsdale Minor has a vagina, and poor old Foxy has no balls at all."

And that's when I saw Meyer. Graham. To my surprise he was talking to Rowntree, who had wandered over to his table. He had a thick, dark beard that was longer than his close-cropped black hair, giving him a severe, slightly Slavic demeanour, though he and Rowntree were laughing heartily enough at some shared joke. My surgeon had vanished so, intrigued, I decided to wander over. As I got closer I noticed a walking frame behind Graham's chair and realised that he was the man I had seen getting into the lift on the way upstairs.

I sat down directly across the table from them and, as one, they looked at me and stopped laughing. I assumed they had not recognised me, which was understandable given that this was the first such event I'd been to since leaving school, so I told them my name. Graham's face was a little lopsided. "Frobisher, seventy-six to eighty-one. For my sins." I wondered if his thick beard hid some kind of facial disfigurement.

"I know," said Graham. "You were over there talking to Craig Hartnell."

"I didn't expect to see you here."

"Why not?" said Graham. His expression was blank.

"Well, you didn't have the happiest time at school." He nodded and tilted his head slightly as if digesting this but said nothing. "It's good to see you nevertheless."

"Is it?" asked Graham.

Rowntree leant back in his chair and smiled broadly and I got the unnerving feeling that he was preparing to be entertained by the reunion between Graham and myself.

I held up my hands. "I'm sorry. I barged in and interrupted your conversation. My apologies."

"No apologies needed," said Rowntree smoothly, knitting his fingers over his belly and crossing his legs.

"So . . ." I was at a loss for words. I wanted to slip away but I felt trapped. I turned to Graham and tried to sound as warm as I could. "What are you doing with yourself these days?" I had the peculiar sensation I had not felt since those first few weeks at school three and a half decades ago when I was totally at sea among people who instinctively knew the rules I was clumsily breaking.

Graham paused briefly before answering. His tone was weary, as if he'd already told me these things several times and I had forgotten them. He and his wife had three children, all boys. He was the business manager for a large orchestra. They lived in High Wycombe. I waited for him to ask about me in turn but he didn't. He let the silence run in the way that Fairfax used to let silences run so as to keep his audience on the back foot.

I said, "I have obviously said or done the wrong thing. I'm not sure what it is but . . . my apologies."

Graham laughed noiselessly to himself. I remembered seeing him for the first time all those years ago in the house foyer, the trunk, the polished shoes, the too-small jacket, his inability to use his size to his advantage. Paradoxically, now that he walked using a frame, and despite the fact that he was sitting down, his physical presence was an imposing one, threatening almost when combined with his current stony glare.

He leant forward with his elbows on the table. "You see, I remember a conversation we had a very long time ago. In a tree of all places. I told you about a letter my father had sent me, and I asked you not to tell anyone else about it. But you told everyone about it and, well . . ." He indicated the legs which no longer worked properly. "Here we are."

When I first told Martina about Graham she said, "You can't put children in a place like that and expect them to behave like choirboys. You were fighting for survival." I remember how moved I was by hearing someone else saying this out loud. I wanted to say the same thing right now but it sounded petulant and self-centred.

Graham seemed to be reading my thoughts. "It all started with you though, didn't it. If you hadn't told them about the letter none of this would have happened. They'd have got bored and picked on someone else. And I might still be able to walk."

I was disturbed by this unexpected attack, but equally disturbed by the fact that Rowntree was still smiling contentedly, as if the two of them were a team and I was the victim of a game they had cooked up together.

I couldn't help myself. I gestured towards Rowntree and said, "He kicked the bloody chair away." I regretted saying it immediately. I sounded like a child.

Rowntree chuckled and slapped his knee as if he'd just won a bet that I would say precisely this. Graham's expression didn't change. He slowly folded his serviette into four and placed it down beside his half-full wine glass. "You always saw yourself as just that little bit better than everyone else, didn't you. Drifting at some Olympian height above the rest of us. Passing judgement."

"That's not fair."

In the corner of the room two men had removed their jackets and were climbing onto the backs of two other jacketless men preparatory, I assumed, to a piggyback-joust. I thought about the small green exercise book with its sugar-paper cover and graph-paper pages and wondered what had become of it.

Graham ignored my complaint. "Why did you come here?"

What was I meant to say? That I was bored? That I was lonely?

"This is not a restaurant. You don't just swan in and out. This is a community of people who look after one another."

I shifted in my chair preparatory to getting up and walking away but Graham's tone hardened and I found myself frozen and unable to move. "For month after month after month boys told me that they thought about my mother when they were wanking, that they thought about fucking my mother, that they thought about being sucked off by my mother." He sipped his wine and sat back. "She took her own life about five years after that. Stepped in front of a train."

"I don't know what to say."

"Of course you don't." Graham stared at me for an uncomfortably long time. "You're a coward and a bully. Now fuck off and don't come back."

I had an almost uncontrollable urge to reach across the table and grab his lapel and punch him in the face. God alone knows what would have happened if I'd given in to it. I'd never punched anyone in my life. I pushed my chair backwards and came close to falling over it. In the background, several men were chanting, "Fight! Fight! Fight!" as the piggyback jousters charged at one another. I felt giddy and sick. I paused for a moment to regain my composure and make sure that I could walk in a straight line.

"Go on," said Graham. "Get out of here."

I didn't turn round. I was descending the stairs when I realised that my dinner jacket was still on the back of my chair in the function room. I couldn't bring myself to go back and fetch it. I retrieved my little black rucksack from the cloakroom and stepped out into the cold night air. I took my raincoat from my bag, put it on and made my way to the river.

Halfway up the steps of the Golden Jubilee Bridge a very old, very grizzled and very drunk man was playing a battered guitar with only two strings and singing "Stand by Me" completely out of tune. I gave him a fiver and hurried up onto the bridge, wanting only to get to Waterloo and find a train home. Halfway across, however, I stopped and turned upriver to catch my breath and drink in the emptiness and the dark.

I looked down at the water, the sheer volume of it, sliding towards the estuary. Tilbury, Canvey, Isle of Grain. The London Stones, the container ports. The level was high and the river was ebbing fast. The white-painted steel pylons of the bridge were anchored on stone piers, the black water pleating and folding around them as it found its way under the bridge. Some old fear rose up inside me of deep water from when I was a child, of getting trapped below the surface, my swimming costume snagged on a rock or my fingers stuck in a grating, unable to free myself, the light above me near but unreachable.

The London Eye had stopped for the night, the unlit pods pinned to the glowing blue wheel. Airliners slowed overhead, flaps up, wheels down. A police launch came under the bridge and made its way upstream, a bright little windowed room moving steadily on the black water. I watched it plough the tide in the direction of the Houses of Parliament, shrinking steadily until it was swallowed by the darkness.

I remembered Fairfax ruffling my hair during that first visit to the school with my father. *Don't worry, we'll give him a sound thrashing if he steps out of line.*

I looked up into the starless sky. I was starting to shiver. I needed to get going but I did not know where.

D.O.G.Z.

Clamare libebat
"Actaeon ego sum, dominum cognoscite vestrum!"
Verba animo desunt

He wanted to cry out,
"I'm your master Actaeon, don't you recognise me?"
but the words wouldn't come.

Ovid, *Metamorphoses* Book III, ll. 229–31

He steps into the circle of baying dogs. *Back! Stay back!* The wounded boar sinks to her knees as if his brazen closeness were the final arrow to enter her shaggy flank. She is big for a sow, the weight of two men by the look of her. The dogs go quiet and he can hear the sucking rattle of her breath. He puts his boot against the muscled hump of her shoulders and pushes and she rolls onto her side as easily as a three-legged stool. Standing on her neck he levers and twists the shaft of his own arrow. The double barb leaves the lip of the wound ragged as it comes free with a wet slurp. Breath leaks in bloody bubbles from the new hole. He wipes the arrow clean on the rough, blonde hairs of her belly, then gestures to the pair of waiting slaves who jog over, rope her ankles, thread the pole between them, squat, shoulder the pole and hoist her ingloriously into the air. The pole sags and creaks and the weight of her own stretched carcass squeezes the final air from her lungs like the wind from an emptying bagpipe. Her head swings, lifeless.

He scratches Blackfoot, the nearest bitch, behind the ears. She squirms and pushes back against his knuckles to make him scratch harder. The boar is carried to the makeshift hecatomb which contains a further five of her kind, ten hares, six deer and more rabbits than he can count. The eagle his brother-in-law transfixed midflight in the most extraordinary piece of marksmanship is laid separately on a cream cloak befitting its status, wings outstretched in a tawny crucifix. The kennelman is roughly butchering several of the hares to share among the dogs, just enough to whet their appetites and keep them hungry for the afternoon's hunting. *Go. Join your friends*. He pats Blackfoot and she lopes away with her pack mates.

The men are in high spirits, eating flatbreads, drinking watered wine from leather bottles and sharing stories of the morning's adventures with which they alternately mock and flatter one another. A slave he does not recognise mends a hole in one of the hoof-torn nets, another slave who might well be the first slave's twin brother cleans bloody spearheads with a cloth. Actaeon wipes his brow with the back of his hand. It is almost exactly midday. The trees stand plumb on their shadows and the distant hills shimmer in the heat haze. Only the thinnest flag of white cloud trails downwind of Cithaeron's summit. A lizard skitters from crack to crack over the lichened belly of a boulder. Desiring suddenly to be alone, he turns and walks downhill towards the dark ribbon of pine and cypress that fringes the valley's rim, where yellowed grass gives way to great walls of sandstone and pumice. A thousand cicadas rasp in unison as if the dry, shimmering air were rubbing against itself. Behind him the dogs yelp and scrabble.

There is something inside his head, halfway between a pain and a noise so high in pitch it lies on the very edge of his hearing. On any other day he might pause to ask himself whether this were not some obscure warning, the way a gold ring can vibrate or one's hair stand on end in the moments before a lightning strike, but the morning's exertions have sapped so much of his energy that his mind is little sharper than the minds of his quarry. Besides, he is convinced that there is a stream among the trees, a pool or a spring, and the idea of kneeling at its pebbled rim and drinking cold, clean water from his cupped hands is intensely seductive. Indeed, as he gets nearer to the trees . . . yes, he is certain now, he can hear a faint bathhouse echo, the slap and chime of tumbling water. He climbs down a moraine of crumbling stone and dwarf lemon trees and walks towards the edge of the little wood. There are women's voices, too.

He does not stop to ask himself why he can hear women playing in this high valley a good half-day's walk from the nearest village, where he has hunted before on thirty or forty occasions meeting no one but the occasional solitary shepherd. He steps into the shade between the trunks and the change in temperature is itself like a draught of cool water. He pauses so that his eyes can grow accustomed to the sudden darkness. The air is heavy with the scent of resin. Dry needles crunch underfoot. There is a flash of something between the trunks up ahead, pale, luminous. He moves deeper into the trees. Another flash. He can hear the women more clearly now. A part of him knows that he should turn around and quietly retrace his steps, but the erotic and the dangerous are, for him, such similar flavours that, in this present moment, when everything is so out of kilter he is unable clearly to distinguish one from the other. He moves closer to the hidden glade. There are splashes and laughs, the sound of women in private, relaxed and safe in one another's company, unobserved by men, a sound he has only ever heard over walls and through closed doors. But the taboos he would never dream of breaking on those occasions seem weaker in this alien place.

He is only a few steps away from the sunlit pool. Between the trees he sees a plump thigh, the fleshy S of a back, a white nape and hands squeezing water from a shock of black hair as thick as a horse's tail. Directly in front of him there is a gap in the trees the exact size of a good stone doorway leading from darkness into light, and he knows now for certain that something is very wrong, not just because there is green, sweet grass ahead despite the relentless summer heat of the last month but because on the green, sweet grass is a pile of discarded clothing, of bows, javelins and full quivers. It no longer matters whether he feels aroused or terrified for he is like the swimmer who realises the current is too strong and too fast only when they are wholly in its grip. The story has its own momentum now. His mis-step, the day's hunt, his life are now only small parts in something bigger over which he has no control.

He steps through the doorway. There is a stone arch overhead, so geometrically clean it is hard to believe that it was not made by human hands, though it must have been carved by the clean, clear stream which flows beneath it, over a lip of tufa and into a great basin. There are perhaps eighteen women, some sitting, some standing, some tenderly washing themselves, two splashing one another like children. Are they beautiful? He does not know. He has seen naked women before but only up close in stuttering lamplight in darkened rooms, not like this, out of doors, naked and without embarrassment, like animals or men. He feels so many things that it is impossible to untangle them. He knows that this is the most extraordinary moment in his life and that if he is not very careful it might be his last.

He assumes that one of the women will see him and scream and cover herself and that the others, hearing the noise, will turn and do the same but this is not what happens. The woman who sees him first becomes very still, the way a deer will freeze when it is aware of your presence, not wanting to draw attention, bolting only when you begin moving towards it, but the woman does not bolt, nor does she cover herself. She holds his eyes, turns slowly to face him and stands upright, straightening her back, and though she neither makes a noise nor gives a signal of any kind the women around her all do the same thing—turn towards him, stand upright and hold his eye.

And this is when he sees her, at the back of the group, a good head taller than all her companions. It hurts to look at her, the way it hurts to look into the sun, but he cannot take his eyes off her. She raises a hand towards him as if she were lifting a bow and that piercing pain, that high note on the edge of his hearing which had been briefly pushed to the side of his mind, swings back into the centre of his attention and consumes him.

"You have seen what no man should ever see." He does not hear the words as such, rather feels them branded in smoking letters onto some soft, internal membrane. "Go on, then. Run away and tell everyone about it." She starts to laugh. All of them start to laugh. "If you can."

He staggers back towards the opening in the trees, hoping against hope that he has had a lucky escape, but as he is about to enter the shade someone, or something, grabs his head and twists it hard, throwing him to the ground. The mocking laughter behind him grows louder. Only when he kneels up does he register the unexpected weight of his head. He lifts a hand to his scalp, touches something rough and wrong, and flinches as if he has grasped a thistle. He gets to his feet. His head is even heavier now. He steels himself and lifts his hands to investigate but stops when he sees that he is wearing gloves made of tawny bristle. His fingers have shrunk to stumps. He turns his hands over and sees that his palms are tough and yellow like an old man's toenails.

A sudden pain folds him in two. Something terrible is happening inside his body, as if another man has been stitched inside him and is fighting his way out of this cramped and bloody prison. His spine straightens before arching backwards in a violent rictus. Then they hit him, the smells, all of them at once—pine resin, cypress leaves, bracket fungus, mallow, thyme, lemon, fox shit, wolf piss, boar's blood, hare's blood, the scent of every individual dog, his brother-in-law's sweat . . . He can smell himself, too. He no longer smells like a man. Finally he understands. It was his antlers which snagged on the pine trunks and knocked him to the ground. Fear simplifies his thoughts. He must put the horrifying reality to one side in the way that he would step carefully back from a precipice. His only possible salvation lies in getting away from here as quickly as possible, through the trees and out into the mundane sunlight, to his friends and his fellow hunters. He hears, from inside his own body, a creaking like the creaking of a ship's mast under pressure of a gale. The rictus eases. He is on all fours now.

He cannot see the shape of his antlers, so he turns and reverses through the trees to stop them snagging on the branches. The path is narrow. The antlers scrape and clatter and jam. He leans backwards with all his weight until the branches bend and snap. Another spasm grips him. He waits and breathes. He pushes backwards again and his antlers clatter free, spilling him out of the trees and into the daylight.

He spins round and sees, a single stone's throw away, his friends, his brother-in-law, the dogs, the dead animals. The familiarity of it makes him want to weep with relief. He starts to run up the slope of cracked earth and yellow grass. He vaults the broken stone and the dwarf lemon trees. Then the dogs see him. It is a sight of profound pleasure. He loves them more than he loves most of the men. And they have recognised him. He longs to have them jump up at him and lick his face, and this once he will not discipline them for doing so. But the dogs have not recognised him, they have seen a stag. His new body understands this before his old mind does.

Panic roars through it like a fire through dry rushes. He rears up onto his hind legs to show his attackers how tall he is and comes down hard on his front hooves. He tries to cry out, "I'm Actaeon. I'm your master!" but the only sound he can make is a deep, hollow bark. Heart hammering, he starts to run, up the valley, towards the treeline, into the mountains. He must find stony ground where the dogs are not at home, gullies and fissures he can jump more easily than they can. This knowledge is written deep into his new bones.

They give chase. He does not need to look round. His hearing is so acute that he knows exactly where every dog is from their yelps and their panting and the clattering of their claws on the dry earth—Storm, Hunter and Wingfoot out in front, Blanche and Little Wolf at the back. Harpy who injured her paw on a thorn this morning has given up the chase already. But it is Tracer and Flash who are the greatest danger, older, wiser animals who run always in the centre of the pack, letting the younger ones set the pace, saving their own energy for the kill.

He passes through the pungent trail of another stag and three female deer who came this way the previous day, and bounds up a great shelving slab of cracked limestone, and in all the terror and confusion there is something thrilling about what this body can do, its absolute sure-footedness, the clack of hoof on stone, the arc of these great bounds. And if he were pure stag he might throw the dogs off, if every particle of his energy were committed to running, but there remains some small human part of him which cries out even in the privacy of his own mind—*Why is this happening to me? What have I done to deserve this?*—and this is an indulgence an animal in flight cannot afford, when the mind must shrink to nothing and the body must be as committed as a thrown spear or a falling rock. Momentarily he loses his footing, a front hoof slipping sideways on a scattering of pebbles. The leg folds under him, his entire body pitching forward and his bony knee smacking the gravel hard.

He rolls sideways, his antlers clacking loudly on the ground. The pain stuns him for no more than a fraction of a second but the pack is moving like the wind and he has just got back to his feet when Storm sinks his teeth into Actaeon's rump. Again he cries out. "I'm human! Do you not recognise me?" But his lungs and throat and tongue can form nothing beyond that wordless, scraping bark. So he kicks out, throwing Storm off, then kicks again, striking the dog a crunching blow to the ribs. But the time spent doing this has enabled another dog, Wingfoot, to lock her jaw around the meat of the other rear leg. A third dog has jumped onto his back. It is Little Wolf. He swings his head but he cannot reach her to catch her and throw her off with his antlers. He gets to his feet and starts to run. It is now his only hope. But he is heavier with one dog on his back and another clamped to his thigh and while he can feel no pain from his rear legs they are already damaged and will not carry out his commands properly. He is so distracted by this that he is caught by surprise when another three dogs—he can no longer work out which is which—run at him from the side like a single animal and knock his front legs out from under him.

He topples sideways and hits the ground for a second time. He hears an antler snap and cries out. No words now, even inside his head, just raw animal sorrow. The dogs are on him. His legs flex and kick but no longer with the same force so that they simply jump between them or come at him from the other side, the younger animals leaving Hunter and Storm space to tear and scrabble at the soft section between his ribs and genitals where there are no bones to protect his inner organs. Storm grips a fold of flesh and fur and thrashes his jaws from side to side to rip his way in.

Actaeon is now surrounded entirely by dogs, like swine around a feeding trough. Suddenly Snow is in front of his face. He remembers her as a puppy. Her mother died giving birth and her twin sister a few minutes later. He is not sentimental about most of the dogs but she touched his heart. It was winter so he let her sleep in a basket by the fire in the main house, feeding her milk from a clay bottle with a rag in its mouth. But she is fully grown now and there is a murderous blankness in her eyes which he has never seen before. She leans in and bites right through his upper lip and twists it back and forth to try and rip it free. Faintly, in the distance, he can hear the shouts of his hunting companions calling out his name, half-excited that the dogs have brought down such a magnificent animal, half-exasperated by their friend's ill-timed solitary wander.

"Actaeon . . . ? Actaeon . . . !"

There is a spray of blood as the treasure chest of his belly is opened up, Hunter and Storm forcing their snouts in among the packed, wet organs, other claws and teeth pulling the skin back to widen the opening so that they can all feast. There is pain, there is unbearable pain, but some salving substance is flowing through his veins meaning that he and the pain are not quite in the same place. Hunter yanks a purple loop of intestines free and bites through it. He can smell his own faeces. He has a brief vision of his childhood, three images of supernatural brightness and clarity. His sister's hair catching fire when she leans too close to a lamp. Maggots churning in the eyes of a dead sheep. The weight of his own head against his nurse's shoulder as she carries him to his bedroom. These thoughts are the stuttering embers of a dying fire. The last featherweight spark is lifted skywards on the frail column of its meagre heat and is briefly the brilliant centre of all this surrounding dark. Then there is nothing.

And this is where the story ends for Ovid. Actaeon has stumbled on the goddess Diana bathing and seen her naked. She has turned him into a stag as punishment and he has been eaten by his own dogs. The metamorphosis is complete. Why linger? But what if Actaeon were not the true subject of the story? What if there were other transformations which have only just begun? What if the story were really about the dogs? Actaeon is the only human character to whom Ovid gives a name. Thirty-three of the dogs are given names. Some of them have their heritage appended, too, as if they were Homeric warriors: Blackfoot is a Spartan; Tracer is from Knossos; Glutton, Quicksight and Surefoot are all from Arcady. Ovid devotes more time to the dogs than he does even to Diana's nymphs, only six of whom are given names.

The final image of the story in Ovid's telling is that of Actaeon's corpse, but there is an earlier version of the story written by Acusilaus in which, having finished eating, the dogs start looking for their master, howling miserably when they can't see him. And this is how I always picture them, meat-drunk, bellies fat, the fur of their legs, chests and faces gluey with blood already hardening to a scabby crust in the sun's heat. Like revellers who have drunk themselves into a stupor they now stagger, hungover, into the harsh glare of dawn, their satisfaction souring slowly into regret. Their master has abandoned them. The other hunters, now genuinely worried, have spread out across the valley to look for their vanished friend, assuming that he must have met with some kind of accident. None of them are thinking about the dogs. The dogs can wait. The dogs are not important right now.

But something extraordinary has happened to these animals. It is not simply that they have eaten their master alive. They have eaten their master just after he stepped through the veil and looked on the divine. If this carcass were nothing more than a stag then the dogs might lope off to the nearest patch of shade, lick themselves clean and doze away the bloated minutes till their injured master was found and they were gathered in. But they are no longer entirely at home in themselves. The discarded bone, the bed of straw, the plump rat skittering over the flagstones between kitchen and stables . . . these things will no longer possess the ability to fill the world to its brim. When the dogs dream tonight they will dream not just of what has happened today and in the days before but of things that might happen tomorrow and in the days ahead, image laid over image laid over image, a pentimento of possibilities.

Restless and hungry for something, yet ignorant of what that something is, they begin to disperse, some in small groups, some in twos and threes, a small number alone, some heading down the valley towards the villages and towns, some heading to the cooler temperatures above the tree line, some working their way along the limestone spine of the range from meadow to meadow through cols and saddles, some north towards Boeotia, some south into Attica.

And it would be easy to leave the story here instead, on this dying minor chord, but the transformations have only just begun, so allow yourself to rise into the hard, bright sky above Attica and the Peloponnese until you reach the very lowest of the celestial spheres and find yourself a vantage point in one of those seats reserved for minor gods and dying heroes. Lean forward and rest your forearms on your own little arc of that great handrail and look down at the stag being taken to pieces in nature's scrapyard. Marsh harriers and black-winged kites tearing away the final shreds of meat from the stag's cadaver, beaks searching out crannies that tongues and claws couldn't scrape clean. Bacteria burning down the cathedral of each cell. At night foxes, stoats and owls. See the skeleton being hauled away piece by piece to be smashed for marrow in holts and setts.

Listen closely as the stories inspired by Actaeon's puzzling disappearance spread and mutate. He was killed and torn apart by wild animals (but why was no body found?). His friends murdered him (but they had no motive). He ran away and is now living under a new name (but how can someone whom we loved so much love us so little?). He was abducted by a god (there is some soothing flattery in this preposterous possibility) . . .

His family grieves. His hunting companions blame themselves. His friends are dejected. His horses stand idle. But life is relentless and has no care for the individual and, in the absence of new clues, mysteries become rapidly uninteresting, for there are marriages to be made and fights to be picked and money to be earned.

So sit back and take in the long view. Barley and dates are harvested, snow comes and goes on the high peaks. The trade winds revolve in their chains. Towns expand, reaching out to one another like fungus throwing off tendrils. Cumulus, nimbus, stratus are endlessly reconfigured. Forests are eaten away and the cities are visible at night now, tangerine and cadmium orange. Even at this height you can smell the new poisons in the atmosphere—sulphur dioxide, methane, compounds of lead and mercury . . .

But what of Blackfoot and Tracer, Little Wolf and Blanche? What of the transformation? That glimpse of the divine?

Zoom in on Judge Miller's place in the Santa Clara Valley and see the patient, naive Buck, one hundred and forty pounds of him, half St. Bernard, half Scotch shepherd, being taken to the College Park train station by Manuel, soon to be sold off to finance the treacherous gardener's gambling habit. Spin the globe back the other way and bring it to a halt so that you can see Dartmoor at night where a coal-black hound, *large as a small lioness,* its muzzle, hackles and dewlaps outlined by the flickering flame of the phosphorus with which it has been painted, lies riddled with five bullets, alongside Sir Henry Baskerville whose throat it would have ripped out had Holmes been a less impressive sprinter. Move a little further east and here is Jip emerging from his Chinese house by the fire to lie down at David Copperfield's feet only to *stretch himself out as if to sleep, and with a plaintive cry* expire because his beloved mistress, Dora, has this very minute died in the bedroom overhead. And there is Flush lying at the feet of Miss Barrett in the cushioned cave they share on Wimpole Street, the traffic droning on outside with muffled reverberations, sometimes a jangle of organ music, sometimes a voice calling out, "Old chairs and baskets to mend!," a pure-bred cocker spaniel darting around the room on windy autumn days, unable to stop himself chasing the partridges he knows will be scattering right now over the stubbled fields of England.

Here is Landseer's *Jack in Office* presiding over his master's meat barrow and keeping the starved mongrels at bay. Here is the greyhound Laertes laying his damp jaw on the knee of Julie Manet. Here is Goya's nameless hound whom we seem to glimpse over the rim of a volcano in a scene so devoid of detail it could be anywhere from Carabanchel to the lower circles of hell. And here, flowing through the dark between the trees are Uccello's hounds, neither touching the flower-covered ground beneath them nor possessed of shadows but pouring like smoke, together with their masters and their master's mounts, towards the vanishing point in the centre of the canvas as if their quarry were the dark itself.

Here is the fox terrier Nipper listening patiently with a cocked head to a wind-up Edison-Bell phonograph (hold your breath and lean in close and you may just be able to hear, deep in the crackling fuzz, Dame Nellie Melba singing "*Voi Che Sapete*" from *The Marriage of Figaro*). Here are Snoopy and Dougal, Junkers and Krypto, Mutley and Sorry-oo and others *quosque referre mora est*, all of whom it would take too long to name.

But what of flesh-and-blood dogs, Dobermanns and Dalmatians, mongrels and Maltese? Can we see in their eyes that faint glow of the divine? Or are they still no more than tools for bringing quarry to the hecatomb?

Zoom in again on a cellar at the Russian Space Research Institute and a small band of mongrels who have been lifted from the Moscow streets in the hope that their outdoor lives have made them impervious to cold and hunger. They are being trained to live in tiny cages. They are being trained to withstand the sound of jet engines. They are spun in centrifuges. They are fed meat jelly from a tube.

Three of them are chosen for the mission. Mushka will be the control, Albina will be her backup, Laika will go into space. On that final morning Vladimir Yazdovsky, wanting to do something nice for her since she has so little time left to live, takes Laika home to play with his children. The girls have a red rubber ball which they throw to one another over her head while she tries to catch it, her claws skittering on the polished linoleum.

The dogs are flown from Moscow to Tashkent, then from Tashkent to Tyuratam. They are driven to the Cosmodrome in a military truck. It is cold, a fierce blue sky and puddles splintering underfoot. Laika is separated from Mushka and Albina. Tubes are inserted into her ankles and chest. Patches of fur are shaved away and the bare skin swabbed with iodine so that electrodes can be fitted. She is washed down with alcohol. They strap her into her leather harness and put her inside the same metal canister she's been locked inside so many times before that it seems ordinary and safe. There is a bag behind her to catch her shit and a feeding tube next to her mouth.

Oleg Gazenko closes the door and everything goes black. She is not afraid. She trusts Oleg and Vladimir. They always make sure that she comes to no harm.

There is a roar like the roar of a great fire, the volume rising so rapidly that she can no longer hear her own howling. The canister is thrown violently from side to side. Where are Oleg and Vladimir? Some unseen force presses her to the floor and holds her there. She feels sick and dizzy. Gradually the noise lessens, the canister tilts to one side and the mysterious force slowly releases its grip. The shaking stops and the roar dies down so that she can hear only her own breathing, the dull hammer of her heart and the muffled tick of machinery. Her paws can no longer find the floor. She floats in her leather harness.

Outside, the sky turns black and the horizon bends slowly into a circle. The atmosphere is peach fuzz on the curve of the earth. Below, the forests of the Taiga, the great ochre belt of the Sahara, the relentless dirty blue of the Pacific. Cumulus, nimbus, stratus. There is no window. Laika can see none of this. She thinks that she is still at the Cosmodrome but she can hear no voices outside the canister, no noises of any kind. Instead there is an absolute silence that makes her feel profoundly lost. Has something terrible happened? Are Oleg and Vladimir safe? She thinks about Mushka, about Albina.

An insulation panel was ripped away during the ascent and as a result, the canister is heating up. When they closed the door on her it had been a bitter October day, but now she is trapped in a tiny metal box in high summer heat. She is panting hard. She scratches at the walls of the canister but can get no purchase on the aluminium panels. She tries to bite her harness but it is buckled too tight. She barks until her throat is raw and she can bark no more. She circles the earth four times and dies at some point during the fifth revolution. Her body goes on to orbit the earth another two and a half thousand times over the next six months, a little lower each time until the atmosphere finally snags this lazy satellite and she and it burn up somewhere over Mexico and are transformed into nothing more than the tiniest change in the colour of the rain falling on a single mountainside.

THE WILDERNESS

It happens like this. She is distracted momentarily by lime-green sunlight blazing on a mossed erratic behind the curtain of pines to her right. It is the most unexpected and the most beautiful thing she has seen in several days of unbroken forest and she looks at it for a fraction too long. She is going downhill at the time, not fast but fast enough. Her front wheel drops into a hard rut which narrows rapidly, clamping the wheel so that she is thrown over the handlebars. She cartwheels into the undergrowth between two trunks on the opposite side of the track, then down a steep incline. Time slows as it does at such moments and she watches two things happen in great detail before she loses consciousness. The first is her right hand reaching out instinctively to soften her landing but finding, instead, the narrow gap between two thick tree roots. She can see what is going to happen but does not have the time to prevent it. The gap between the roots grips her hand much as the rut gripped her tyre. Her body keeps tumbling down the slope and the snap of her jammed forearm is audible. The second thing happens after she has come to rest, lying on her back, her broken arm yanked free and lying beside her. It is her bike flying down the same slope, several metres above her head, perfectly upright, as if piloted by a ghost rider until it hits a tree, spins sideways and vanishes from sight. She counts at least ten subsequent rattling concussions getting progressively quieter and quieter and knows without having to look that the slope is steep and long and the bike has fallen a very long way down and is now irretrievable.

She tries to move her arm but cannot. Some emergency override or shutdown seems to have become engaged. Everything is very still. She hears the sound of a woodpecker like marbles dropping into a wooden box. She thinks, *And soon the pain will come*, and is impatient to get through this unnatural calm which is, she knows, only an overture. The sky above the trees is a perfect blue.

There is a violent fizz which is unlike anything she has experienced before, not wholly a noise nor wholly a bodily sensation, then the world disintegrates into scratches and blocks like the picture on an old television screen when the aerial loses the signal. She goes blind, the pain sweeps through her like fire through corn and she blacks out.

The world comes back slowly and in pieces, like a jigsaw being put together by a clumsy child. Nothing fits properly for a while. She sees that her forearm is bent. She knows that this is bad. A displaced bone means that blood vessels and nerves might be crushed or pinched or severed. Ideally someone should put the bone back in place before getting her to a hospital. But that's not going to happen any time soon so she must move the arm as little as possible to prevent any further damage.

She is comprehensively fucked. The panniers on the back of the bike contained everything—water, food, phone, first aid. It's hard to tell how far she has fallen from the logging road but the likelihood of anyone passing in the next few days seems low given the waist-high grass along the midline which suggests that nothing on four wheels has been this way since before the spring. Every time she moves, trying to make herself a little more comfortable on the stony ground, her arm screams. It will take her several days to learn not to move at all.

That first night she bangs two stones together to keep any bears away until the darkness and the rhythm and the exhaustion let her drift into some distant cousin of sleep from which she is woken by the absolute conviction that a great clawed hand is dipping into her guts like a bear emptying a honey jar in a children's story. She lashes out to protect herself and the pain in her arm rips the world away. The TV effect all over again. She is somewhere else for an unmeasurable period of time and when she comes back to the forest she can see only darkness and tiny patches of indigo above her head and she has no memory of where she is and this is as terrifying as the conviction that she was being eaten alive.

Dawn finally comes and with it a halo of midges and blackfly that will not leave her alone so that soon enough she gives up trying to wave them away and lets them settle and bite. At some point during the morning she hears a squeaky crunch like celery stalks being broken and sees a dead pine some eight or ten metres away bending and splitting. With a gunshot crack it topples sideways, spikes of pale heartwood bursting from the exploded trunk. A butter-yellow splinter tumbles from the air and lands moth-like on her arm. The silence afterwards is the deepest she has ever heard, the silence you might hear when the power fails in deep space, and the laughter of a crow that breaks it is as welcome as the sound of good friends in the next room.

Later that day she sees, through gaps in the canopy, a big raptor circling. Buzzard? Vulture? It takes her a long time to realise that she is the wounded animal it can smell. She hopes she's dead before it starts on her eyes. Her hands and arms and lower legs are now pebbled with bites. Mary J will be panicking after two days without a reassuring text. She can hear her saying, *Why do you always need to prove yourself, Tegan? Why do you always take things too far?*

That night she hears wolves calling to one another, or imagines that she hears wolves calling to one another. She no longer has the strength to bang stones together and the idea of being killed quickly is beginning to seem more blessing than horror.

By the following morning two fingers and their knuckles have become infected, the skin red and shiny, the flesh so puffy that she can no longer make a fist with that hand. There is a low, loud, steady buzzing in her head. The blue of the previous day's sky has been replaced by a thick lid of porridge white. She is cold and can no longer measure the passing of the hours using the angle of the sun. Along with the buzzing there is now a thin halo of cream light round every object, breaking into starbursts here and there. She longs for rain so that she might be able to drink a little moisture but it will not come. Her dry lips are cracked and covered with a sticky crust.

She hasn't heard a human noise since the accident—no truck, no logging chainsaw, no plane overhead, no explosives.

At night there is an electrical storm, so far away that she hears no thunder and sees only soft, spectral pulses in the dark. She weeps. She is not a person who weeps and is angry at herself for this pointless display of self-pity. She feels an overpowering need to be back in her childhood bedroom, her father sitting on the wicker chair with a cup of sugary coffee and a blister pack of paracetamol, a need so strong she can smell shoe polish and cat piss and dried lavender and feel the cool cotton of the pillow under her cheek.

She is losing her mind. She has to hold tightly to the night-time forest because that's where her living body is located but she is in no pain in this other place which is, she knows, an anteroom to a vast, cold, empty universe from which there will be no return. She mustn't close her eyes and sink into that pillow.

The sun comes up and hauls her back into the brutal, singular world. There is a new pain in her head, on account of the dehydration probably, like a steel circlip around her skull. With her right eye she can see only a pale fog through which coloured vapours swim. Over the next few hours an unexpected resignation grows. Dying will mean an end to the pain, to the fear, to the succession of dreaded nights. Everything and everyone has to die at some time, these trees, that circling bird. Adrian is dead. Her grandparents are all dead. The old house was bulldozed ten years ago. Better to go when you were young and fit, no chemo, no care home.

Later that day she is fourteen or fifteen years old and she is having an argument with her sister on a beach in Malta, the scene peculiarly detailed despite the family never having been there—a towel patterned like giraffe skin, candles in coloured glass jars hanging from the ceiling of a beach bar. She hears a dog barking. The dog is not in Malta, the dog is in the forest. She turns her head so that she can look in the direction of the noise using her one good eye and is surprised to find a Dobermann looking down at her, panting, its fat, ham-coloured tongue lolling. She can smell its meaty breath.

"This is all I fucking need." There is a man standing behind the dog. She has to squint hard to see him with any clarity. He is wearing a Pantera T-shirt and grey work pants with black kneepads. He has a ponytail and a good week of stubble. He gazes up at the treetops, breathes in slowly and breathes out slowly. He says, "Let's put you out of your misery," braces the butt of a rifle against his shoulder and aims at her head.

"Stop." She can't remember how to say words out loud and it's possible that she says this only in her head. "Wait." She raises her one functioning hand as if she can deflect the bullet.

The dog looks at the man and barks softly. The man looks at the dog and the barrel of the rifle drops. The dog barks softly for a second time. The man slings the rifle back over his shoulder. "Have it your way." He squats and puts a hand behind her shoulders to force her into a sitting position.

"Careful." She knows that she says this out loud because she hears her own voice and briefly wonders who's talking. "My arm's broken."

He thrusts his other arm under her knees and hoists her so that her broken arm swings free. The TV screen of the world flickers and disintegrates and goes black.

She comes round lying in a bed in a clean white room, gazing up at a skylight set into a sloping roof beyond which clouds evolve slowly against a washed-out sky. The air smells of cedarwood and a cleaning fluid she remembers from school. There is a wooden chair and a small wooden table, and a cast on her right arm for reasons that are not immediately obvious. A window to her left gives onto another wooden building. A memory comes back of being driven through a forest on a rough, rocky road. She starts to shake and cry. Somehow this is connected to the roughness of the road. In its wake a second memory comes back. *Let's put you out of your misery*. The dog, the ponytail.

She doesn't want to think about these things so she pushes them away. It's like moving a heavy chest of drawers across a wooden floor. And now the memories and the unpleasant emotions attached to them sit some way off, still there but unable to reach her. She wonders if she has been given strong painkillers.

She pushes off the sheet and blanket and turns gingerly onto her side before sitting up, cradling her broken arm in the absence of a sling. The room sways back and forth a few times before stabilising. She's wearing a pair of baggy, pale green pyjamas she's never seen before. The cycling kit she was wearing when she had the accident sits washed and folded on the table beside what looks like a set of khaki coveralls. She gets carefully to her feet. She must let Mary J know that she's safe. She needs to call her parents.

She feels a little jag of worry, wondering if the room is locked, but is reassured when the handle turns smoothly and the door opens onto a corridor. One wall is painted white, the other is made of pale wooden planks onto which a symbol which rings the vaguest of bells has been darkly branded.

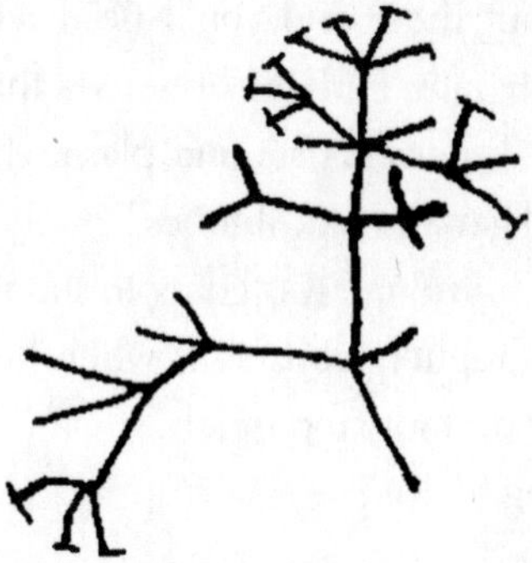

She walks unsteadily down the corridor holding her broken arm like a baby, pushes open the door at the far end with her shoulder and finds herself in the open air looking at ten or twelve other blocks in similar pale planking with sedum roofs, none of them more than a couple of years old at most. Over the roofs she can see trees and, beyond them, two forested peaks. Between two buildings she can see a high wall topped with coils of razor wire.

A young man is walking towards her, dark skin and a trim black beard, clean, crumpled, white cotton shirt tucked into jeans, sleeves folded carefully above his elbows, ostentatiously urban. "You're awake." As if they are friends on holiday together.

"Where am I?"

"It's good to see you up and about."

"What is this place?" Her tongue is thick in her mouth. The steel circlip has been loosened but not removed.

"You were lucky someone found you."

"I'm really grateful to be alive, but I need to get in touch with my partner. I need to get in touch with my family."

"I understand that."

A game is being played here, the rules of which she can't discern. "Just a couple of phone calls."

"Another day out there and you'd be dead." She can hear a threat in this simple fact. Perhaps he senses that he has crossed a line. "My name is Tanweer. I set and plastered your arm. I filled you with fluids and gave you antibiotics."

"The man who found me was going to shoot me."

"You were only vaguely conscious when he brought you in. I wouldn't trust your memory too much."

She says nothing.

"And your name?"

If she speaks it will be obvious that she is angry and upset.

"You came in with nothing. We're all wondering what you were doing out there. It was only thanks to the dog that he found you."

She counts down silently from five to one. "Deborah Deacon." Deborah was a housemate in Edinburgh, a small, angry woman who smelt vaguely of petrol and never washed up after herself. The lie makes her feel a little more in control. "I was cycling. The bike went into the ravine."

He stands next to her and turns so that they are both looking out over the compound. "We're off the map here, as in literally not on the map. Also, no phone signal. In ten days we get our next vanload of supplies. The driver can take you to Prospect on the return journey."

"People are looking for me."

"It could be a lot worse." He pauses. "You will have to sign some legal paperwork before you go."

"So this place is . . . ?"

"Just try not to ask that kind of question."

"The razor wire . . . ?"

"The upside is that we have a refectory. The food is better than you might expect for the middle of nowhere. And you must be starving."

Tanweer is right. The chicken wrap and the coffee are excellent though any food would doubtless taste good at this point. She is wearing the khaki coveralls from the table in her room, the right sleeve of which has been thoughtfully scissored so that she can slip her cast through it, together with a sling of bandage she found folded with the coveralls. There are ten wooden tables with wooden benches in the refectory, the same branching sign branded into the wood at the end of each table, and a long window onto a wildflower square. It could be a youth hostel were it not for the people sitting at other tables, security staff in navy uniforms who carry holstered revolvers and a younger group who would look more at home in a university science department.

She starts to feel calmer as the calories come online, her body a little warmer, her thinking more logical. She's had a narrow escape. It doesn't matter what this place is. She'll see Mary J again, she'll see her parents and her sister again. She imagines Mary J holding her and saying, "You are a complete fucking idiot, you know that, don't you?" and she starts to cry.

She wipes her eyes and takes a forkful of the cheesecake and a man she has not seen before swings his legs over the bench and sits himself down on the far side of the table. One of the science group though a decade or so older than the others, a little jowly, a distressed but clean denim jacket over a black T-shirt.

"And you are?"

"John Magnusson. You're Deborah Deacon, I gather."

It takes half a second for her to remember. "Call me Deb." She hopes the detail makes up for the fumble, though if she were called Deborah she would never allow anyone to call her Deb. "And your job here? Assuming that's a question I'm allowed to ask."

He laughs without opening his mouth. "I like you. You're quick. I'm the director of this . . . let's call it a facility. Tell me how you ended up here. Not *here*." He waves his hand towards the ceiling. "But out there." He has a spray of acne across his forehead, as if he's never quite shaken off the teenage boy he once was.

"I was cycling round the world." *The best lies are those closest to the truth* is Mary J's rule and she's a master.

"Because . . . ?"

She takes a long in-breath. "My brother died. Of glioblastoma. It's a kind of—"

"Brain tumour, particularly aggressive, very hard to treat, pretty much always recurs." He seems very pleased with himself for knowing this.

"He was training to be an architect. The cancer was discovered in his final year. He kept having these blinding headaches. We thought he was working too hard. Then he started having epileptic fits. It was seven weeks between his diagnosis and his death."

"Seven weeks." He nods.

"Life is shorter than you think. If you want to do something, do it."

"Or perhaps you're running away." He seems equally pleased with himself for this insight. "From grief, from mortality."

"You'd get on well with my mother."

"Oh, I doubt it."

She fails to read some people but John Magnusson is peculiarly transparent. He means, *I have no interest in people who are of no use to me*. She neither trusts this man nor likes him but she has missed this kind of banter. "You're probably right. Very few people get on well with my mother. Cats get on well with my mother. Cats are not great judges of character in my experience."

"Degree?" he asks.

"Me?"

"You."

"Politics and sociology. BA."

He smiles to himself. "I think you can tell a great deal about someone from simply looking at them, even when they're unconscious."

She doesn't like the image of him standing beside her bed. "There are some very stupid people with degrees."

"But I don't think you're one of them. For which I'm grateful."

"Because . . . ?"

"The opportunity for intelligent conversation?"

"I get the impression that you're surrounded by a lot of intelligent people here."

"Whom I've come to know a little too well over the past eighteen months."

At that precise moment she sees that he is no longer interested in her. It is as clear as a light changing from green to red. He swings his legs back over the bench. Before standing, however, he pauses, as if he has been reminded by a voice coming through an earpiece. "I'm sorry about your brother." Then he is gone.

She finishes eating, borrows a couple of dog-eared paperbacks from the swapping library in the adjacent social room—*The Stars My Destination*, *The Gunslinger*—and spends the evening reading in her room.

She wakes that night to the sound of howling and, seeing stars through the skylight over the bed, thinks for a few terrifying moments that she is still lying in the forest. She looks around the speckled gloaming of the unlit room and anchors herself to the table, the chair, her cast. The howling continues. She gets out of bed. The burst of adrenaline that woke her is not subsiding so she slips the coveralls on over her pyjamas, steps into her trainers and makes her way out into the corridor. When she opens the outer door onto the decking she realises that the sound is not just howling. There are dog barks, too, human shouts and a clanging like pots and pans being banged together. A picture springs to mind of wolves attacking the compound and people making noises to drive them away. Two armed security staff jog past. Like Tegan they seem to have woken in the last few minutes, one still buckling the belt that holds his revolver, the other dropping his navy baseball cap, glancing backwards briefly and deciding that he hasn't got time to retrieve it. They vanish into the shadow between two blocks.

Nothing else moves in the dark compound. A half-moon floats among trembling stars. The noise continues for another thirty seconds, then three gunshots ring out. She feels light-headed and has to lower herself carefully to the floor. Blood drums in the arteries of her neck, sweat beads on her arms and forehead. She is not someone who panics any more than she is someone who weeps. Something has happened to her since the accident and she doesn't like it.

It seems unwise to risk being discovered here. Better to pretend she slept through the whole event, whatever it was. She gets to her feet, makes her way back inside, takes off the coveralls and lies down, but the panic is still churning, her body saying, *Do something! Act now! Move!* so she tries to calm herself by taking an imaginary journey through the ground floor of the house where she grew up—the dried thistles in the vase of green glass, the missing banister, the godawful psychedelic fish painting . . . until it merges into a nightmare about wolves and a sinking boat and she struggles through a troubled half-sleep from which she eventually wakes feeling ragged and unrefreshed.

If she was on heavy painkillers the day before they have left her system now and there is a constant throbbing ache in her arm. She washes, dresses and heads over to the refectory with *The Gunslinger* to get a coffee and some oatmeal. She feels a little saner in the daylight, but the urgent restlessness of last night has not dissipated entirely so after breakfast she starts walking round the facility, little circuits of the wildflower square outside the refectory at first, then further afield. She tells herself that she's getting exercise so she can sleep better. A week ago she was cycling between fifty and ninety miles a day and this sedentary existence is unnatural. But the truth is that she can't let go of what she heard in the night, she doesn't trust these people and has always been uneasy with the idea of waiting passively for someone else to get her out of any difficult situation. She wants to know what's in the rest of the compound.

The open gate sits between two slate-grey concrete walls. The gate itself is heavy-duty wire mesh on a solid frame of tubular steel and stands ajar, an open steel padlock swinging from the hole in the retracted bolt. There is a zoo smell coming from the passageway on the far side, dung and urine on hard floors, the waxy residue on your hands after you've been stroking pigs or horses. She hears the scratching of claws and a muffled shriek.

She should walk away. She has to think of Mary J, of her parents, but she can't stop herself. And she can see no security cameras. *Do something! Act now!* She manoeuvres herself sideways through the gate, the ammoniac smell thickening as she makes her way down the concrete passageway. The walls are bare except for a single cable linking a chain of heavy-duty lights bolted onto the concrete at waist height. The roof is ridged, translucent plastic which reminds her of her father's home-made conservatory, dappled light falling through the moss and leaves which have gathered on the top surface. There is a single crimson smear on the floor which might or might not be blood.

She turns a corner into a wider corridor with cells on either side. The two nearest cells contain chimpanzees together with heaps of sawdust and plastic bowls of food—chopped apple, celery, damp pellets in mottled pink like tiny sausages. The chimpanzee to her right sits slumped against the door of its cell, its arm flopping between the bars and reaching lazily towards her, palm upturned like that of an old man begging for money in the street. The chimpanzee to her left takes a moment to register her presence, then grips the bars and screams, setting off a chain reaction of shrieks and yells which echo down the long room until the air is thick with noise. She braces herself, certain that whoever left the door open will come running to find out what the commotion is.

No one comes, and slowly the noise dies down. She walks the length of the room. The next few cells contain primates of other kinds—an orangutan, a marmoset, a gibbon. The orangutan is sitting with its face pressed against the wall as if in sullen protest against the spartan conditions. The gibbon is playing some kind of game with a bucket, rolling it in circles in the sawdust and spilt food. The cells after that contain dogs—an Alsatian, a spaniel, one of those big Anatolian hunting hounds she remembers from Istanbul. The last two cells contain a sheep and a goat.

Turning a second corner she finds herself in a similar room with two layers of smaller cells on each side—cats, rabbits, a couple of snakes behind glass instead of bars. She stops and listens. There are voices coming from a further room. They don't sound like the voices of any of the people she's seen since her arrival. It's hard to make out individual words but someone is cursing loudly and another person is singing sarcastically the way children sing to mock one another.

A third turn takes her into another room of full-height cells. Is this what she is not meant to see? Is this the reason why the place is off the map, surrounded by razor wire? There is a woman in the cell to her left, curled up in a foetal position on the bed which runs along the wall. The woman in the cell to her right is staring at Tegan through the bars. They are wearing the same khaki coveralls she has on.

"The fuck you staring at?"

The mocking song has stopped. From the end of the room she can hear another woman muttering loudly to herself. She thinks briefly that the woman is speaking in a language she does not recognise but it's English, chopped into fragments that make no sense. ". . . marvels . . . them all . . . rock find me . . . chut chut chut . . . baby man car . . ." The woman sounds psychotic or brain-damaged.

"Who the fuck are you? Out there. In that." She waves a hand at Tegan's coveralls. "Bitch, I'm talking to you." The woman's sleeves are rolled up and two ladders of scar climb the soft flesh on the insides of her forearms.

There is a strong taste of aniseed in Tegan's mouth, and she can feel pins and needles in her left arm and left leg.

"Bitch." The woman clicks her fingers. "Look at me. You one of them or one of us?"

There is a bang like a metal bucket being dropped nearby, or maybe it's inside her head. The taste of aniseed is so strong that she is close to vomiting. She turns and runs back into the room of small animals but she is light-headed and a little dizzy and falls sideways as she re-enters the first room, hitting her right shoulder hard against the bars of the nearest cage, then twisting away to protect her broken forearm as she goes down. Inside its cage the goat shrieks and leaps away, pinballing between the walls of its cell. She gets up onto her knees, vomits a little into the back of her mouth and swallows it down again. Other animals are shrieking, barking and hooting. She holds on to the bars of the goat's cell to get to her feet. The aniseed is receding but her left side is still numb and tingling. Carefully, so as not to fall again, she makes her way out into the entryway, through the open gate and onto the gravel path.

She retraces her steps back past the refectory and from there to her room. Her shoulder hurts from where she fell and she has too much adrenaline coursing through her system to lie down. She takes long, deep breaths and plays the country game. *Morocco, Western Sahara, Mauritania, Senegal, The Gambia, Senegal again, Guinea-Bissau* . . . No one saw her, she was an idiot but no one saw her. Sign the papers and get out of here. Deal with it all later.

The taste, the pins and needles. Did something happen to her in the accident? Has the dehydration permanently messed with her brain?

She sits at the desk and picks up *The Stars My Destination*. "This was a Golden Age, a time of high adventure, rich living and hard dying . . ." She closes the book and puts it down.

There is a knock at her door. She does not respond. There is a second knock. "It's Tanweer. Are you OK?"

She takes a deep breath and tells him to come in.

"How are you getting on?"

If she met him in the outside world she could imagine them being friends on account of the warmth he radiates. She wants to tell him what she has just seen. She has to remind herself that he is involved in what she's just seen.

"I'm . . . not feeling very good."

"I'm sorry to hear that." He asks if he can check her pulse and blood pressure, then take a blood sample.

"Why?" She doesn't want anyone to touch her, let alone put a needle into her arm.

"Your recovery has been remarkable in the circumstances but I'd like to check that you're continuing in the same direction."

He's a doctor, at least, or says he's a doctor. "OK."

Her pulse and blood pressure are high.

"I slipped and fell over." She nods towards the bathroom. "Hurt my shoulder."

"You be careful. Two plastered arms is something you very much do not want. Now . . ."

She watches him closely, to make sure the syringe is empty and that he's taking blood out rather than putting something in.

"If you hold that down . . ."

She presses the little puff of cotton wool and he fixes it in place with a strip of plaster, then stands back and looks at her as if seeing her for the first time. "You seem . . . troubled."

It catches her off guard. She waits for a few seconds before speaking. "I'm four thousand miles from home. My partner and my family will be going out of their minds . . ." If she carries on in this direction she will lose control. "I'll feel better when I know I'm getting out of here."

"I'll ask and see if we can give you a date."

"Thank you."

He holds up the syringe of blood. "Thank *you*."

She had an argument with Mary J only days before she set off. *You're playing Russian roulette. You feel bad because Adrian died so you're sticking your life on the line. "Are you sure it wasn't me you wanted?" Why can't you grieve like a normal human being and cry and get drunk and smash things? There are other people in your life.*

It's not just the numbness and the aniseed. Thoughts and feelings pour through her head like ticker tape. She needs a project. Something bad is happening in this place. She can do nothing about it till she gets out. She can't write anything down so she needs to remember it in as much detail as she can. She starts with a mental map—the layout of the buildings, the wildflower square, the refectory and the social room, the generator block, the little office where the guards hang out, the cage of propane tanks . . . She adds the directions of sunrise and sunset, the silhouettes of the mountains she can see in the distance. She walks round the place in her head, fixing it, then zooming in on detail—the light fittings, the furniture, the shape branded into the walls and tables.

The night is hard. Her mind loses structure as the light falls and the world outside vanishes. She is exhausted and there is only so much walking round an imaginary version of this place that she can do. The room feels like a bathyscaphe lowered to some unimaginable depth, linked to the world by the thinnest of cables. Her exhaustion is not a lack of energy but a restless, grinding fatigue that will not hand her over to sleep. The dark scares her. *Fear is what stops us doing stupid shit, Tegan*. But Mary J is wrong. Fear is not good. It's like nausea or migraine, it squats in the very centre of her body and will not be ignored, and coming off it like smoke are these crazy, unhelpful thoughts, the conviction that she's a victim or about to become a victim, that there are hidden things nearby which mean her harm.

At some point in the small hours she has stomach cramps and gets to the toilet just in time before her bowels loosen and empty. What comes out is almost completely liquid. The smell is foul and alien and made worse by the taste of aniseed which is suddenly back in her mouth. The cramps come again even though her bowels are now empty. She stays sitting on the toilet for another fifteen, twenty minutes. She should shower but she doesn't have the energy to do it while keeping the cast dry so she wipes herself as well as she can, flushes and makes her way back to bed.

Adrian is dead. She will never see him again, never talk to him again. She hasn't quite realised this before. She will never hear him butcher "Cavatina" on an acoustic guitar, never swear at him for welding scrambled egg onto the base of a non-stick pan. His head sunk into that pillow, the tubes, the smell of disinfectant and the other smells it never quite hid. She is crying in a way she hasn't cried since she was a child, not even at the funeral. That surreal moment when her mother went into the garden after hearing the news and squatted and howled like an animal giving birth, a theatrical performance or so it seemed to Tegan, to compensate for not wanting to be at Adrian's bedside because it was all *too upsetting*. She understands now. This force washing through her, the size of the void.

Mary J is wrong. She didn't make this journey to offer herself up in exchange for Adrian. She came to break the dam that held these feelings back. She wants to tell Mary J this. She has never felt so alone in her life.

She wakes with her head at the foot of her bed and thinks for way too long that the entire building has been rotated. She feels wrung out and her guts ache, but she is hungry, too. The pins and needles are back. She goes to the bathroom and runs the shower till it's warm. She will get a flight home and see a doctor. The coming week is just one more part of the ride, another snowstorm, another climb into mountains. She steps under the falling water, plastered arm outstretched to keep it dry, and starts to feel more human.

Fortified by oatmeal, coffee and orange juice she decides to take matters into her own hands and ask Tanweer or John Magnusson for a definite date and is spooked when, leaving the refectory, she sees John walking towards her as if summoned.

"I was coming to find you."

"Follow me. I have something interesting to show you."

He leads her to a recessed door on the far side of the wildflower square, then up the stairs to an office behind a locked door on the first floor. There is a revolving chair. There are two postcards pinned to the wall, an Escher staircase print and a photo of a Lisbon tram. There is a bundle of what look like master keys on a hook and a mug bearing the slogan, *There are two types of people in the world—1. Those who can extrapolate from incomplete data.* The long window running down one side of the room looks out over the sedum roofs and the blocks containing the animals and the women to the five peaks of a mountain horizon of which she could previously see only a small part. She adds the outline to the map in her memory.

"So," he says, "what do you think is going on here?"

"I thought that was the kind of question I wasn't allowed to ask."

"But you don't like being told to follow rules, do you?"

"I don't understand."

He flips up the screen of a MacBook on his desk. "Come closer." In one of the windows is a rectangle of black-and-white CCTV footage. She is looking down at the first room of animal cages. He presses PLAY. She feels sick. She sees herself walk into shot.

"Cameras are very small these days."

"I saw the door had been left open."

"It's what I would have done in your situation."

She needs to stay on his good side but she doesn't know what's going on here and her mind is not working as well or as quickly as it should.

"Are you not going to ask?"

"About what?"

"The apes, the dogs, the women . . ."

He is a child with a secret he wants both to keep and to tell. She nearly says, *I just want to go home*, but she senses that he would be disappointed by this and that disappointing him would be the wrong move. She says, "Tell me about the apes and the dogs and the women."

He turns to the window and looks into the distance. "What do you know about gene-editing?"

"Very little."

"There is a protein called Cas9. It evolved in certain bacteria as a defence against viruses. It keeps snapshots of tiny sections of the DNA in harmful viruses, like a rogues' gallery, and whenever it sees those sections again it cuts them out." She wonders, initially, if he is talking metaphorically about this whole place, or perhaps about himself. "Now, DNA is very good at repairing itself. It has to be. It gets damaged all the time. Sunlight, radiation, toxins, random mutations. So every time a strand of the double helix breaks it looks to the other, identical strand to know how to mend itself. But Cas9 has cut out both sections because they're identical. The DNA is irreparably damaged. And the harmful virus is destroyed. However . . ." He turns back from the window and looks at her. "What's extraordinary about Cas9 is that we can add our own pictures to the rogues' gallery and programme it to look for specific sections of any DNA and cut it out. What's more—thank you, Nobel Prize winners Emmanuelle Charpentier and Jennifer Doudna—we can attach a model that the damaged DNA will use to mend itself. In short, we can take any gene out, and we can put any gene in its place." He spreads his hands as if he has just performed this magic trick himself. "We're doing it with plants, with animals. We're doing it, tentatively, with human beings, with blood to cure sickle cell, with the pancreas to cure diabetes. Brains . . . are more complicated. And legal systems are innately conservative."

"So these women . . ." The baying at night, the gunshots. "You infect them with this . . ." The word won't come. The aniseed is back together with something nastier like sour milk. The pins and needles, too.

"More often than not nothing happens but sometimes . . ." He pops up a new window on the Mac and swivels it towards Tegan.

A woman in khaki coveralls sits on the floor, pressed into the corner of a white room, arms around her knees, rocking gently back and forth. A female member of staff comes in, pushes a chair to one side and crouches. Her words are inaudible but her posture is the one you'd adopt with a sad and reluctant child. The woman in the coveralls stares unmoving, then lunges, knocking the staff member backwards. And this Tegan can hear. The woman is barking like a dog. It is not an affectation. The energy of the attack, the way she moves her body. She is on all fours, her teeth locked into the screaming woman's shoulder. There is a clatter of footsteps and two of the armed men in dark blue uniforms run into shot and pull the dog-woman off.

John folds the screen down. "The results are crude but we are, as far as I know, the first people to have done this." He pauses. Is he waiting for congratulations or just observing her reaction?

"What did you do to her?"

"Come on." It's like a party game. She's failing to guess the obvious answer.

She knows what they have done to the woman but when she imagines the words they sound preposterous.

He sighs wearily. "We injected her with a neutralised monkey flu virus carrying this exquisite piece of molecular machinery"—he turns his left hand over and holds a tiny, invisible object the size of a marble between his thumb and forefinger—"which makes its way through her brain chopping out carefully chosen genetic sequences from cell after cell after cell, replacing them with the equivalent genetic sequences from those of a dog. Is it not extraordinary?" He is not going to allow her lack of response to undercut his performance. "It's all guesswork at the moment. But every success lights up some tiny area of a vast, uncharted continent."

"You're treating these women's brains like . . ." She can't think of the right word. Her leg is entirely numb. She wants to get away from here but if she stands up now she will fall over.

"You think we got to the moon and cured cancer by being *nice*? Do you know how many tens of thousands of dogs and monkeys have died so we can do heart surgery?"

The aniseed, the sour milk, the pins and needles. Have they done it to her? Is some piece of exquisite machinery working its way through her brain right now, chopping out pieces of DNA and inserting fuck knows what in its place?

"Besides, I wouldn't shed too many tears for these women. They're not people you'd want to meet in a dark alley." He leans forward a little as if the two of them are friends and he is about to share something he shouldn't. "Five months ago a group of them escaped. They killed one of the guards. Cut his throat with a broken plate. Blinded another." He gestures towards the forest, the mountains. "And for what? It's sixty miles to the nearest town." He puts air quotes around the word "town" to show how small it is. "There's a reason we're out here. Wolves, cougars, bears. I doubt they lasted long."

She needs air and space. She gets to her feet without thinking, her numb leg giving way so that she stumbles sideways and has to catch herself on the desk. He reaches forward instinctively to help and she roars at him and doesn't know if it is because she is turning into an animal or whether she is too preoccupied to summon actual words. He backs off and she limps towards the door. She makes her way downstairs, gripping the handrail, and pushes open the door to drink down the cold and the sunlight.

Only when she is back in her room does it dawn on her, that

whatever might or might not be going on in her brain, they will not be taking her to Prospect. Not now.

She is hyperventilating. It is like seeing someone else hyperventilating and wondering what is wrong with them. *Texas, Louisiana, Mississippi, Alabama, Florida, Georgia* . . . She needs a plan. Break it down into stages. With food and water she can do sixty miles. Get out, circle the camp till she finds the road, follow tyre tracks at junctions. Fifteen, twenty miles a day. But she has to go now, before this . . . this problem in her head gets worse.

She goes to the refectory for lunch and fills her pockets with cereal bars when the woman behind the counter is not watching. She takes three bottles of water back to her room and stays there all afternoon, keeping her head down. She can't read so she tears pages from *The Gunslinger* and makes an origami swan, an origami turtle, an origami fox. She will leave after dark. Over the wire behind the propane tanks, using the cage as a ladder. *Colombia, Venezuela, Guyana, Suriname, French Guiana* . . . Walk for a couple of hours and the area becomes too big to search. πr^2. After two miles the circle of possible locations covers twelve square miles. Assuming they bother searching at all.

She does stretching exercises. She thinks about Deborah Deacon, her fake self, the string of homeless guys she went out with, that fucked-up saviour complex. Danny with the cats. The ginger Viking with the amazing tenor voice and the facial burns.

She eats a big supper at the refectory, slips two knives into her pocket, more cereal bars, more bottled water.

She waits till dark, then goes to the laundry block where a dryer still tumbles in the unlit room. That smell, the warmth and moisture, like an engine room or a nursing home. She takes T-shirts, a hoody, jeans and thick socks from a hamper of dirty clothes. Sweat and perfume. She wants a waterproof but can't find one. From a cupboard she takes twine, bleach and a holdall she can use as a rudimentary backpack.

Back in her room she dresses in several layers of clothing, darkest on top, and fills the holdall with cereal bars, water, spare clothes and the blanket from the bed. She turns off the light and closes the curtains. An hour? Measuring time is one of the many things she's finding increasingly difficult.

She lifts the bag onto her back, a loop over each shoulder, takes the rug from the floor, rolls it and tucks it under her arm. Once outside she hears the faint crunch of gravel and steps back into the porch as a security guard walks past with a loose, off-duty saunter. Moonlight and deep shadow. A single room-light burning low.

She moves between wedges of darkness round the wildflower square to the cage that protects the propane tanks, puts a toe of her trainer into one of the diamond-shaped holes of the mesh and starts to climb. It's difficult with only one fully functioning arm but she moves slowly, holding on lightly with the fingers of her right hand while she reaches up with her left.

From the roof she can see the surrounding forest, the vastness of it. The great disc of sky. Luminous blackness. Wind sighs in the black trees on the far side of the fence. Pine sap and wood rot, the smell of oil and the muffled chug of machinery in the adjacent building. Two trunks squeak against one another. A shooting star is a brief, white scratch on the sky. She throws the rug onto the razor wire. One movement—roll over and drop down. It's going to hurt. Go now, before someone sees her.

A cry, far off—animal or human, she can't tell which.

She knots the loops of the bag together and throws it into the darkness, clamps her plastered arm to her chest and puts her free hand under her armpit so she doesn't reach out and shred her fingers. *Go*. She falls forward, shoulder onto the rug. The wire dips and twangs like a diving board. A single barb rips her coveralls and pierces her shoulder. A flash of pain like that shooting star. She spills into the tumbling night. It's like the accident all over again. Half a second of nothing, then she plunges into dense undergrowth, branches and brambles snagging and slowing her. She comes to a halt. Like floating in a cloud of needles. Above her she sees the rug still pinned to the barbed wire, like a sign saying, *She went this way*. Nothing she can do about it now. Thorns in her face. Aniseed again and that fizz down her right-hand side. She paddles with her feet until they find solid ground. Blood is running into her right eye and her hair has snagged on something behind her. She wraps her fist in her sleeve and fights her way out of the brush, coveralls ripping again.

So much darker down here than she expected. She retrieves the bag and swings it onto her shoulders, then circumnavigates the fat trunk of a big fir, her good eye getting slowly used to the gritty un-light. Go straight ahead, keep the compound lights behind her, get as far away as she can. Tomorrow she can swing anticlockwise towards the road.

She can see a little more now, nettles and undergrowth giving way to rocks and roots, the ground sloping sharply to her right. She stops and turns. No voices, no sirens, no torches. She follows the edge of the escarpment, taking small steps, not wanting to fall.

An hour or so of walking, then clouds slide over the moon. Real darkness on all sides, only the faintest rags of indigo overhead. It's too dangerous to go any further. This will have to be enough. She wraps herself in the blanket and sits against a tree. An owl hoots, then hoots again. The ground is hard but she's shattered. She's at Logan airport. She's on a swing in the garden of that French house. *Sonnez les matines! Sonnez les matines!* Mary J's face in close-up. The lemony soap smell. She lets the dark take her.

. . .

She wakes to find a hand over her mouth. A woman is sitting on top of her. Dawn light. Forest. Where is she? She tries to push the woman off.

"Lady, lady, lady. Whoa. Calm down."

The woman is strong. She is holding a big stone aloft like she's about to split Tegan's head.

"You gonna stop struggling? 'Cause we need to talk. And we can't talk if you're acting like this."

She had an accident on the bike. No, that was way back. The woman on top of her is filthy, khaki coveralls streaked and stained with mud, hair matted.

"I'm gonna take my hand off your mouth and you're gonna tell me your name and how come you're out here and if everything goes well we're gonna be friends but if you shout or fight back we are very much not gonna be friends. Sound like a deal to you?"

The compound, the chimpanzee virus. Tegan nods. The woman takes her hand away from Tegan's mouth. She doesn't put the stone down.

"Tell me your name."

It takes whole seconds to remember. "Tegan. My name's Tegan."

"Cherry." She lowers the stone. "How come you're out here?"

"I escaped."

"On your own?" The woman doesn't believe her.

"I wasn't . . . I didn't . . ." She has to slow down otherwise her thoughts get tangled. "I wasn't locked up."

The woman looks at her, quizzical, sceptical.

"I climbed . . . jumped . . . over the wire."

"You on your own?"

Tegan nods.

Cherry puts her hand over Tegan's mouth and scans the forest slowly, listening hard. She takes her hand away. "The arm. They do that to you?"

"Accident."

"OK. Let's get you up. I'm gonna take you somewhere."

As they walk the woman chants quietly to herself. Tegan can hear only parts of it. ". . . *there came a great wind from the wilderness, and smote the four corners of the house* . . . Give me the bag." Tegan gives Cherry the bag. ". . . *At destruction and famine thou shalt laugh: neither shalt thou be afraid of the beasts of the earth* . . ."

In the centre of a clearing a second woman tends a little fire dancing in a circle of rocks while a third is using a sharp stone to skin a dead animal the size of a baby deer hanging from a branch. Both wear the same khaki coveralls, equally battered and soiled. A rudimentary awning of branches and leaves has been built around a big boulder whose overhang creates a simple shelter. Burning sticks crackle and soft grey smoke tumbles into the canopy. The women turn to look at Cherry and Tegan.

"Shona—" Cherry points at the woman by the fire, then at the woman butchering the animal—"Bree. Least that's what we call her. She don't talk."

Shona says, "What you doing bringing someone back here?"

"You want me to leave her to die out there?"

Tegan wants to say, *I wasn't going to die. I had a plan*, but the conversation is moving too fast for her to form the words and say them at the right time.

"She on her own?"

"Far as I can tell."

"No one following her?"

"Far as I can tell."

"Maybe you ask us first about crazy plans like this."

"You gonna say no?"

"What's in the bag?" Shona takes it from Cherry. Looks inside.

"My . . . stuff," says Tegan, panicking. She shouldn't have agreed to come here.

Shona is holding two cereal bars. "This is quality shit."

"I need it." Tegan hobbles over and grabs Shona's arm. "Put it . . . Put it . . ."

Shona stares at her. "Don't fuck with me. Seriously do not fuck with me."

Tegan lets go. "I need it . . . to go home . . . I need it."

"You insane?" Shona tilts her head to one side. "You think you gonna *walk* out of here?"

Bree is pushing sharpened sticks through lumps of meat and balancing them above the flames.

"I cycled . . . I cycled . . ." *Three thousand miles.* She can see the words written down, she just can't work out how to say them.

"*For thou shalt be in league with the stones of the field,*" says Cherry, "*and the beasts of the field shall be at peace with thee.*"

"I want . . ." Tegan pauses and takes a deep breath. "I think . . . I think they did something to me. When I was . . ." She's looking for the longer word, the more scientific one but she can't bring it to mind. ". . . sleeping."

"Welcome to the club," says Shona.

If she waits until nightfall perhaps she can steal some of her belongings back and start walking. But in which direction? She can no longer see the mountains and has lost any sense of where the compound was.

She sits hypnotised by the flames and loses track of time, not daydreaming or failing to concentrate but something stranger and more abrupt, as if she were a machine that someone has turned off and then turned on again.

Bree hands her a skewer with three small chunks of meat on it.

Cherry looks at Shona warily. Shona holds her hand up like she's surrendering. Tegan finds this language of signs hard to understand. She takes the skewer and thanks Bree. The meat is part burnt, part raw. It tastes of ash and blood and woodsmoke.

The four women eat. Unseen birds chitter. Her left-hand side is fizzy. "*Where is the house of the prince?*" says Cherry. "*And where are the dwelling places of the wicked?*"

Bree hands Tegan one of her own water bottles. She drinks. Bree takes the bottle back.

She must fall asleep at some point because Adrian is standing in a gap between the trees. He is desperately thin, trailing plastic tubes or white ribbons, oddly bridal. He is illuminated by a creamy glow which comes from inside his chest. Tegan knows that he is asking her to take his hand and let him lead her to the heart of the forest. She wants to go with him but she has to get home. She has to see Mary J, she has to see her father.

When she comes round they are all inside the shelter and a light rain is falling. Shona and Cherry are talking.

"She a dead weight."

"She's a child of God."

"She a child of God who ain't no use to anyone."

"What d'you want to do? You tell me."

"This ain't a charity."

"She's awake. She can hear you."

"So she can hear me. I ain't ashamed. I'm just looking to stay alive here long as I can. This ain't Sunday school."

Then she's gone again.

"Same story all round," says Shona. The rain is no longer falling. Bree is building a new fire. "None of us got family on the outside. We get a transfer and we in that van for a *long* time. Then we here. We just meat."

. . .

She's woken by a gunshot, or a tree falling and snapping. The other women are asleep. Maybe she imagined it. Embers rise into the dark. Somewhere nearby she can hear children singing, *Frère Jacques, Frère Jacques, Dormez-vous? Dormez-vous?*

They are sitting beside a stream as it tumbles over rocks. There is a ragged strip of sky overhead where the water has cut a path through the forest over hundreds of years. Bree is fishing with a shirtsleeve knotted at one end. She sweeps it through the pool in figures of eight then pours away the excess water before emptying it into the grass. Tiny fish flex and flash between the green blades.

A shadow makes Tegan look up. A big hawk is crossing the road of light above them. It vanishes, then crosses back again. Once upon a time there was a hawk which was waiting to eat her when she died but she did not die. When was that?

She looks down and sees that Bree has the head and face of a wolf. This seems entirely normal. Then it seems very wrong. Tegan squeezes her eyes shut and opens them. Bree looks like Bree again.

"I'd do it all over," says Shona. "No way I was going to let him do that shit to someone else."

A bear circles the camp at night. She bangs two stones together to keep it away.

There are two graves in a further clearing, flat barrows of earth parallel to one another, a cross made of little stones above the face of each dead woman.

. . .

"I don't believe her," Shona says. "That girl's brain is super fucked up. She full of imaginary shit."

Tegan says, "No. Listen. There's a big . . . a big . . ." She mimes holding them in her hand, shaking them, making them jangle. ". . . of master keys. On the desk in his office . . . First floor . . . Door next to the refectory."

Shona and Cherry look at one another for a long time. Cherry says, "We could get them out. Shay. Martina. Everyone."

"How we gonna feed them?" says Shona. "And what if they been . . ." She taps her head. "What if they like that Taylor girl and we have to . . . I do not want to go there again."

"You want to live out here for ever? Use a hole in the ground for a toilet? Wait for a wound to go septic? We haven't even had a winter yet."

"They got guns. What we got? Sticks?"

"Burn the buildings," says Bree. It is the first thing she's said since Tegan arrived. Shona and Cherry stare at her. It's clearly the first thing Shona and Cherry have ever heard her say. Shona's mouth is hanging open. "The buildings are more important to them than the women."

Tegan turns a rotten log over and finds a smear of fungus. She looks closer and sees a miniature landscape of yellow spheres on white stalks. It is like flying above a city on an alien planet. There is such beauty in the world. She never noticed it before. She was moving too fast. She is seeing everything clearly for the first time.

Cherry says, "Are you crying? Don't let Shona see you crying. She's not a fan of that stuff."

Bree is lying on the floor, shaking. Shona is kneeling beside her, stroking her hair. "C'mon, baby. It's gonna be all right." Like the two of them are lovers. It is the first time she's seen Shona be tender. The fit comes to an end. Shona puts Bree in the recovery position, sits beside her, waits.

They clear an area of earth. Tegan uses sticks and stones to make the map. It is easier than talking. She needs only a handful of words. Her room, the refectory, the wildflower square, the cages, the propane tanks, the office.

Cherry says, "*When I looked for good, then evil came unto me: and when I waited for light, there came darkness.*"

"Come on," says Adrian. "It's no fun playing on my own."

He has angled a long plank against a crate to make a ramp. When he rides over the ramp the bike will rotate forward, he will hit the handlebars with his face and snap his two front teeth in half. It will be her fault for letting him do something stupid.

They set out after nightfall. The pins and needles and the numbness make it hard for Tegan to walk and she hangs on to Cherry's sleeve to help her balance and stop them getting ahead of her. They see the lights of the compound from far off, a glow at first, hardening to chunks of brightness chopped into fragments by silhouetted trunks and branches.

They crouch and wait and listen. Tegan is gone and then she is back again. The compound is silent. The moon hangs like a lamp in the canopy. So strange to think that there's a world up there, boot-prints of astronauts and aluminium spiders with feet like dinner plates. A deer barks in the distance, a sound she remembers from her childhood. The woods behind the house, bows and arrows, condoms and lager cans.

"Let's go," says Shona. They move through the undergrowth between the trees, towards the fence.

Shona lays the makeshift ladder against the razor wire, which twangs and scrapes as she puts her feet on the lowest rungs. The deer barks again. Tegan feels like a character in a story. She need only let this happen. There are no decisions left for her to take. Besides, Adrian is watching from among the trees. He will keep her safe.

Cherry climbs up after Shona, stepping gingerly over the razor wire onto the cage around the propane tanks. Cherry climbs the ladder, then Bree climbs behind Tegan, reassuring her, moving her numb foot into the right place when she can't find the rung.

They clamber down the meshed netting into the shadowed gap between the tanks and the adjacent building, Shona catching Tegan when she misses her foothold. There is no alarm, no one has appeared to challenge them. Tegan wonders if the whole place has been abandoned and they are surrounded by empty buildings. Bree strikes two flints until a spark falls onto the dry moss cupped in her palm, becoming a tender, green flame. She lays it against the splayed, fat-soaked splinters at the end of the first brand. Nothing happens and nothing happens and then, suddenly, the head of the brand is wrapped in a bubble of blue light that smells of meat and pine sap. They light the three other brands.

Tegan leads Shona to the office. Shona doesn't pause to see if the outer door is unlocked but kicks it hard with the flat of her foot the way you might kick someone in the chest or stomach if you were athletic and you knew about fighting. Inside, the entryway comes alive with tangerine light, heat bouncing back off the walls. There is a thrilling wrongness to uncontained fire inside a building. Tegan looks up and sees loops and swirls of soot on the white ceiling painted by the black smoke spilling from the tips of their flames.

Shona runs upstairs and by the time Tegan reaches the landing Shona is kicking away the remains of the splintered door whose latch and hinge remain attached but which has split down the centre.

"Where?"

Tegan steps inside and points to the keys. The siren starts as soon as Shona lifts them from the hook, as if it were the keys themselves which were alarmed. The whine gets higher and louder like an air-raid warning in a Second World War film, quaintly analogue, as if someone is cranking the machine that generates it. Tegan thinks, *I'm Deborah Deacon so it will be Deborah Deacon who dies if this all goes wrong*. Shona takes the keys and runs. Tegan looks down at the desk. She touches a sheaf of paper with her brand. The flame is a bright liquid she is pouring onto the desk like milk into a saucer. A sheaf of paperwork at the edge of the desk catches fire and individual leaves start to take flight, black and orange birds rising into a thunderstorm. The siren is steady and insistent now.

By the time she reaches the foot of the stairs and steps outside there are people everywhere, in pyjamas, in dressing gowns, in dark blue coveralls. One man is wearing nothing but boxer shorts. A distant building is alight, flames clambering raggedly into the sky from behind the silhouette of a nearby roof. She walks into the centre of the wildflower square. Adrian says, "You have to be really sad for two months after I'm gone. Then you can stop. Is that a deal?" Two security guards carrying fire extinguishers run into the doorway from which Tegan has just emerged. A goat zigzags out from between two buildings, bleating and skipping. There is a gunshot and the goat is knocked sideways. A woman screams, hands to both cheeks like a character in a cartoon. The goat lies on its side, bleeding from a wound in its neck, still kicking, still trying to run. Tegan thinks that this could be a funny story if she told it right. *I was standing right there but they shot the goat*.

She sees John Magnusson. He turns to look at her. She thinks, *If the goat can escape then the women can escape, too*. Magnusson opens his mouth to say something to her but this is the moment when one of the propane tanks explodes. There is a sudden, stunning brightness, as if someone has turned the sun on at the wrong time, then, a fraction of a second later, they are all thrown to the ground. It is like being hit by a car made of heat and light. She opens her eyes. A man in dark blue coveralls is lying on the ground with a bent metal pole through his abdomen. She hears a scream that is both human and not human, but it is not coming from this man. He seems merely puzzled that this strange thing has happened to him. The scream is coming from a monkey on a roof which is shrieking and bouncing as if it started all this chaos and it is the best fun ever.

Then she sees them, the women. Ten? Twelve? Walking out from the gap between two blazing buildings, one of them staggering a little, held up by the two walking on either side of her. She recognises the barking woman from the video. The big Anatolian hunting dog from the cages trots beside them like the coven's familiar. One of the women is Mary J. Tegan falls in beside her and takes her hand.

John Magnusson gets unsteadily to his feet and watches them cross the wildflower square. None of them turn to look at him. The guard with the metal pole through his abdomen is no longer moving. There are several other people lying on the grass. One of them is the man wearing nothing but boxer shorts. A guard in navy blue overalls raises a handgun towards the women, then thinks better of it and lowers his arm.

The women walk past the refectory, past the door to the laundry, past the window of what was once Tegan's room, the fire ballooning behind them, the heat on their backs. The hunting dog barks, a deep, rasping boom that she can feel in her abdomen.

Shona tries several of the master keys on the padlock holding the main gate shut before the women grow restless and start heaving the whole thing back and forth until the upper hinge wrenches free and the entire gate twists and falls, the lower hinge snapping as it does so. The women stamp noisily over it, into the dark and up the road between night-blue trees as it winds towards the top of the hill, the temperature falling as they move slowly further and further from the fire. Tegan stops and turns to see the entire compound ablaze, a fat, black root of smoke pouring up into the stars. She turns back and carries on walking beside Mary J. Cherry says, "*I am a brother to dragons, and a companion to owls, my skin is black upon me, and my bones are burnt with heat*." They turn a corner and the compound is no longer visible. The hunting dog growls. It is starting to rain. They walk on into the dark.

THE TEMPTATION OF ST. ANTHONY

The shattered mosaic floor on the far side of the courtyard wobbled and blurred in the blistering heat. He had woken at dawn and been praying ever since. He had not eaten today nor had he drunk. He would wait until the craving had passed, then allow himself to do both when it had become a choice, not a lost battle in his long war against the base needs of the body. There was grit under his knees. The pain was mortality made manifest. It demonstrated the shape and strength of that which he must rise above.

For eighteen years he had lived inside the ruins of this little Roman fort in the desert past Krokodilopolis, devoting himself to worship and contemplation, wearing rags and depending entirely on the charity of nearby villagers for sustenance. The original roof was long gone, but the walls, though partially collapsed in places, were still high enough to hide the surrounding landscape so that he could see nothing beyond the fort but sky. There was little protection from the sun during the day and no protection from the cold at night. The worst of the wind was kept out at least. He stored his food and water in the slim wedges of shade inside the perimeter of the compound and relieved himself at the far corner where scavenging insects consumed his excrement before it was dry.

The Devil had tempted him forcefully and relentlessly. A rain of gold coins lay on the ground for days, finally evaporating when he refused to touch them. Every so often a great trestle table of pies and tarts and wine would appear in the centre of the courtyard. The Devil himself would sit in his ear for days on end talking softly about all the pleasurable and profitable things he could do with his life. Daemonic women had appeared in the small hours and invited him to join them in a range of sexual acts that beggared belief. Angered by his persistent refusal to weaken, the Devil had sent a swarm of tiny, blood-red demons with spines like needles and razor teeth who tore his flesh to shreds, leaving his body permanently peppered and striped with scars.

A fat, brown scorpion sidled onto a rock beside him, its tail vibrating. It looked like a real scorpion but it was hard to be certain about such things, and he had to be on his guard. In the corner of his eye he could see a vulture turning overhead. One had landed on him a few months ago, puncturing his left shoulder with its talons and hacking out a chunk of his scalp with its beak. He had flinched and cried out and the bird had flown sullenly away.

The scorpion descended from its rock and scuttled off.

He could hear distant voices, a faint whoop and the slap of leather on powdery stone. He would not turn immediately. He would not allow himself to be steered by mere events. Neither, however, must he be ungracious. Bringing his prayers to a decorous pause, he got slowly to his feet. His knees were like the rusted hinges of an old door. He assumed the villagers were delivering bread and water, and indeed, when he turned, he saw the silhouette of the boy, Jarwal, standing in the notch in the southern wall that must at one time have been a window. But Jarwal was reaching down and hoisting a second person up beside him.

Another ogler come to see the hermit? He had asked that such people be gently dissuaded wherever possible, but some were wealthy, the villagers were poor, and he relied upon their goodwill.

The second silhouette was that of a robed woman, and if she was an ogler then she was a very insistent one because Jarwal was helping her climb down the slope of tumbled stones to the floor of the courtyard. He raised his hand intending to shout, "Stop!" but he had not talked, let alone cried out, for a very long time and no sound came from his mouth.

The woman was walking towards him carrying a basket. He did not want to be in the company of a woman. She was, thank God, not one of the phantoms who stepped naked from the shadows in the middle of the night. If the visitor were a man he might have been carrying news of sufficient weight to justify breaking the intrusion, but no one would entrust a woman with a task of such import.

She stopped a few paces in front of him and put the basket down. Ten loaves and three leather bottles of water. "I gather these are yours." The voice was so familiar it could have emanated from inside his own head. She pushed her hood back and looked around. "I had heard that it was austere but I did not expect quite this level of ostentatious self-flagellation."

He felt giddy. His sister had become a woman. "You . . ." He sounded like a raven. He coughed to clear this throat and tried again. "You should be in the convent."

"Don't worry. I'll be going back."

"As for ostentation . . ." He coughed again.

"I have no money of my own. You gifted the order the little wealth you did not give away. They are, in consequence, the only people who will look after me. Unless I can find myself a husband. Which is not easy from inside a convent."

He was about to defend himself but she cut him off for a second time. "You sold me to nuns."

"I didn't sell you to anyone." His sister seemed as unwilling to take instruction as she had been when she was a child, and the convent had not improved her. Arguing was pointless.

She sat down on a crumbled pediment, uncorked one of the goatskins, hoisted it to take a generous swig, then tore the end from one of the loaves. It was hard to tell whether she was genuinely hungry or whether she was trying to goad him. He refused to rise to the bait.

"Father indulged you too much. You grew up thinking that constant praise was normal and that other people were unimportant."

"I care little for your opinions about me, but you should not speak ill of our father."

"The nuns are vile, by the way." She picked a tiny stone from the bread and flicked it away. "Unsurprisingly. The majority were deposited there by rich families who wanted them out of the way. It has made them very bitter."

"A life devoted to Christ . . ."

"The ones with vocations are worse. Vinegary little witches. They need our money but they hate our company."

He took a deep breath. "Did you come here with some serious purpose?"

"Then Father died and there was no one to revere you. You couldn't sing, you couldn't paint, you couldn't argue fluently. You had fallen off a horse so many times we lost count. You were neither intelligent enough to practise law nor diligent enough to handle other people's money. But you had to be better than everyone else, didn't you." She looked around scornfully. "So you picked a challenge too pointless for anyone else to better."

She looked up at him and he saw that she was crying. "I could have been happy. I could have been a mother. You threw my life away in return for this." She hurled the remaining crust across the courtyard where it cartwheeled to a halt and lay in the little cloud of dry dust it had raised.

He was angry that she was so wilfully misinterpreting everything he had done. He was angry that she was dismissing his years of sacrifice as self-indulgence. He was angry most of all that she was able to stir up these violent emotions.

Then he was not angry. He was overwhelmed instead by a memory of standing in a sunlit courtyard. He was fifteen years old, his sister seven or eight. It was spring or autumn, the air neither too cool nor too hot. His mother was weaving on a small hand loom, yarns of indigo, turmeric, kermes red. He could hear the splash and slap of the servant girls washing clothes in the trough in the adjacent courtyard. His father was elsewhere in a dark room, poring over diagrams and accounts. His sister sat cross-legged in front of his mother. She had arranged two clay people and a little clay horse on the stone in front of her and was making them act out some ridiculous drama. The sun falling through the quince tree littered the ground in the centre of the courtyard with tiny overlapping circles of brightness like fallen blossom.

Within three years it would be gone, his father left paralysed by a seizure, then wasting away over the following months, barely able to eat or drink, his mother dying shortly after from the annual fever which swept through the city in the damp heat of summer.

His sister was right. He had been so consumed by his own grief that he had not considered hers. They had both lost their parents. He had been a young man, but she was still a child. How was it possible to be so blind for so long to such obvious facts?

An uprush of warmth towards his sister was overtaken by his shame at never having felt it before. He walked over and knelt in front her. "I am profoundly sorry. I treated you very badly indeed. I told myself that everything I did was done to serve the Lord. I should have remembered that serving the Lord means, first and foremost, looking after one's own family." He felt better for having simply spoken the words out loud.

She stared blankly at him as if he had spoken in a language she did not understand. "I am forced to sleep on a straw mattress in a room with five other women. One of them has lost her mind and whines constantly like a sick child."

"You have every right to be angry with me and I am painfully aware of my having no means of recompense for the wrong I have done you."

He paused. He couldn't say, at first, what caught his attention. Some animal faculty was warning him of danger. He remained perfectly still for a few moments. He could hear his sister breathing, the soft hush of wind-borne sand moving across stones and, every few seconds, the clang of a goat bell.

Then he smelt it, the faintest trace, the stink he had not smelt since the day some months back when a hyrax died and burst and oozed and dried out in the courtyard, felled by a disease so vile that even the birds of prey would not touch the corpse. He felt sick in both body and spirit.

"Brother . . . ? Something is wrong."

He forced himself to ignore the voice of doubt. He had to do this and he had to do it quickly. He stood up, lifted his arm and struck his sister hard across the face so that she was thrown onto the ground by the force of the blow. She lay there not moving for what felt like a very long time indeed, then lifted herself slowly back onto the pediment, the red print of his hand bright on her cheek. "And this is how the famous holy man behaves to his own sister."

"You are not my sister."

He wondered briefly whether he had made the most terrible error, then she let out a long growl and her eyes turned black. Her skin smoked and crackled and split and peeled away like the skin of a rabbit being roasted over an open fire. The same stink but overpowering now. He stepped backwards. She had been transformed into a hairy, snarling ape, spittle flying from her mouth. She sprang onto his chest, knocked him to the ground and fastened her sinewy hands around his neck. "You doubted. For a few minutes you doubted everything. I came *so* close. Next time I will shatter you completely."

There was a bang as loud as a house collapsing and the creature exploded, covering him in clumps of brown fur and gobbets of sticky fat bearing the same foul stink, which he had to peel away one by one before washing himself with a mixture of dust and precious water.

He felt wounded over the following weeks in a way that he had not felt wounded before, and it took longer for him to heal. He had been blindsided. He had won the battle but the margin by which he had done so was terrifyingly thin. There were nights when he began to question his vocation, bitterly regretting that he had so thoroughly detached himself from his previous life that now his only choice was between religious poverty or poverty with neither meaning nor purpose. Gradually, however, the same lack of choice gave him comfort and encouragement. There was a single path open to him. He did not need to waste time and effort in pointless debates with himself, he need only put one foot in front of the other. So he applied himself to his daily routine with redoubled vigour, he consoled himself that any mental bruises were useful reminders of his all-too-human failings and he gave thanks to God for pointing out his self-centredness.

It had rained sparsely and infrequently during the years of his confinement, but that winter a deluge fell from a night sky rumbling with thunder and cracked by bolts of lightning, turning the entire fort into a pool of freezing water. He knelt in it, praying until his frozen legs were too numb to support him and he was forced to stumble and splash through the absolute dark and take refuge on a fallen column. A burst of blue-white fire revealed, for the briefest moment, two rats sitting beside him, equally sodden and perplexed.

Drying off in the sun the following day he began to see the storm as a divine cleansing, of earth, of body, of soul. Whilst he tried very hard not to make predictions or draw conclusions or, worst of all, congratulate himself, it seemed to mark a turning point in his journey, a summit after which the path became easier and the landscape ahead more clearly visible. There were difficult dreams and days of doubt, but the Devil no longer appeared to him in person. He heard no bodiless voices, met with no animals who seemed anything more than creatures seeking shade or taking shelter or trying to steal his bread.

The oglers came in steadily increasing numbers but he accepted their appearances with as good a grace as he could muster, even when some of them refused to leave and put up tents and lean-tos outside the fort. The quiet and the calm he had enjoyed for so long was now interrupted not simply by the wind and the cries of birds and the bleating of goats but by the faint sounds of human conversation, the slap of canvas, the clink of pans and the clatter of wheels. Occasionally he saw a thin column of smoke rising above the wall and smelt meat being cooked.

When some of these men—for they were all men—came into the compound to ask for guidance he would instruct them to commune in silence with their Maker, to abjure the demands of the body and to live as simply as possible. He would point out, in addition, that they could do these things anywhere. They did not need to be near him, they needed to be near God.

According to Jarwal there were now some sixty or seventy of them camped round about. He could feel their presence even in the silence of the night, the way they pressed against his solitude, the way they made the heavens smaller. He had left the city and gone into the desert to escape everything that might distract his attention from his holy vocation, but the city had finally tracked him down and was in the process of swallowing him up again.

He forced himself to rise above his petty grievance. This piece of land, these ruins, had not been given to him for his sole use. All men stood in the same relation to God and no one had precedence over another. God neither spoke to him alone, nor cared for him alone. They were not impeding his religious self-betterment, he was impeding theirs. It might seem arrogant to suppose that he had anything to teach these . . . He could think of no word that did not make him feel uncomfortable. Followers? Acolytes? Disciples? But was it not more arrogant for him to refuse to help them?

He came slowly to accept that this phase of his life was over. He had a new calling and the fact that he did not want this calling was of no relevance. He was a servant of the Lord and it was not his place to dictate the tasks he was called on to perform. His distaste for company, for conversation, for noise, for activity, these things were no different from the physical pains he had previously taught himself to overcome in pursuit of a higher purpose. He would grieve for the loss of his solitary life, but he had already put one life behind him entirely. He could do it again.

He took the decision that he would leave the compound shortly after Easter so that he might, for one last time, celebrate Christ's death and rebirth on his own before re-entering the world. He spent the period of Lent fasting, sleeping little and praying constantly, asking God to give him strength and wisdom for the new and challenging task ahead.

He climbed the wall at dawn on Easter Monday, hoping that few of his followers would be awake and that the shock of re-entering the world would not be doubled by the shock of finding himself at the centre of a crowd.

It was not the makeshift village that troubled him most, large as it was—a wide, jumbled moraine of temporary dwellings which ringed the fort entirely—nor Krokodilopolis in the distance, nor the silver slice of the oasis, nor the seemingly endless desert beyond, but the sheer wheeling monstrosity of space which contained these things. He stooped and placed his hands on the dusty stone, as one might do travelling in the back of a cart along a rutted road, until the vertigo receded.

Getting to his feet again he saw a man squatting to relieve himself, thawb bunched around his waist. The man looked up and cried out and within moments numberless other men were clambering up and circling him like hunting dogs around a felled quarry. He could not hear what they were saying. He had not listened to people talking over one another since entering the fort. The warm, animal smell of them, the shock of being touched, the vastness of the horizon, then this press of bodies. But they were further away now, their voices had become muffled, the sun was dimming as if it were evening and he was falling backwards very slowly.

"He is unwell," shouted one man. "Give him space."

He was hazily aware of being carried into a shady tent and laid on a bed of terrible softness, and whilst he wanted to protest at a luxury dangerous both to him and to them, he did not have the energy and, in truth, he was relieved to be in a cool, dark space with only two men.

"Drink," said one, holding a clay cup to his lips.

He drank and slept and woke some hours later. He insisted that he must not lie in the shade but must be outside praying in the heat of the sun. When he went outside to do so, however, he found himself mobbed. He asked those around him to join him in prayer and some of them did so, but the noise and press of those further away, by whom they were surrounded, made quiet contemplation impossible. He tried to call out to these men but his voice had become a small thing over the years and they could not hear him. He felt overwhelmed, as if he were sinking in an ocean of humanity and were going to drown if he did not climb onto dry land. Eventually he returned to the cool of the tent, exhausted, ashamed and perplexed.

His cravings for stillness, for space, for empty hours, these were simple things to overcome. Dealing with other people was a great deal harder. He had forgotten how difficult it was to understand what was going on in another man's mind. He had forgotten that one could be on good terms with two men who hated one another. He had forgotten how well people lied, to others and to themselves. He had forgotten their capacity for saying one thing and doing another and being utterly unaware of the contradiction.

He constructed a regimen that would act like a map to get him through the difficult weeks ahead. He slept and ate in the company of different men every night so that none might count themselves as favourites or be counted as favourites by others. He spoke to, and prayed with, small groups in tents so that they might at least be able to hear one another clearly and find some relative peace. He tried to be a friend to all and to treat the whole encampment as his home.

He began, gradually, to feel more at ease in company, less disturbed by the noises and smells, the distractions and demands. His voice grew stronger. On a couple of occasions he clambered up onto the wall of the fort and spoke to those gathered below him, and this soon became a weekly, then a daily act.

"Let us not think, as we look at the world, that we have renounced anything of much consequence, for the whole earth is very small compared with heaven."

He instructed his followers to put aside the eating of meat and the drinking of wine and commit themselves to the simple diet of bread and water that had sustained him for nearly two decades. He instructed them to live without the false comforts of warmth and cleanliness. He instructed them to pray constantly and not waste energy in idle talk amongst themselves. He instructed them to undertake tasks that would purge the body of sinfulness, to remain still for long periods, to pass nights without sleep and days without food. Some of them submitted to his edicts, others were unable to rise to the challenge and returned to the world, but they were soon replaced by a growing number of others.

He shared with the increasing crowds the story of his own experiences so that it might prove an example. He told the stories of the gold and the pies and the daemonic women and the tiny, blood-red demons. He described how Satan had appeared to him in the guise of his sister.

"So let us intensify our discipline against the Devil, for a good life and faith in God are great weapons. Christ has given us power to tread upon serpents and scorpions, and upon all the power of the enemy."

Not all those who left the encampment did so because they found the rigours of this ascetic life too hard to bear. A handful not only embraced his teaching but walked even further out into the emptiness of the desert to find places of solitude where they, in turn, might come closer to their Maker, and it was the news of these men that, more than anything, persuaded him of the rightness of his decision to abandon his solitary life in order to preach.

Spring became summer, summer became winter, winter became spring. He had lived among his followers for nearly a year, by which time he had gathered about him a community of a thousand men or more, all devoted to living a holy life.

As Lent began he was acutely aware of the difference between this year and the last. He still felt a yearning when he recalled his final month inside the fort, pushing his body past fatigue, past discomfort, past doubt, past wilfulness into that place of profound stillness which seemed to lie just beyond the borders of the material world. But he had discovered a new and different joy in a vocation shared, the holy power of a community united in a single spiritual aim. Over those four weeks of penance, mortification, repentance and self-denial he felt every man slowly finding his place, like blocks being shaped and fitted by a master mason so that their individual bodies could be used to build a cathedral of souls.

The night before Easter Sunday they all remained awake in prayer, and in that communal silence he felt closer to God than he had ever done in his years of seclusion.

When the first splinter of sun blazed at the desert's far edge he rose and drank a little water and broke a crust of bread with those around him. Then he ascended to his usual spot on the ruined wall from which he could be seen by everyone in order to preach from the Gospel according to Mark, which was written, like much of the New Testament, on the pages of his heart.

"Now when the Sabbath was past, Mary Magdalene, Mary the mother of James, and Salome bought spices, that they might come and anoint Him . . ."

It was always his favourite time to preach. His voice seemed to be louder and to reach further, as if the air itself had been rinsed and cleansed by the night of all the sounds it had held during the previous day.

"And they said among themselves, 'Who will roll away the stone from the door of the tomb for us?' But when they looked up, they saw that the stone had been rolled away."

A man with a red beard standing directly below him was laughing. He felt a shiver of irritation but reminded himself that there were those among his followers who were not of sound mind and they should be the object of pity and persuasion, not public correction.

"As they entered the tomb, they saw a young man dressed in a white robe sitting on the right side, and they were alarmed."

Several men on either side of the red-bearded man were laughing now. His first thought was to turn round and see if something was happening behind him or nearby which had occasioned such amusement, but the laughter was spreading and there was a tangible malice in it that was very clearly directed at him.

"*'Don't be alarmed,' he said. 'You are looking for Jesus the Nazarene, who was crucified . . .'*"

Then he smelt it, the hyrax stench, the burst and the ooze of it. A well shaft opened in his bowels. This was surely not possible. A hundred men were laughing now, two hundred, five hundred, a thousand, mouths open, heads thrown back, hands spread theatrically on their bellies and chests. The smell made him retch. The laughter became a roar. He put his hands over his ears. He could neither speak nor run. A thousand pairs of eyes turned black at the same time.

"No, no, no, no, no . . ." He braced himself. There would be some kind of explosion, there would be fire or flood, the men would be transformed into beetles or rats in order to feast on him, or be gathered together into a single daemonic creature of huge proportions.

None of these things happened. The roar began to soften and diminish. The men themselves seemed less substantial, more like pictures of men painted on the air, then coloured mist, then nothing. There was silence.

The sun was fully risen now. He looked around. There were no tents, there were no fire circles, no latrine trenches, no footsteps in the sand, no cart tracks. Everything was exactly as it had been when he entered the compound twenty years before.

"*Pater noster qui es in caelis,*" he recited quietly, "*sanctificetur nomen tuum, adveniat regnum tuum . . .*" But the words were nothing more than sounds coming out of his mouth, as empty as the call of a bird or the bleat of a goat. The whole of the last year had been an illusion. He had thought himself deserving of a thousand followers. The work of his entire life had been rendered worthless by his own vanity. He began to sob. He had not sobbed since he was a small child. He wanted his long-dead mother to pick him up and put her arms around him, and he was terrified by the force of this need and the clarity of the memory.

He was getting to his feet. He had not taken a decision to do this. He was walking along the top of the wall, powerless to stop himself. He had always been powerless to stop himself, that was the truth. He was merely sitting astride the beast of the body as it followed its own base path. Will was an illusion. Control was an illusion. Perhaps God Himself was an illusion.

He was standing at the highest corner of the wall now, below him a field of jagged stones as rough as ploughed earth. He looked into the smoky distance. No habitation, no trees, no animals. Two tiny whirlwinds of dust made their slow progress over the plain. The unpeopled stillness that had previously been a great church was now a howling void. He stepped forward so that his naked toes curled over the edge of the wall. If his head struck the rocks first then he might at least be granted a swift passage to whatever world lay beyond this one. Was it hell that awaited him? He knew only that no hell could be more painful than this existence. He leant forward and tumbled into the empty air like a man falling onto a bed at the end of a hard day's work.

He was not dead. That much was clear. He was in a great deal of pain and someone, or something, was licking his face. He opened his eyes. The something was a stray dog. He pushed it away, then wiped his forehead and found it covered in a sticky paste of blood and dust. The dog cocked its head to one side, examining him. It was a scrawny creature, its fur a dirty, sun-bleached yellow, like pretty much everything else in the landscape.

He forced himself to sit up. For a few moments he had no idea of how he had got here. When the memory returned it was like someone cutting open his abdomen, reaching in and hauling his guts out through the wound. He felt sick and faint. He could not blame the Devil. The Devil had merely opened a door through which he had confidently walked.

He thought briefly about standing up but he could see no reason for making the effort. There was nothing he had to do, no one to whom he could turn, not even God Himself. He had crowned his failings by trying to throw away the most precious of all gifts, his own life. "*. . . and he that shall blaspheme against the Holy Ghost hath never forgiveness, but is in danger of eternal damnation.*"

The dog had a single patch of grubby white fur across its chest and down one leg.

He was painfully hungry and desperately thirsty. He had been painfully hungry and desperately thirsty for twenty years. He lay for a long time looking up into the relentless blue sky. How long would it take for him to die if he did not move? Days? Weeks? Then he remembered that one of the villagers, Jarwal perhaps, would be along sooner or later. He did not want this to happen. If others knew what he had done it would only magnify his shame. He had to leave this place.

Eventually, and with great care, he got to his feet. The world spun and slowed and came eventually to a standstill. He felt very feeble indeed. He had to go somewhere but he had no idea where. Perhaps he should simply walk further into the desert and let the buzzards pick his bones clean.

The dog was still there. It lifted a leg and scratched vigorously behind one ear. He liked the dog's company. It did not judge him. They were both outcasts.

Was it a real dog? He had no strength left to worry about such things.

He remembered the Devil visiting him in the body of his sister. The vision of the courtyard, the light under the quince tree, the sound of the servants washing, indigo and turmeric, the little clay figures his sister was playing with. That uprush of warmth. He wished he had listened to the stories she told herself.

He wanted to see his sister again. He was surprised by the clarity of this thought and the strength of the feelings it stirred up. Was she still alive? The possibility of her having died made him feel panicky and lost.

He calmed himself. If he needed an answer to the question then he could find an answer. It would be a journey of several weeks even if he had money, but it was possible. He had little else to do.

He looked at the dog, half-expecting some kind of agreement, but the dog was lying down in a little strip of shade, oblivious to his dilemma.

And if his sister was alive? If he found her? His welcome might be a very cold one. It did not matter. At the very least he could apologise for what he had done all those years ago, then turn and walk away. He would have tried. He would have settled some small account.

He would start by heading to Krokodilopolis. He would beg for money and use it to buy a place in one of the caravans. If no one gave him money he would work for it. If he had learnt one thing over the last twenty years it was how to put up with discomfort and live frugally.

"Let's go." He said it without thinking.

The dog got lazily to its feet.

He began walking and the dog fell into step beside him.

THE QUIET LIMIT OF THE WORLD

καὶ γάρ π̣[ο]τ̣α̣ Τίθωνον ἔφαντο βροδόπαχυν Αὔων
ἔρωι φ̣.̣ α̣θ̣ειcαν βάμεν’ εἰc ἔcχατα γᾶc φέροιcα[ν,
ἔοντα̣ [κ]ά̣λ̣ο̣ν καὶ νέον, ἀλλ’ αὖτον ὔμωc ἔμαρψε
χρόνωι π̣ό̣λ̣ι̣ο̣ν γῆραc, ἔχ[ο]ν̣τ’ ἀθανάταν ἄκοιτιν.

They say that once upon a time Dawn, with
her rose-coloured arms, fell in love with Tithonus
on account of his beauty and youth, and carried
him to the ends of the world. But grey age caught
up with him in the end.

Sappho, fragment 58

And how is my young man today?" She gently touches his shoulder and bends down so that he can see her without moving his head. Some of the staff say nothing when they're in the room, others talk in loud, kindergarten voices. Judith is the only nurse who talks to him as if he were a friend, telling him about her day, her family, the news, her childhood. "Stop me if I'm boring you." She opens a tub of Hydromol and spreads the ivory-coloured ointment onto the flaking skin of his knees, heels and elbows. Her father broke his neck in a motorcycle accident when she was a girl. "But what can you do? It is the Lord's way." She came over here with her mother and two brothers, both of whom have now returned to Jamaica. She has a son. He cannot remember the young man's name. It is not so much the weakness of his memory as its capacity. New details are so hard to pick out against the mountain range of years which lies behind them.

She closes the tub, washes her hands at the sink, then dries her hands with a paper towel. She puts up a new bag of Nutren. He can't swallow so they've fixed a PEG tube directly into his stomach through the wall of his abdomen. He doesn't want it but he cannot speak and no longer has the energy to signal his refusal. Judith slips a rubber thimble onto his finger to measure his heart rate and blood oxygen level. She wraps a chunky, Velcroed cuff around his arm and takes his temperature by pressing the barrel of what looks like a plastic ray-gun into his left ear. The electric mattress crackles softly under him as it shifts his weight back and forth to stop him getting pressure sores.

They have put him in a side room on his own for which he is thankful, though there seems to be no clear medical reason. Perhaps he scares the other patients. It is many years since he looked into a mirror but the image is not one he will easily forget—solar keratoses, spider veins, warts like fat black beetles, archipelagos of brown lesions. His tissue-paper skin is decorated with scars which cover almost every part of his body like runes from some wild, forgotten language. His ears and nose are too big for his face so that he seems like a very small giant from a very old story. Two fingers are missing from his right hand. No longer able to straighten his back, he lies in a foetal curl. His breath sounds like wind blowing through a little ruined house.

On the whiteboard above his bed and in the absence of any paperwork they have written *Kristof* with a red marker. Kristof was one of the paramedics who brought him in. It is entirely possible that he has been called Kristof at some stage. He has not needed a name for a very long time and can remember only a handful of those he has used. What, in any case, had names ever signified when he could be that person for no more than ten, fifteen, twenty years before he was forced to leave lovers, friends, colleagues behind and go in search of a new life?

"All done and dusted." Before she leaves, Judith squats so that there are only a few inches between their faces. She holds one of his hands and looks into his milky eyes, her voice suddenly serious. "Who are you?"

For how many years had he lain on the sofa as the days and nights came and went on the far side of the window, the sun bleaching and fraying those cheap curtains? He had watched the skyline evolve—chimneys coming down, cranes dancing, towers rising. He missed the stars more than anything, being granted little more than glimpses of the sky proper through the city's airborne dirt on the occasional cold, cloudless night, never a whole constellation. Cepheus, the Dragon, the Falling Eagle . . . They had been his companions throughout the entire journey. Once upon a time all he had to do was to look up after dark and they offered him some small, fixed mark in the desert of time.

But no more. A fine patina of lime-green moss had grown up the glass so that the room now looked like an uncleaned aquarium, filled with a soft green light which dimmed and brightened as the year turned. Rats had scoured the house of anything edible a long time ago and he seldom saw them these days. They never touched him, though they would sometimes sit and stare at him as if he were an insoluble puzzle, which indeed he was. For a period the rug in front of the sofa bred moths but they were gone, along with the rug itself, leaving only a dark oval on the floorboards like the remains of a campfire.

Occasionally there would be a knock at the door or an enquiring shout through the letterbox. Neighbours came and went. For some years a troubled man lived in the adjacent house. Some nights he would yell and rage after drinking, though there were never any voices raised in response. Was there a family who had been cowed into silence or did he, too, live only with ghosts?

When they broke down the front door he assumed it was a dream at first, dreams having become the only place where things of consequence happened, then he heard a conversation about fuses, junction boxes and electrical faults, he opened his eyes and saw a man in dark blue overalls looking down at him, saying, "My sainted fucking aunt, I thought you was dead."

She visits him every day, a little earlier each morning as spring builds to summer, different clothes, always, but the same radiance. Twenty, twenty-two you might say and be unaware of how profoundly wrong you were. Jeans on this occasion, a hooded red sweatshirt, trainers, everything a little scuffed and shabby, her brightness deliberately dimmed so as not to attract too much attention, only a few locks of blonde hair visible.

He thinks, as he often does, of how she must be repulsed by him, then she pulls up a chair and sits down, he feels the force of her absolute attention and is moved to tears. She leans in and dries his cheeks with her hand.

The staff accost her at first since visiting hours don't begin till the afternoon but none of them, despite their seventeen languages, can understand her or make themselves understood. Perhaps there is no one left in the world who can understand her. If the words were written down then doubtless some dry professors toiling in the dusty corners of libraries could parse it, but not if they encountered it like this, sung in the old way. Besides, there is a presumption in her bearing which suggests that she would not take well to being challenged. So they leave her alone. She causes no trouble and there is so little else they can do for him. It is a consolation to know that there is at least one person in the world who recognises him. Great-granddaughter? Great-great-granddaughter? Who knows?

It is the way she vanishes, however, which mystifies them most of all. She's there and then she's not there, just a flash of colour at the end of a hallway, or a shock of blonde hair in the corner of your eye as you glance down into the car park, though even that may be nothing more than light flaring on a newly polished windscreen.

"Not long." She lays the curve of her hand against the translucent skin covering his skull. "Be patient."

Will you stay with me until the end? he thinks.

"I promise," she says. "I will stay with you until the end."

The light which started to fill the room when she arrived is now a bright flood. Only seconds left. In moments the sun will detach itself from the horizon and its blazing circle will be complete.

Don't go. After all this time, the same pointless thought. *I love you*.

And she's gone.

He is washing his hair in the stone trough when it strikes him, a gut conviction that something elemental is about to happen, like the premonition that spooks horses in their stalls before a storm. He turns. She is dawn light poured into the body of a young woman standing on the far side of the stone courtyard. Sandals, cream chiton. A shiver he has only ever felt when seeing a pod of dolphins leap alongside a boat.

He walks over to her and she takes his hand. He flinches as if burnt. She apologises. "I've not done this before."

"Come." She turns and leads him out of the courtyard and through the garden. "Let's be alone together."

They speak little at this first meeting, they do not kiss, yet every moment is more sensual than anything he has ever done or had done to him. He feels like a boy all over again, made speechless by the force of his desire and his fear of losing her. They take a leisurely zigzag down through the vineyard to the stone bench where they can sit and gaze across the valley to the silhouetted hills behind which the growing sunlight looks like fields on fire. Over their heads the final stars are being swallowed by the gathering blue. The lees of the night lie thick and black in the base of the valley.

A cold-eyed observer might say that she is nothing special, that he has simply fallen in love, an experience as common as rain, that she could have a scar across her face or a club foot and it would be beautiful because it was *her* scar, *her* club foot. That same cold-eyed observer might point out that she seems even more tongue-tied than him, that while she is well formed there is something clumsy and unnatural about her movements, as if her body were a borrowed costume recently put on. But perhaps that cold-eyed observer has never fallen utterly in love, for, having been in that state, who could call it *as common as rain*?

Sunlight spills over the hills like liquid iron from the lip of a foundry bucket. They sit for half an hour until the sun is about to detach itself from the horizon.

"I have to go."

"Already?"

"I'll be back tomorrow. No. Don't follow me."

Later he will find a bruise blooming on his shoulder in the exact shape of the small hand she still does not know how to use gently. He obeys her command for no more than a few moments before jumping from the bench and running into the vineyard. Her fragrance hangs on the air—myrtle, almond blossom, oregano. He spins and sees nothing but leaves and earth and sky. The world is like a great brass bowl which has been firmly struck so that it sings. He walks distractedly back towards the main house, realising how chilly the air is, his path a little wayward, as if he were drunk. Did that really happen? He squats and presses his hand into the dust of the roadway to prove to himself that he is awake.

She has spent her life doing little more than playing in the warmth and light of the mountain tops. She has not aged. She has never worked. If she injures herself Paeon cures her wounds and ailments as quickly as fig sap curdles milk. Everything is possible and in consequence nothing matters. Small wonder that her clan squabble like children while, down below, under the inconstant weather, their little counterfeits whose lives come and go as swiftly as those of mayflies act as if love and honour and goodness are eternal truths, all the while knowing that they will be crushed under chariot wheels or sputter like candle flames in their ageing bodies. Who then could fail to be jealous of the way that, in spite of this, they fight so desperately to create something that might outlive them—a city, a poem, their own good names?

And there he is, awake before his sisters, dunking his head in the limestone water trough in the Heron courtyard, that muscled back, the animal confidence in his own body, his youthful ignorance of how soon the bloom will be gone. The same cold-eyed observer might say that he could be replaced by any of a thousand young men, that she wants only youth and beauty, to be made thrillingly self-aware, to feel the dew under her naked feet, but isn't that precisely what love is, the excitement of being in a body, the miracle by means of which another person makes every dull thing shine? Does it matter why you love one person and not another? Is a metaphorical arrow from a fat, winged boy any more ridiculous than looking down into that stone courtyard and saying, "I choose you?"

She puts her hand on his chest and feels, under her fingers, the soft, double thump of the heart's shuttle as it weaves the blood back and forth. She looks into his eyes and sees a tiny image of the young girl she has temporarily become floating in the black wells of his pupils.

She comes again the following morning and the morning after that. Expectation wakes him in the small hours, the fear that he might sleep in and miss her. He washes himself and oils his skin and goes outside to wait in the blue of moonlight and the black of moonshadow, wrapped in his woollen cloak, willing the heavens to spin faster, listening to the cries of nightjars and foxes and the wind running its soft hands over the oaks and alders. And every time, when she appears, he feels the same breath-taking surprise at her beauty.

His sisters mock him. He is in love, surely—his moping, his distraction, those aimless wanders in the hills, his lack of interest in hunting with his cousins and his father's account books. But what can he say in return that will not sound deranged and grandiose? In any case, he cares little what they think. Their chatter is like cow bells or rain on a roof.

On the tenth morning—if it is indeed the tenth morning, for he is already becoming unmoored from human time—she leads him back into the house and they walk along the L-shaped corridor to his bedchamber, hand in hand. She feels a giddy panic at first, the shock of real darkness, these borrowed human eyes hungry for light but flooded only by this grainy monochrome nothing.

"In here."

He ushers her through a doorway and she hears the changed acoustic in the slap of their sandals against the stone floor. When he closes the door the squeal of the double hinge and the rush of displaced air make it almost visible. They sit on the bed and the squeaky give of the knotted ropes and the hay scent of the mattress form a picture in her mind and she understands for the first time that seeing happens in many different languages.

Then they are lying beside one another, their mouths and tongues together, hands exploring one another's bodies, and it doesn't matter that he is clumsy in his way and that she is clumsy in her different way for they are both experiencing the thrilling disorientation that comes when the boundaries between one's body and another body dissolve so that they feel less like two separate people than a single creature pleasuring itself.

Afterwards she lies in the growing half-light, conscious of the breath entering and leaving her body. She can control it or she can let it happen. She is breathing, then she is being breathed. She is on the very border between spirit and matter. Is it possible that she could let go, become mere body and never find her way back, never know there was a way back, never know anything, just *be*?

She has been visiting him for several months now and slowly the great bowl of the world has stopped ringing. Compared to the transcendent hour they spend together the remainder of his day is drab. The cry of a cockerel sounds harsh and mechanical, the sky is a vast and tawdry marquee, the dog that greets him when he stands in the empty doorway reminds him of a beggar, the smell, the neediness. Nothing else matters apart from that brief ecstasy. Because he wakes so early he is constantly tired and distracted. He attends family meals less and less. Increasingly he prefers the company of creeks and hills which, unlike people, demand nothing of him.

His youngest sister falls badly from a spooked horse, landing on a locked arm that snaps, leaving the shattered end of her radius poking through the skin. He acts as if he cannot hear her screams. He lays her on her back, braces a foot in her armpit and hauls on her wrist as if he were roping a heavy barge to a stone quay. He tells the groom to align the bones, then slowly lets go of her wrist when it is in the right place. His sister stops screaming in the middle of this process and removes herself to some distant place from which she does not return for several days. The whole event is witnessed by other members of the household drawn by the noise and whilst it is generally agreed that he saved his sister's life the cold blood which made it possible is talked about as if it were a form of sorcery.

There is no more laughter. His other sisters no longer tease him. If a girl is the cause of this unsettling state of mind then they pity her.

He can no longer summon interest in leases, stocktakes, taxes. His exasperated father loses patience. "I don't give a damn about you. This is about your mother, about your sisters, about these buildings, the tenants, this land. What happens if I die tomorrow? Does everything drift onto the rocks because duty and gratitude mean nothing to you, because family and honour mean nothing?"

He cares. Or rather he knows that he should care. He is not an unkind person. Yet how can he explain his situation?

The time it takes to think these thoughts generates a pause long enough to convince his father that he is being ignored. He strikes him hard across the face and the fact that his son does not strike him back is almost a disappointment.

He starts, instead, to share his thoughts about estate business with his oldest daughter and what begins as a piece of domestic theatre intended to shame his son into re-engagement rapidly becomes more serious when she demonstrates more aptitude and interest than his son had shown even when he was fully engaged.

"Are you not happy with me? With this? With us?"

"It's nothing."

"You've changed."

"My father . . ."

When they speak using only their bodies nothing is lost in communication but when they use words the mistakes and misunderstandings which seemed endearing at first are now an aggravation. How do you explain what family means to someone who has never been dependent? How do you explain honour and duty to someone who can simply vanish into the air leaving behind only the scent of almond blossom? "I'm unhappy, but I'm not unhappy because of you."

"You're with me now."

He closes his eyes and puts his head in his hands so that he can think more clearly. "If you are in my life then the rest of that life falls to pieces."

The following morning is the first when he has not woken and washed and waited for her outside. She sits on the edge of his bed. He lies with his eyes closed, turned away from her.

From the very beginning she knew she would lose him. That vulnerability of which he was so blissfully unaware, the brevity of his flowering, they were a part of what made him beautiful. But she expected injury, illness or the dull turning of time itself to be the thief. She did not expect him to reject her, to value his family more than her. Does he not appreciate how far she has lowered herself? She is angry. She wants to destroy him. At the same time she would give anything if it would bring him back.

"I lost my mind."

His mother puts down her needle and holds his eye. "She must be an extraordinary woman, this mystery lover of yours."

He wonders if his mother knows more than she is saying. "I need to apologise to my father." He is standing at the window. Below him, two bird scarers made of pale sacking dance on poles above the tiny furrows in the walled garden.

"You'll need to do more than that." His mother is weaving a tapestry of a skinny red dog vaulting a full moon. "You'll need to prove that you're a better man than your sister."

His father sits him down with a set of accounts for the half-year and asks him to find the evasive error which is throwing everything out of true. He spreads the rolls out on the table and holds the curling corners down with polished green stones from the basket. His sister glares at him from the doorway. He bridles initially at the tedious task but as the morning passes he forgets the weight of his yoke and pulls and turns like a good ox, remembering the pleasure of losing himself in a humdrum task. He asks himself yet again, *Did it really happen?*

He finds the accidental double entry and is pleased to see his father trying to seem unimpressed.

The truth is that she would not give up anything to get him back. Self-denial is not in her nature. She is willing, however, to abase herself a little if the ends justify it.

Her father knows that she wants something. He can smell her need. It is blood in the water for an old predator like him. Before she has spoken five words he knows that she is in love and he despises her for it. He is never in love. He desires, he hunts, he rapes, he discards. He gets pleasure from abusing the weakness of others, so when his daughter asks him to grant immortal life to her lover he feigns magnanimity and grants it immediately, thinking her a fool twice over for not examining the terms, as one should always do with any contract, especially one meant to last this long.

He digests what she has told him, then staggers out into the soft light of the night's end and leans against the wall of the stables. The sweet, ammoniac scent of dung, faint snorts and bridle chimes. He was caught in a storm at sea a long time ago, travelling with his father on a chartered cargo vessel. They were trying to reach the safety of a port's breakwater before nightfall, the hull yawing and twisting, the light at the harbour mouth now to one side, now to the other as they tacked into the gale. Then lightning struck the mast. Hard white light, the bowel-shaking *crack*, sails, booms and mast on fire. He knew with complete certainty that they were going to die.

She has followed him outside. "Are you not grateful?"

Now that he is faced with the opposite possibility that he might never die he feels the same wheeling terror. Everyone he has ever known will be taken from him. His parents will die, his sisters, his friends. Every tree will fall, every building crumble. How long does a language last? A mountain? "I don't believe you." He feels nauseous. "I can't believe you."

She says, very slowly, as if she were talking to a child for whom an idea must be put into simpler words. "We will never be separated."

"No," he says, holding his hand up to keep her at a distance. "No."

The gift for which she humiliated herself in front of her father is being thrown back at her. She walks away and rubs her eyes and turns to look at him and that little distance is enough for her to see him as he is, just a man, not greatly different from other men. Pull back a little further and you can see thousands of them barking and mewling in market squares, hunkering in their houses at night with their mates and litters. Their presumption at giving themselves names when there is so little difference between this one and the next, no more than the difference between two rabbits or two rooks.

Why did she love him? It seems delusional now, one of those idiotic yearnings for something different from which nothing good ever comes, not so different in principle from the sordid adventures of her own father, though this is not a thought she will share with anyone.

She is suddenly aware of the tightness and smallness of the human body she is trapped inside, mortal time cranking like a poorly oiled wheel, both too slow and too fast. How dull these stones are, these leaves. The day is coming. She can bear it no longer. She turns away from him and steps into the air and is gone.

He knuckles down to the business of living and there are days, weeks, months sometimes, when his experience is little different from the experience of those around him, for everyone has secrets, and don't we all exist in the shadow of vast and indigestible facts that we must try to ignore for fear that they may overwhelm us? But there are moments when he lets his guard down and is ambushed by images so bright they seem to have happened only yesterday: the hand-shaped bruise on his shoulder; the curve and sweetness of her belly as he ran his tongue across it in the darkened bedchamber. He remembers her promise of eternal life and feels a panic that crushes his chest so tightly he has to drop to his hands and knees and fight for each breath.

He marries a plump woman with dark brown skin and a mane of black, corkscrew hair. She is the daughter of a neighbouring landowner and it is a politic match which he enters into by taking the path of least resistance. He is distant but makes few demands. Her fathers and brothers were angry, selfish and sometimes violent men so his coolness comes as a relief. She bears him twin girls and then, a year and half later, a boy and he finds in their company something close to real joy, playing with them in a way that few parents do, building dens, taking on fantastical roles in make-believe games—a giant, a horse, a river god. There is a furious intensity to their experience, and he finds that if he gives himself over to this way of thinking then the magical cave of their days becomes the universe. He builds them a rope swing, he builds a raft.

One morning his father is unable to get out of bed. He can

neither raise his right arm nor feel his right leg nor access certain words. Names are particularly elusive. He is unaware of anything happening to his right side. His condition deteriorates over the following week, robbing him of speech altogether, then robbing him of the ability to walk unaided. He chokes if he tries to eat solid food and every meal must be softened to a pulp and spooned into his mouth by a servant. His father will remain in this state for a decade and he will never know whether the father he remembers is trapped inside this damaged body unable to communicate with the world or whether they are tending a useless vessel his father has vacated.

He takes over the running of the estate but he cannot summon sufficient belief in its importance to do the job well. The possibility that he might not die has put a distance between him and everyone and everything around him. *This will all pass away*. The formula no longer has for him the consolation intended by the poets but instead leaches everything of meaning, of urgency. His attitude spreads like an infection. The estate becomes less and less a community where workers, tenants and family members think of themselves as contributing to some shared enterprise, and increasingly a group of individuals resenting their mutual entanglement. Roofs tumble, yields fall, bills are left unpaid, disagreements fester. His wife no longer feels so lucky to have escaped her father's house.

His oldest sister is angry. She knows that she could do a better job. He knows it too but he is unwilling to take his hands from the tiller for if he has no distractions what is to stop him wandering to the cliff edge and looking over?

One of the twins dies. She is ten years old. She has a fit in the presence of her sister who can only watch as she lies on the ground twitching, eyes rolled back into their sockets, breathing in her own vomit. Those around him think he is broken by grief. He is broken by his lack of grief. It does not matter, he thinks. None of it matters.

It is late autumn, the end of a dry week. He is walking in the grounds when he comes across a great bonfire in which the gardeners are burning a summer's worth of dead leaves and sticks, several old barrels, a broken cartwheel. The conflagration sits at the centre of a raked circle of bare earth to prevent it spreading. The heat is extraordinary. The hot, swaying air, the angry snapping crackle, above it all a fat column of drunken smoke. He stands for a long time looking into the luminous heart of it. He thinks, *I am dead wood. I am a broken wheel.*

It is not a decision, it simply happens. He closes his eyes, steps into the flames and falls forward, the way you might if you were diving into a river or a lake. He thinks, briefly, *It is all over now,* and the thought brings him exquisite relief for a few moments before the pain occupies him so completely that he is unaware of someone grabbing his heels and dragging him backwards, then rolling him over and over in the dust for want of a water butt or a cloak to smother the flames.

He spends the next nine weeks in a single, darkened room. His face, his chest, his belly, the fronts of his legs and arms one open wound. With the help of two nurses his wife applies honey every morning to the weeping flesh to prevent it becoming infected, then re-covers it in clean bandages.

The story is put about that this was a terrible accident but his wife knows better. Something is rotten inside him. She resents him for thinking he could just step out of the world and away from his responsibilities. She does not care if he cries out when she cleans and re-dresses his wounds. Causing him pain feels like some small recompense. She forces him to stand and walk. The single wound becomes many smaller wounds which heal and scab and split and ooze and re-heal. She leaves them open to the air for longer and longer periods, sitting beside him to swat away the flies.

It is assumed, at first, that he will die. When he does not it is assumed that he will be permanently disfigured. But this is not what happens. He loses the two smallest fingers on his right hand, the remaining knuckles melted to nubs, but over many months his arms, abdomen, chest and face all return to perfect health. If anything he looks better than he did before the supposed accident, which confirms suspicions some have already begun to harbour. It is not noticeable in most circumstances for who can remember in detail even their spouse's face from six months ago, a year ago, two years? But when he stands beside his sisters it is unarguable. He is not ageing in the same way. And what might have begun as grounds for envy or congratulations is tipping into something more sinister.

He knows it too. She was telling the truth. Throw himself into a churning torrent and he would find himself being pulled out of the water downstream by a couple of goatherds who happen to be passing. Swallow poison and he would throw it up moments later. He will not die. Instead the world will die around him. He looks at his father and wonders how much difference there is between them. Is this a life he is leading, or merely an empty vessel which looks like a life?

She does not think of him for many years. Or perhaps it is only minutes. The distinction means nothing. Mortal days are like the blur of a dragonfly's wings. She looks down occasionally out of little more than boredom and curiosity. She sees him listening to his daughter play the flute. She sees him arguing with his wife. She sees him drinking alone when the rest of the household have retired to bed, his only companion a hearth of dying embers. She sees—and it is this detail which snags and holds her attention—his crippled hand, the missing fingers, the smooth red misshapen knuckles. It is ugly but the imperfection touches her.

. . .

His mother blames him for everything—his father's paralysis, the decline of the estate's fortunes, his daughter's death, his own unhappy marriage. And there is a general truth to this which makes any protest about the details pointless. When she becomes ill herself this too is indirectly his fault. "If I hadn't had to look after your father these past years . . ." She is constantly exhausted and short of breath. Climbing stairs is an effort. It is hard to listen to the same charges every day without taking them on board. He killed his father. He killed his daughter. He drove the family to the edge of ruin.

His mother can no longer walk. She is confined to her bed. She starts to lose her mind. She believes that she is living under the sea. She describes the octopus and mackerel and rays swimming around her and the boats passing overhead. She falls asleep one night and does not wake. His father is carried to the funeral on a simple stretcher covered in soft cream sheepskin and laid near the grave. When his wife is lowered into the ground he speaks for the first time in many months, saying, clearly, "We are here for such a short time. I know where we go to, but where do we come from?" The gap in the clouds closes as swiftly as it opened and he never speaks again.

After the funeral, her tongue loosened by grief and by the strangeness of the event, his youngest sister, the one whose broken arm he once helped set, gently touches the smooth skin of his cheek and says, "Everything that ages us makes you younger. You feed on our suffering."

He packs a bag with food and a sturdy cape. He takes a spear, a knife and a bow and says that he is going hunting. He is not going hunting. He simply wants to be away from those who blame him for everything that has gone wrong in their lives. He wants to be in a place where he can no longer hurt people. He wants not to feel guilty.

He walks for many miles. He spends the night rolled in his cape under a rocky outcrop in a gully he has passed through many times over the years. His sleep is deep and long and dreamless and he wakes feeling refreshed in a way that he has not felt for a long time. He keeps walking. He kills two partridges and cooks them over an open fire, eating one and smoking and drying the meat of the other to eat later. He gathers handfuls of tiny wild strawberries. He spends a second night sleeping in the open. He lies awake for a while watching clouds, visible only because they blot out the Milky Way as they pass across it, great sliding holes in the heavens. He wakes in the night to see a bird perched on a rock only a few paces away. It is surely too big even for an eagle but the low light plays tricks and he drifts back to sleep not knowing if he was awake or whether the creature had visited him in a dream.

He reaches a river which marks the limit of the territory he knows. He wades the flood where it is wide and shallow and when he steps onto the far bank he feels something heavy fall from him.

He never thinks, *I am abandoning my family.* He thinks, *I can always turn round and go back.* He thinks, *They are better off without me.* He thinks, *They can come and find me if they need me.*

He bathes in streams. He meets shepherds, hunters, farmers, and finds unexpected pleasure in conversations with strangers who know nothing of his story. He moves northwards and inland, away from the coast, onto higher ground.

He is attacked by wolves one night, waking only when a big male sinks its teeth into his calf. Without thinking he grabs the wolf's head and presses his thumbs into its eyes as his father taught him to do. It backs off, snarling. His leg is badly wounded but he cannot feel the pain yet. He grabs a knife and gets to his feet to show how tall he is. The wolf bristles and quivers, then springs onto him. He hoists the knife into the wolf's chest as hard and as high as he can. The two of them twist together in the air and hit the ground hard. A paw slashes his face but the animal's movements are random now, more spasm than attack, so he pulls his knife out and rolls away and sees that the wolf cannot get to its feet and that its companions have dissolved into the shadows.

When the pain starts to ebb he sees that a wedge of wet, red flesh has been hacked from his calf. He is in the middle of nowhere with no clean dressings. It is a day since he last saw another person, a solitary hunter, and two days since he passed any buildings. He wants very badly to be at home again, to know that he will be looked after. He is going to die and those same wolves will return to take their time finishing their interrupted meal. He will become a pile of scattered and unidentifiable bones and no one will know how he left the world.

He lies back on the cold, bristly grass, trying not to move his injured leg. He stares up into the vastness of the night and only then does he remember his burns. He has walked so far out of his old life that he has forgotten his own story. The pain eases a little. He realises how much of hurt is a fear of what it portends. He wonders what he can use to bind the wound while it heals. He wonders whether he even needs to do this. A ghoulish part of him considers filling the wound with ash from last night's fire, with earth and crumbled bark and dried leaves to test this power with which he has been cursed.

He leaves the wound undressed and uses his knife to skin the wolf. He does this slowly and carefully so as to save the pelt. He cooks the meat, eats some and dries some. The bleeding slows and stops. He does not walk far over the next few days but he walks nevertheless, the wound crusting slowly. In two weeks the gash has healed, leaving a single scar, a lopsided pink omicron.

Over those same two weeks, however, the turning seasons and the rising ground mean that it is no longer so pleasurable to sleep out, despite the wolf pelt under him and the cloak on top. It rains on three consecutive days and he can find nowhere dry to shelter. On the fourth day he comes to a small town and makes the mistake of telling the owner of the one tavern that he is literate and numerate, that he can do bookkeeping and copy documents in a fine hand, and the tavern owner asks him why, if he can do these things, he is on the run. Several days later he comes to another town and asks in the bakery where he might find work as a labourer.

He tells a local landowner that he can build walls. He has underestimated the skill of the workers he once underpaid. He cannot build a wall. The foreman beats him with the stick he uses for driving cattle. He fights back, two slaves intervene and he is shackled in a cowshed. The foreman feeds him brackish water and bowls of cold grey bean soup and makes it clear that he will be released when he "learns his place." The chains force him to shit on the dirt floor and when the foreman sees what he has done he whips him like a dog. On several nights the man comes in drunk and urinates on him.

Days pass. His beaten back bleeds constantly. The knowledge that he will not die reduces the pain but does nothing to reduce the humiliation and the anger. Eventually the landowner visits him. He is weak from lack of food and it is hard, at first, to tell whether this is really happening. He must show that he and this man have things in common. He says, as calmly as he can, "I am grateful, at least, that a long-winged eagle has not been set to eat away at my immortal liver every day." The man's expression is unreadable. He turns and leaves without speaking. Has he made himself more vulnerable? Might it be thought too dangerous to let an educated man free after such treatment?

The foreman reappears, a knife in one hand and a key in the

other. "I'm going to release you. Fight and I swear to the gods I will gut you. Understand?"

He cannot bring himself even to nod in agreement.

The foreman shakes his head, spits on the stone floor and unlocks the shackles. "Go. Get out of here."

He holds the man's eye. The man grabs his jaw and holds it tight. "Don't push me, boy."

He walks until he is out of sight, then kneels and places his hands flat on the earth and exhales, opening the furnace of anger which he has been holding tightly closed.

He washes himself in a stream and waits till nightfall. He returns to the farmhouse and retrieves his bag and wolf skin. He breaks into the store and takes a knife and a staff. He heaps up dry straw, pours linseed oil over it, then sets it alight. He watches the fire from a stony promontory which marks one corner of the property. At first it is just a glowing door floating in the darkness. Then the roof falls with an audible crunch and a cow on fire breaks through the shed door, the burning animal bellowing piteously before it staggers and falls. He hears screams and sees two human silhouettes, black puppets against the flames. The foreman and his family live adjacent to the cowshed. Other buildings are on fire now. It's been dry for over a fortnight. It is entirely possible that come morning everything belonging to his supposed employer will be turned to charcoal and warm black stone.

He walks for hours. Dawn comes and the sleep that swallows him up when he lies down wrapped in the wolf skin is the most delicious he has experienced for a very long time.

In a tavern overlooking the market square of the largest town he has seen for a very long time he says, "I got into a fight and killed a man. I can write. I can do accounts," and finds himself working for a Cyrenean woman who is trying to run her recently deceased husband's import and export business. He assumes that she trusts him because he, too, is an outsider, but it takes only a few days before he realises that his supposed outlaw status is their bond. She might not have murdered someone but it seems possible that her husband was murdered, given the number of people he defrauded, the tax he has avoided and the stack of unpaid bills. He is not greatly troubled. He can see now, from his peculiar vantage point on the outside of everything, that morality and laws are little more than the rules of the wealthy validated by philosophical packaging. His daughter died. His mother died. His father will die. His father is very possibly dead already. There is no final judgement. Everything just fades away.

Silk, ivory, glass, copper, onyx, saffron, cardamom . . . He writes threatening letters and keeps parallel account books, one for the authorities, one in a locked trunk. His employer is generous and funny and good company and untroubled by the suffering of other human beings if she does not know their names and cannot see their faces. She has a lover half her age who is convinced that he will inherit this unsavoury little empire.

He has a straw mattress and a dry room with a fire in the grate whenever he needs it. If he cannot see the harbour he can smell the salt air, the tar and the fish. There is ocean light above the terracotta roofs and a grey-headed gull with a yellow beak that sits on his sill to feed on the crumbs he leaves in a tin bowl. He learns about shipping, about legislation, about bribery.

His best guess is that his employer's nemesis will be the state's tax collectors or the victim of a fraudulent scheme whose venom they have underestimated, so he is taken by surprise one morning when she appears in his office covered in blood. The kernel of a jumbled story is that her lover is now lying in a room downstairs badly injured. "Just go and . . ." She makes a hand-cleaning gesture which means, he suspects, ". . . finish him off and dispose of the body."

He fills a saddlebag with his most valuable possessions, buys a loaf of bread and two poppy seed cakes and takes the coast road south on his employer's cream gelding. It is clear and cool, a beautiful day for riding. Out on the choppy sunlit water three boats are heading home after a night of fishing, each under a halo of gulls eager for scraps.

Several days later the road tops the brow of a low hill and he is surprised by the sight of the family estate in the valley below. He did not know that this was the direction in which he had been riding. *Home*. Is he allowed to use that word any more? His children are down there. A fish hook snags at his heart. How long has it been? He feels a sudden, painful need to belong to people who are his people in a place on the earth which is his place on the earth. It has been a hard lesson to learn and he has been a poor student. He spurs the horse.

A slave opens the great door and asks him to wait. He feels uneasy. He deserves to feel uneasy. It is the first instalment of a large price that he must pay. A man he does not recognise appears. Has the property been sold?

The man uses his name. "Your sister and I married shortly after you disappeared." A vague memory of the man's face floats back. "Come in. We need to talk."

He hears running water and the clang of a ladle against a metal cooking vessel. A bird crosses a bright blue window. His brother-in-law leads him through the inner courtyard to what was once a bedroom. His sister sits at a long table.

"I have to apologise—"

His brother-in-law holds up his hand. "We don't want to hear what you have to say."

"—and explain." Can he explain? He must try at least. "I know I have behaved badly."

"I said, give him the benefit of the doubt. He's lost a daughter, he's lost his mother. None of us knows what another person is suffering. But they said, he'll wander back in here in six months, a year, two years, as if he had gone to deliver a letter or buy a pair of sandals. And"—his brother-in-law spreads his hands—"here you are."

"A great deal has happened to me." He will tell them about being imprisoned. That is a good story. There is no need to tell them other things.

"Your personal possessions have been placed in a storeroom. You can take away as many as you wish. The rest will be burnt."

He is finding it hard to maintain his intended deference in the face of this treatment. "I'll listen to my sister. Not to someone talking for her."

His sister gathers herself and says, "Talking to you is an unpleasant chore that my husband kindly offered to perform on my behalf."

"I want to see my wife."

"Your wife does not want to see you," says his brother-in-law.

"How do I know that?"

"You'll have to trust me."

"My son and daughter . . ."

It is his sister who speaks. "We told them you were dead. It seemed kinder. Who wants to know that they were abandoned?"

The brother-in-law walks up to him and stands uncomfortably close. "We think we can read cruelty in a face but it hasn't left a single mark." He drops his hand. "Take your possessions and go."

. . .

He takes nothing. His mind is a stew of so many feelings he cannot distinguish one from another. His previous inability to be touched by what happens round him seems like a loan he took out in ignorance which must now be paid back immediately and in full. He weeps as he rides. He will not see his children again. There are no people to whom he belongs. There is no longer a place on the earth he can call home.

He does not know where he is going. He does not see the landscape around him. He rides, eats little, drinks little, sleeps fitfully. He does not wash, he does not change his clothes.

She looks down from above. She can see his sister and her husband. She can see his wife and his two remaining children, though there is a faint sickly haze around the boy which suggests that he will not be spending long in this world. She can see that his parents are both dead. But her former lover is nowhere to be seen. She feels a queasy flutter which is only magnified by its strangeness. Worry is not something she does. It is a weakness and she does not like it.

Like an eagle gaining height and scanning for prey she pulls back and takes in a widening panorama of the human world. The fields and the temples, the busy wharves and crowded alleys. Rabbits and rooks.

She finds him twice and looks away, thinking she is mistaken. Then she remembers the missing fingers on his right hand and looks more closely. He is lying in an alley and both he and his ragged clothes are filthy. She is angry that a beautiful thing that belongs to her has been treated in this disrespectful manner.

When she manifests before him he assumes that she is merely the most solid of many hallucinations which have taken this form. He has a savage hangover. He turns and covers his eyes to shield them from the dawn light. She bends down and squeezes his arm too hard. He yelps and twists round.

"Did someone do this to you?" She can smell the sweat and urine dried into his clothes.

He takes a long time to reply. "You are real."

"Or have you done this to yourself?"

He is ashamed, of what he looks like, of the state he has fallen into. But he is angry too. He feels like a small boy, vulnerable, overwrought, unable to control his feelings. "You left me."

"I offered to be with you for ever and you were horrified." She is tempted to turn and leave right now, but something nags at her. She wants to know how her plan went so badly wrong. "What happened to your hand?"

"I walked into a fire."

"Why?"

"I don't want to live for ever." The anger wells up. How can she be so powerful and yet so stupid? "I don't want to watch everything taken away from me piece by piece." His head is spinning and he feels sick. "I lost my home. I lost my family." He knows what he is going to say next and he knows that it is going make him sound pathetic but he cannot stop himself. "And I lost you." His stomach convulses. He turns back to the wall and vomits, too drunk, too tired and too lacking in self-respect to avoid soiling his hand and tunic.

She feels as if she is falling. Is this sadness? Is this tenderness? She tells herself that she is going to solve this problem. That is all, no more. She must remain in control. A mistake was made. She is going to put it right.

She puts her arms beneath him and lifts him off the ground. It is late spring, dawn comes early and only a handful of people stop to stare at the young woman dressed in spotless white linen carrying a gaunt and filthy young man down the paved rake of the gloomy lanes to the harbour.

She manoeuvres him gingerly down the steps to where the clear green water sways between the stone and a painted hull. A fat crab sidles away from her foot and spins slowly down into the dark. Two bracelets of cold rise up her legs. The vividness of these mortal details. A belt of cold around her waist.

The shock sobers him a little. His head throbs. He is ashamed of his dirty state, his dependency, but it is a long time since anyone cared for him in any way, let alone this intimately. He puts his feet on the silky weed of the lowest steps to support his own weight. He says, "I burnt a farmhouse down. I think I may have killed some people inside."

She does not know what to say. She has killed people. It was like brushing flies away. She removes his dirty clothes and lets them float off. He has lost a great deal of weight but he has not aged. Beard apart, he looks like a teenage boy whose bones have grown suddenly. She leans him backwards so that she can rinse his knotted hair.

Sunlight is filling the harbour now, the colours of the fishing boats coming alive one by one—rose, cream, olive, khaki. He has imagined this meeting many times and in every scenario he begged her to let him die but now that she is in front of him . . . That face, those eyes, the body he can see so clearly under the wet linen . . . He flinches.

"Your hair is full of knots and I have never done this before."

"Please come again tomorrow." He is too tired to be angry. She is the one person in the world who has some small knowledge of what he is going through. He cannot bear the prospect of losing her again.

"Hold your breath." She pushes him under the water to wet his face, then cleans the grime away. "I will bring scissors and cut your hair." She laughs. "And I will do it very badly."

. . .

She leaves him her chiton when she disappears and he fashions it into a rudimentary skirt which dries in the first few hours of sunlight. If he were old or crippled in some way he might be able to beg alms from the trickle of pilgrims who disembark here to visit the shrine carved into the cliff behind the town but his persistent good looks suggest to passers-by that laziness must surely be the reason for his poverty. So he spends the morning in the hot square at the back of the market where labourers offer themselves for short-term hire and finds a few hours' work at the end of the afternoon cleaning the market itself, split melons, fish oil and bloody sawdust. It earns him enough for a loaf of bread.

She comes the following morning, bringing scissors and a robe in raw cotton both of which she has stolen, an act she describes with the excitement of a boy who has just run from an angry gardener with arms full of apples. She cuts his hair badly, as promised. The knots are gone at least. She trims his beard.

She says, "Tell me everything that happened to you."

He is surprised to find that her genuine interest is worth more than the apology he has given up hoping for, the beginning of something new rather than the wrapping up of something old. He tells her about the fire and the wolves, the cowshed and the double accounts, his burnt possessions, the children who have been told that their father is dead. The stories trouble her. It is not guilt, for she is no more capable of guilt than she is of apology. In large part it is the shock of realising her own ignorance, discovering the drama that has gone on in her absence.

"Your children." Like her father, she has an unerring instinct for the weakest and least well-defended places. "Tell me about your children."

He tells her about the twins and their secret language which might or might not have been simple nonsense. He tells her about their fear of the dark which came upon them like a fever just after their third birthday and the story he told them about the night being a blanket laid over the world at night to keep it safe and warm. He starts to talk about his daughter's death. "She had a seizure . . ." He cannot speak. There are tears in his eyes. Why is he so moved now, after all this time?

She should be repulsed. It was his strength she fell in love with, his blithe self-confidence. Nevertheless she wraps her arms around him. He hugs her in return and for a period he weeps more, as if this body of hers, which can give him so much pleasure, were making him even sadder. Then a profound calm comes over him, so powerful that she feels it spread through her own body. How strange to think that for all her boundless power this is something which lies beyond her reach unless she inhabits these limbs, these hands.

She makes a decision. She will come back every morning. It is not love, or not something she is willing to call love. She tells herself that she is honouring a contract, making this experiment work. In truth she is unsure what she feels. And perhaps it is this which compels her more than anything. The experience of opening a door in one's own mind and finding rooms one has never entered before. It is an adventure of a kind she never expected. She tells him none of this. She will not appear subservient

"I have to go. I will see you tomorrow."

Prospective employers see a new self-possession. He climbs a ladder of increasingly better-paid jobs—labourer, guard, companion, tutor, accountant. She offers to help him. It would be the simplest thing. The contents of a locked box in a town four hundred leagues away could vanish and he could be in possession of a small fortune. But he cannot allow himself to become her creature. She promises not to help him.

. . .

They no longer make love every morning. The excitement fades, but there remains always an intensity to their time together, knowing that the same hourglass has been flipped every time they meet.

Her body becomes the landscape in which he is at home, the thing that anchors him to the physical world. The two moles that sit inside one collarbone like tiny beans which have come to rest in the dip. The spire of fine curls which rises from her pudenda almost to her belly button. The faintest onion smell of her armpits on a hot summer morning after they have exerted themselves. The knotted skin of her belly button, as if someone has tied it from the inside.

He works as a fixer for the town's corrupt praetor, a gaunt, wealthy, pockmarked, irascible man who is vain, wholly lacking in self-awareness and so susceptible to well-judged flattery that he can be played like a musical instrument. Political change sweeps through the province and the man takes poison to pre-empt a less dignified end, by which time his fixer is already a day's ride away with the coin-weighted saddlebag which will become a repeating motif in his life. (Many centuries later, when the council clear the flat after his final admission to hospital, two of these same silver coins—an Ephesian electrum embossed with a stag's head and a stater from Aegina with an embossed Pegasus—will be found in a cutlery drawer.)

The problem, he realises, is not foreknowledge. Everyone knows what is coming. He sees this over and over. It is not even money. Leaving with the clothes on your back is better than being raped or butchered or enslaved. It is the letting go which proves too hard. But letting go is his way of life.

He becomes a blacksmith. He trades in gemstones, in wheat, in oils of many kinds—walnut, olive, palm, coconut, hempseed. He learns Farsi, Akkadian, Hebrew. He buys a small farm with a view of the Gulf of Corinth and grows plums and quinces. He joins the prodromoi of Aretes, fighting for a number of years with the armies of Alexander against Darius lll. The knowledge that he will not be killed lends him a daredevil courage that earns him the respect and distrust of his fellow soldiers. It is reassuring to fight alongside him knowing that he will never swerve from an attack, but it is all too easy to forget that the circle of protection which seems to surround him embraces no one else. At the Battle of Issus he receives a prodigious abdominal wound through which half his gut has to be shovelled back into his body cavity, the slimy purple bags gritty with the dirt and filth of the plain. His companions ferry him back to the Macedonian camp slumped over a horse's rump, thinking only that he deserves the dignity of a proper burial.

Several hours later someone sees the chest of his supposed corpse rising and falling and he is transferred to a bed. Fever becomes coma. The grotesque wound begins to heal. Stranger still is the rumour that every morning a beautiful young girl is to be found sitting beside his bed and those who challenge her find themselves frozen in the doorway, held back by some force which is both nebulous and monumental.

He is fit enough to fight again at the siege of Tyre. His infamous recovery makes the other men uneasy. He has no friends, he reads a great deal and seems happy with his own company.

He fights, for the last time, at Gaugamela. He is aware of little beyond the loud and bloody bubble he fights inside. The sight of a downed war elephant, however, will remain in his mind for the rest of his life. He thinks it is a great rock until he gets close and sees legs as thick as temple columns and skin like tree bark. The smashed turret is still belted to its back, a Persian warhorse crushed beneath it. Five or six long pikes protrude from bloody wounds in the animal's belly and one of its tusks has been snapped off. Its cries sound like blasts on a great horn.

The current of the battle sweeps him away and, late in the afternoon, he finds himself at the western edge of the fray. He has no idea of the outcome and no longer greatly cares. It is the sight of the elephant, perhaps. Something profoundly out of kilter about it. The lack of distinction between monster and miracle. He rides to the river's edge, drops his armour and swims across on horseback. He reaches the shallows of the far shore and he rides back into the great shadow where the torch beam of recorded history does not reach.

A man approaches him in a steam room at Leptis Parva, places a hand on his chest and presses him against the mosaic of battling Lapiths and centaurs. The gesture is both aggressive and gentle. The man leans in close and kisses him, pulls back and locks eyes for a few seconds, as if to say, *Remember me.* The man is dark-skinned, stocky, handsome and possessed of a stony, unreadable expression. His name is Hannikar. It is one of the very few he will remember. They do not meet for another three weeks. Then they become lovers.

He does not tell her, unsure whether she will be blasé or incandescent. Certainly part of the pleasure in making love with a human being is having a secret, being less dependent on her, fleshing out the part of his life which can too easily become mere waiting.

The liaison does not last long. The end was readable in that first touch, if he had only known the language. Hannikar takes pleasure in roughness and the roughness is too vivid a reminder of the foreman who chained him up in the cowshed.

He takes other lovers. Men, mostly. The prejudices against such relationships, that wax and wane over his long life, have forced such men to learn an ability to let go which he has learnt for different reasons. He cannot, in any case, risk a long marriage with a woman who notices that her husband is not ageing, nor does he want to father children he must abandon. He will not forget the last trip he made to the estate where he grew up, a pair of scraggy goats grazing in the rectangle of fallen stone marking the room where he was born. He asked for news of the family in the nearest village and found himself, later that same day, standing beside the graves not just of his children, but of his grandchildren and great-grandchildren.

He moves slowly south-east along the southern half of the Persian empire—Babirush, Uvja, Parsa, Zranka . . . the desert bordering the gulf becoming greener and lusher as he makes his way inland and west towards the Himalayas.

He deals in amber, something liquid and alive become dead and permanent. The most valuable pieces are fully translucent because mortals yearn for purity, but he prefers those with inclusions. A wasp, a leaf, a fragment of bark. Each yellow stone a well shaft sunk deep into the fabric of time itself.

The decades spin past. The blur of dragonfly wings.

He remembers a conversation with a Jain mathematician about zero and infinity and it remains one of the most profound spiritual experiences of his life. He remembers seeing cotton rag paper for the first time and thinking it the most beautiful substance, holding it up to the light, the faintest of veins running through it as if it were an eyelid or the ear of a mouse. He sees a mirror made of glass and gold leaf—he has only ever seen mirrors of polished metal before, a blurred approximation of his face suspended in a cloud of fine scratches—and has the strongest sense that he is looking through a little window onto an entire reversed world which sits invisibly beside this one.

She finds a single white hair on his head. She dismisses it as a meaningless freak until she finds a second a couple of years later, then a third some years after that. She seeks an audience with her father.

He laughs. "Next time ask for eternal life and eternal youth."

There is nothing she can say in response that he will not turn against her so she bites her tongue.

"You are going to spend a long time with a very old man. Or you are going to leave him. It will be interesting to see which choice you make."

There is nothing she can do. She has made a promise, if only to herself, and she must keep her promise because she is not her father.

He buys a Mamluk astrolabe that displays the positions of Mars, Venus and Jupiter. He draws perfect circles of assorted radii with a pair of geometrical compasses. He finds that he is growing a little deaf in one ear.

He is standing in a ruined amphitheatre at dusk, watching the sun go down over the low, barren mountains which ring the plain upon which this abandoned city stands. Three semicircles of stone seats, the higher wooden benches long gone. A vulture revolves above him. He heard about the place while travelling through Hammadid territory and was curious. His Berber guides are twitchy. They say the place was built by giants and do not want to be here after nightfall. He knows better. The city was founded by the emperor Trajan if his reading of the inscription on the triumphal arch is correct, over a thousand years ago and then abandoned for seven, eight hundred. Everything now tumbled and pillaged and covered by sand and thorny shrubs. Digging idly in the dry earth he finds a broken floor mosaic of a child in a cage being used as bait for some mythological winged creature. It is the nightmare he once dreaded, a civilisation forgotten—names, songs, stories, recipes, fashions, letters . . . yet it no longer horrifies him. It is as true of time as it is true of space. Get far enough away, the details vanish and all you see are misty outlines. Giants and dust.

He slips away before elites are overthrown and armies spill across borders but he does not escape the smaller outbreaks of violence that blight every society. He sees a crippled man being eaten alive by a group of hyenas in an alleyway in a small town on the fringes of the desert. He sees a woman being stoned to death by a mob. He sees a young man burnt at the stake for heresy. The man is clearly not well in his mind. He offers up no prayers, no witty final quip, but struggles against the binding ropes and cries out, even as his skin is blistering, "Listen to the horses! For God's sake, listen to the horses!"

He sees people die of the plague in their thousands, wave after wave of the disease sweeping from city to city every decade or so. Fevers, vomiting, racking coughs, blackened feet and hands. During the first few waves he becomes severely ill, dehydrated, feverish, hallucinating wildly, but each time he comes round unharmed except for a single scar where a large bubo has burst and healed poorly.

He nurses five lovers who die of the disease. He tends to neighbours and employees who are sick, runs errands, removes bodies. He prevents a mob torching a house with a sick family inside. He becomes immune.

. . .

He can no longer mount his Arab stallion without standing on a box. He thinks, at first, that it must be some internal tear or strain mending after an injury he has not noticed, but the ability does not return. The thickening brown spots on his forearms, the slight paunch. Slowly the puzzle falls into place.

"You said I would not grow old."

"I did not know how to tell you." She describes the second meeting with her father. "It is my fault. I should not have trusted him."

"So I will lose my hearing. I will lose my eyesight. I will lose the ability to walk. My mind will become soft and slow."

"It will happen very slowly."

"That is not a consolation."

"I am so sorry."

"And you will leave me."

"I will not leave you."

He should be grateful but he is frightened. He says, "I have lovers." He had thought he was saving this revelation for a time when it would cause least damage. Now he is using it to hurt her. She tilts her head on one side to examine him. She looks like a quizzical dog. It is one of the gestures she has not quite learnt correctly but he has always found it too charming to correct. "Should I be angry?"

He thinks at first that she is mocking him but he can see that blankness which enters her eyes sometimes when she is wrestling with the puzzle of being human. "Do you want me to be angry? Because that would be foolish."

Under the terror is profound tiredness. "Will I die? At the end of it all, will I die?"

"You should have died a very long time ago. You got what everyone wants. So you have to grow old. Read poetry. Eat food. Travel. Appreciate this . . ." She opens the little window and a blast of cold air flows in, carrying the voice of a workman singing a song in a language he has yet to learn. He stands beside her and looks down. A barge sits low in the dark furrow of the canal. Tar and dung, burning leaves. Ropes squeal as barrels are hoisted from the belly of the boat onto the quay.

"Is it not beautiful?"

Suddenly it is. And who would not give any number of grey days and bodily aches to have more of this? If only one could take wonder like a potion, swig it back to open the eyes and mind. But there is a dullness not under his control, that even her excitement cannot always defeat, and little by little that dullness is growing.

His lover Samarias is a butcher. His lover Isaïe is the assistant head gardener on a baronial estate who smells of sweat and earth and lavender and the fresh sap of cut branches. Lucas can juggle six lemons. Beatrix is exasperated at having been born a woman. Bookish, with a glass eye, she owns her own house and has taken female lovers too. She is one of only a handful of people to whom he tells the true story of his longevity. She simply nods and tells him in return of how she killed her husband with a flagon of wine, a length of rope and three hungry pigs. They never mention either subject again. She dies of a canker which starts as a dark growth on her neck but consumes her from within over the following two years. He stays with her to the end. During the last few months the smell of rot from her body is almost overpowering. He is the only one willing to bathe her.

She cares about him taking lovers no more than she cares about him having dogs or horses. They come and go like birds taking seeds from an outstretched hand. Besides, the two of them have stopped making love, so why should she care if he does it with someone else? Though she finds it hard to understand what attracts them. When she imagines the body beneath his clothes, she sometimes feels a shiver of physical disgust and has to turn away and find something beautiful to soothe her mind's eye, a winter tree against a cold white sky, the jumbled light passing through a pane of glass, smoke tumbling slowly up a chimney.

Why are mortals and their creations the only ugly things in the world? Even the rotting corpse of a fox is mesmerising. It is one of many things she still does not understand after all this time, and perhaps it is this which makes her promise one she is glad to keep, that he remains a window onto a world which has always seemed smaller, simpler, lesser in every way but which grows more complex and puzzling the closer one looks, like the creatures in a rock pool, like human skin itself.

"Tell me," she says, "tell me about this latest lover of yours."

He reads a copy of Petrarch's *Canzoniere* which has been printed on a machine using the new innovation of movable lead type. A knowledgeable friend points out the new star in Cassiopeia. He is in a small town just south of Regensburg when a whirlwind arrives one November morning, a great tower of angry wind chewing its way through roofs and walls, spraying slates and splinters everywhere and leaving a badly injured mule on a church roof, as if the weather itself were not omen enough.

He sees a tiny clockwork timepiece attached to a man's wrist and it strikes him as the most ridiculous affectation, a kind of pretended ownership of that thing over which mortals have least control.

He wishes that his vast accumulation of years had granted him a wisdom withheld from those who age and die so rapidly around him. He has lived in castles and slums, he has been absurdly rich and desperately poor, he has travelled and traded in more countries and in more languages than he can remember. How have these experiences not given him a better grip on the slippery reins of a human life?

The world seems sometimes like a mere projection, a cavalcade of images which have little to do with him. (He once saw such a thing in a darkened tower in Genoa, a tiny hole in the shutters, a dusty cone of light and the city inverted on the facing wall; a painting, he thought, until an upside-down crow floated into the upside-down sky.) At other times, particularly when he is beset by nagging pains, when his eyes are too tired to read or when he cannot hear the conversation in a crowded room, the world around him feels like a swamp through which he must wade, day by day, year by year, the muddy water dragging at his ankles. Everywhere he turns he sees the old and the dying. How has he been so blind to them before?

There are nights when he wakes in the smallest hours and his racing mind will not let him melt back into sleep. He looks around the room and has to remind himself of where he is—the house, the street, the city—searching desperately for an anchor. "I'm in Lisbon . . ." he will say to himself. "I'm in Basrah . . . I'm in Izmir . . ." Sometimes it takes a terrifyingly long time to remember and an icy claw grips his heart. What happened yesterday? Can he recall the events of any day this past week? Sometimes he throws open a window not knowing what he is going to see on the other side, fearing always that he will see nothing, everyone vanished centuries ago, just a ring of low, barren mountains and a single vulture circling high up.

His eyes are no longer strong enough to read in low light, even with the spectacles he has had fashioned at great expense. So he takes a pot of tea or a glass of wine and sits in a rocking chair beside whatever is left of the fire and waits out the long hours and sometimes, when she finally arrives, the relief is so great that he weeps when she takes his hand. She will put her arms around him and he will feel both comfort and shame, an ageing man being consoled by this beautiful young woman.

The mezzotint, the steam engine. the diving bell, the Leyden jar, the threshing loom . . . There was a time when he felt a boyish thrill about such things. For other people the future was a fantastical world hidden by the impenetrable veil of their own death. He has stepped through the veil. He would live those futures. He would find out what the stars were made of. He would see the plague cured. He would discover how the mysterious liquid engine of the heart worked. But his greatest discovery has been that the endless human capacity for invention is matched only by an equal ability to become bored by those inventions. If people were to fly in airships to the moon he is in no doubt that by the end of the first week they would be complaining about the noise from the new neighbours and the disappointing weather.

Living longer has made him, if anything, more indifferent than those around him, especially now that his energy is flagging. There was a distant time when amazement simply happened to him, when he saw a caged giraffe for the first time, for example, or watched an eclipse in Katowice, the superstitious running for cover as great waves of light and darkness swept across a cobbled square just before the sun was fully blotted out. But he rarely feels surprise these days and amazement requires effort.

It is age and infirmity in part, but it is disappointment too. Human beings can circumnavigate a world they now know to be a vast sphere of rock spinning around the sun. They have mapped the vessels of the body. They can trap lightning in a box. But their capacity for cruelty does not diminish, it just takes new forms. It seems incomprehensible to him that Christians should make pariahs of Jews when they share a holy book, that a war is always brewing somewhere like the pus inside a great boil. He has lived under three Roman emperors from Africa—many of his lovers, including Hannikar, were African—but now the descendants of those same men are stolen and traded and bred like cattle and shipped across the ocean to work in chains, if they are not thrown overboard like unwanted fish. More and more he thinks there is a deep need for people to believe that *we* are chosen and *they* are damned. He knows for certain that if those fantastical airships ever reach the moon and there are creatures who already inhabit that cold, white world they will be eaten or made to work, and the choice will depend only on the taste of their flesh and the profit to be made from either possibility.

He is on the western shore of the Caspian Sea when an earthquake strikes. He is crossing a small ornamental park in the centre of a small town and stops in his tracks as the sky fills suddenly with birds in their thousands rising simultaneously from their disparate perches. Then the entire town moves sideways as if it were a scale model some oaf had stumbled against. He is lying down and the air is full of screaming and rumbling and dust and when the latter clears he can see that most of the buildings are lying down too.

He is losing the sight in his left eye courtesy of a persistent fog in the centre of his field of vision which is surrounded by a mocking ring of clarity. His left hip is regularly sore and he is finding it increasingly hard to ride for long periods. The idea of moving to a different city, as he has done every ten or twenty years for longer than he is able to remember, seems a greater burden every time. He no longer has the energy for trading across borders, one of the few lucrative professions open to someone who must always keep moving. He has made investments over the years, in everything from gemstones to bonds to property, knowing that this time would come, but it is arriving sooner than he expected and he does not know how many more years he will be doomed to live. He hopes, at least, that he can keep a roof over his head, but is haunted by the possibility that he will find himself penniless and homeless once more, this time without the robustness of youth and lacking any saleable skills, blind, decrepit and sleeping in an alley.

It would be the easiest thing in the world for her to leave him, like closing a door or snuffing a candle. That formerly angled face is long buried in jowls and creases, the luxurious black hair shrunken to a fluffy grey crescent around the back of his head. Saggy belly, scrawny shanks. He can neither see nor hear well. He moves slowly and with visible discomfort. He has lost his appetite for anything different or challenging, and he moans about this state of affairs, as if it were all part of some great injustice which might be reversed if the right person were to hear his plea, as if he has not already been given more life than any other human being. She could choose a younger lover. She could be finished with the irksome business of mortal entanglement altogether. But she comes back every morning, partly to prove that this useless loyalty which is second nature to her mortal inferiors is not beyond her, partly to make some small amends for having placed him in this unenviable position. But she feels, too, a genuine fondness for this old man with whom she has shared so much life. Her rabbit, her rook. Having spent so many mornings learning how to accommodate herself to the narrow confines of this body and these senses, she is learning to fit herself inside something smaller still, this love for someone who is day by day less present, less available, less able to give.

He travels by steamboat and locomotive for the first time, on the same day. He crosses the Channel and finds himself a small house some twenty miles from London. He is like a bear preparing for a final hibernation, knowing that spring will not wake him. Were he to listen simply to his appetites he would travel south where it is warmer and drier, where he can lie in the sun during the summer months and where winters are temperate, but he can feel the faint tremors of some coming cataclysm on the horizon and must hope that he has placed himself sufficiently far away from its epicentre.

He engages and fires four servants before finding not someone he can trust absolutely—for if he has learnt nothing else over all this time it is that everyone bends in the right wind, everyone breaks under pressure applied in the right way—but someone with whom he can share an understanding. Peter is an ex-soldier, invalided after a fall from a horse that has left him with a limp. He says to Peter, "There is a young woman who will come to visit me every morning. I am afraid that I will never be able to explain who she is," and Peter accepts this because he has a locked room of his own. It is possible that even Peter himself does not know what is in this room.

Peter washes his clothes and cooks his tiny meals and reads him the newspaper and grows vegetables in the back garden and guides him outside on sunny days.

He reads Ferdowsi's *Shahnameh*, trying to keep his rusty Persian alive, but grinds to a halt only a quarter of the way through. He reads *Revelations of Divine Love* by Julian of Norwich and whilst he forgets almost everything he reads there is a passage in this last work that will stay with him almost to the end, where the Lord shows Julian "a little thing, the quantity of a hazelnut, in the palm of my hand; and it was as round as a ball." Julian asks what it might be and the Lord answers, "It is all that is made." He reads the first few chapters of *Armadale* by Wilkie Collins and is finally forced to admit defeat. His eyes are not good enough. He will never read again.

. . .

Peter buys him a gramophone which plays celluloid cylinders and they listen to crackly renditions of "*Air des bijoux*" from Gounod's *Faust*, and Hans Kronold playing the aria "*Ombra mai fu*" from Handel's *Xerxes*. He remembers the last time he heard live music, some clunky piano sonatas performed by a beautiful young man with unfashionably long hair. It was warm, a trio of high windows were open and in the silence between movements you could just hear the chatter of the town's inhabitants beginning their evening's passeggiata. The young man, he remembers, had grown his hair to cover a terrible burn on the right side of his face.

Peter takes him to a local hall where they are showing moving pictures. *Alice in Wonderland* and A *Daring Daylight Burglary*. His eyesight is poor and his back aches on the hard chairs. The pictures are jittery and monochrome and he thinks how much more he would pay to be able to sit by the sea for half an hour, or lay his hands against the warm flank of a good horse.

The cataclysm comes. Peter has a cousin who is killed by shrapnel when a munitions truck explodes near Bapaume. Otherwise the war barely touches them. Peter takes him out to see a Gotha G.IV which has crashed in a nearby park. The pilot and the nose gunner are dead but two beleaguered policemen are trying to protect the badly injured dorsal gunner from a group of men too old for active service who do not want to pass up the chance of killing a German. He is more interested in the Gotha. It is the first aeroplane he has ever seen. Peter wheels him to the tip of the broken wing. It is covered in simple plywood, yet it has crossed the Channel, thousands of feet in the air.

. . .

London creeps closer. The road outside becomes a cul-de-sac when, over a summer of yelling and hammering and air thick with dust, one end is blocked by a train line. Peter buys a radio. He likes the music more than the schoolmasterly announcers, but best of all he likes the gentle fizz that comes from the speakers after the end of the day's programmes. It is perhaps no more than an artefact of the machine itself but he likes to imagine that he is listening to invisible waves breaking and retreating on the beach that marks the very edge of the material world.

She asks for an audience with her father.

"And how is your old man?"

"I want him to die."

"You're finally bored of him."

"I am."

He looks puzzled. Is she telling the truth or is she lying because she wants to spare her lover the pains of old age? For once he cannot read her mind.

He nods. "I have an idea."

Has he taken pity on her or worked out a new way to twist the knife? Asking the question will only make the latter more likely. She thanks him and retreats.

He has a bed in the front room and sleeps for several hours in the middle of the day. He walks slowly and with some difficulty, using two canes of polished walnut. He is losing the languages he once possessed. Words with no meanings float in his head, like brightly coloured fish in a pond. Casco . . . Alshita . . . Motýl . . . Ghiaccio . . .

Most mornings she simply sits silently in the growing half-light. Sometimes she looks at him as if he were a fallen apple or a fly stuck in a web. What did her father have in mind? Will he die? How will it happen and how long will it take? Then he reaches out and takes her hand and she remembers that they were lovers once upon a time. The bloom on him, the glitter of sweat on the downy hairs in the small of his back in the dim light of that bedroom long ago. And, for a moment, there is a lump in this borrowed mortal chest.

One morning Peter does not appear. He cannot climb the stairs to find out what has happened but he manages to open the front door and hail a neighbour with whom he has not spoken for many months. Peter's body is carried down by two sons of the family who live next door and taken to a local undertaker.

He is unsure what he feels. He is unsure whether he feels anything at all. He has lost so many people. It is like the rain. One waits until it is over. He remembers, a very long time ago, that one of his twin daughters died unexpectedly of what they would now call an epileptic fit. Breathing in her own vomit. He cannot remember her name. He should be sad about losing the man who has looked after him for these past five decades, but it is the fact that he cannot remember his own daughter's name which makes him cry. *Dust to dust*. That fine, colourless powder you wipe away without a second thought.

The neighbours bring him food and help him place an advert for a servant in the local paper. Millie is in her fifties, a portly woman who has a limp freakishly similar to Peter's. She is good company but he does not trust her, recognising something in her that might have bound them together in a world long before she was born. She will betray him, he knows it with absolute certainty. Perhaps it will accelerate his demise. He has little choice in the matter so he will embrace it. She is an excellent cook. Rich stews and steamed puddings are her speciality. It is only a pity that his appetite is so small.

. . .

The world convulses again.

There is a communal shelter in an underground station a quarter of a mile away but Millie is convinced that the house will not be struck, according to the cards that earned her grandmother a living at county fairs. It seems no less ludicrous to him than priests divining the will of the gods from the entrails of butchered animals, or men in clipped accents pontificating on the wireless. He lies awake in the small hours, held from sleep by the intermittent thump of explosions, a part of him calling out to those nameless pilots high up in the dark, assuming that whatever occult mechanism has been keeping him alive all this time surely cannot be a match for a two-hundred-pound crude-oil bomb coming through the roof. But the cards are correct and while they are woken one morning by an explosion which reduces the two terraced houses opposite to rubble and blows out all the windows from the front of their own, they remain untouched.

Millie tells him that she had two children out of wedlock who were taken from her and given to *good families*. She has no idea where they are or what names they have been given. When her youngest was taken she became distraught and was placed in an asylum. The story of her escape sounds too melodramatic to be entirely true but the core of undeniable truth is so cruel that she has surely earned the right to embroider it howsoever she wants. And now he knows. She will protect herself against a world that has only ever used her. He will be collateral damage.

A single bomb dropped on Japan kills more than a hundred thousand people. Three days later a second bomb is dropped.

. . .

Millie assumes that his story of the young woman who visits him every morning is a delusion. Then they meet. It is a late dawn, several winters after the war's end. She hears a voice she does not recognise and opens the door without knocking.

"And who on earth are you?"

The young girl stands and turns, and it is not that she shines more brightly but something burns in the room and anyone else would back away immediately but Millie holds her ground for ten, fifteen seconds, grimacing as if struck by a fierce migraine, before she turns and leaves.

She vanishes that night. She takes the money from the loft and the money from the back of a drawer in the dining room along with two clear stones of amber from the same drawer. She leaves a stockpile of black market tinned food she built up steadily throughout the war—Imperial luncheon beef, Del Monte pear halves in syrup, Hunters royal pork sausages . . . She will send him a letter some years later, apologising for what she has done. It will lie unopened in the growing slope of post that covers the floor of the front hall.

The radio stops working. From this point on he will hear nothing about the world outside the house.

The gas and electricity are cut off. She fetches blankets from upstairs. She is breaking her long-held promise not to help him but it seems unimportant now. She trims the veil of sparse white hair at the back of his head with a pair of rusty scissors from the kitchen. Every few mornings she opens another tin of food for him and refills the glass of water. He eats and drinks little. Some days he eats and drinks nothing at all.

. . .

The winters are hard at first, the cold and the pains in his arthritic joints nag at him through the long nights. Slowly, however, the sensations in the small world of his body start to recede into the distance just as events in the greater world have receded. He is drifting a long way from the shore on some dark, interior sea.

Two of the upstairs windows are shattered by children throwing stones. A storm lifts seven slates from the roof so that it leaks in heavy rain. Pigeons roost in the bedroom and lay down a carpet of sticky grey and white excrement. He knocks over the water glass, it rolls onto the floor and smashes. Does it matter? He has drunk nothing for a long time now. In any case, the house no longer has running water. She leaves the shards scattered on the floor. Some winter mornings the low sun catches them and they light up against the darkness of the rotted carpet and make her think of the Pleiades.

He remembers a rectangle of hot blue suspended on a cool, black wall. He remembers gold leaf on stone columns, almonds and goat's milk. He remembers how cold the water was in the stone trough before the sun came up. He remembers riding horses with shoulders and thighs like mahogany, the clink of the bridles, piles of dung steaming in the summer stables. He remembers the smell of thyme and gorse. He remembers the skitter of the dogs' claws on flagstones. He remembers turning to see her standing in the Heron courtyard for the first time. He remembers the tiny moles which sat just inside her collarbone.

She touches his arm. "I'm still here."

Every so often there is a knock at the door or an enquiring shout through the letterbox. Sometimes he can hear the neighbours faintly talking. For some years a man in the adjacent house rages late at night, after drinking, presumably. He hears no voices raised in response. Has the man cowed his family into silence, or does he, too, live only with ghosts?

When they break down the front door he assumes it is a dream at first, dreams having become the only place where things of consequence happen. Then he hears a conversation about fuses, junction boxes and electrical faults, he opens his eyes and sees a man in dark blue overalls looking down at him, saying, "My sainted fucking aunt, I thought you was dead."

Too much is happening and everything hurts, the lights, the noise. He cannot remember what country he is in. A woman squeezes his wrist and wraps a stiff black sash round his arm.

"Can you tell me your name?" The language is English but he does not recognise the accent.

What was the last name he used? He cannot remember. He opens his mouth but no sound comes out.

They slide him onto a stretcher. He has been lying on the same sofa for many decades and the pains from which he has slowly learnt to detach himself crash back into him like stones. He squeezes his eyes shut to keep out the hot flare of daylight. He is placed in a moving carriage but the interior is as white and clean as the sky. There is a mask of some kind over his face. An engine rumbles and he rocks from side to side. He wonders if he is flying. Those plywood wings. That crow above Genoa. Are they crossing the Channel? Perhaps he is going home. The giant, the horse and the river god. The rope swing and the raft.

"You're in St. George's."

His sight is foggy but he can see that the world has changed in his absence. The hard, bright illumination. More vivid colours. Novel sounds, too, mechanical, clipped. Some are machinery, he thinks, some are music. Some could be either. The languages and accents of those around him are so jumbled that he catches himself thinking he is in a warren of market stalls in Palmyra or Ekbatana.

They try to make him drink cold, sweet broth from a spouted cup but he has not swallowed anything for a very long time and it makes him choke. They put needles in his arms and a tube up his nose. Someone lifts his eyelids and shines a torch into his eyes as if he were a deep well into which a lost child might have fallen.

She comes the following morning. In truth he is no longer sure she is there. It does not matter. She has become synonymous with the dawn, with first light, with the night's end.

What does she think of this new world? If she hears his imagined question she does not answer. That magnificent disdain of hers. He understands now. The blur of wings. This is merely one of numberless worlds that come and go. A little thing, no bigger than a hazelnut in the palm of one's hand. Like leaves on the tree, like trees in the forest, like forests on the changing earth. The dying elephant, the child in the cage, the sails on fire. Time swallows them all.

"Not long now." She strokes the fragile skin covering his bald head.

Will you stay with me until the end?

"I will stay with you until the end."

Light fills the room.

Judith is the first to find Kristof's bed empty. She's grown fond of the old man and wants to say goodbye on her way home at the end of an early shift. She assumes, at first, that he has been portered elsewhere for a procedure of some kind. Then she sees that whoever has taken him has detached him from the PEG tube and the saline, both of which now dangle from their stands. Something is very wrong. She swings back to the nursing station and a panic breaks out because it is not good to lose a frail, elderly patient.

She cannot go home. He was her responsibility. She needs to know that he is safe. So she returns to his room in the hope that whoever took him has left a clue of some kind. If they have, then she cannot see it. A grey, kidney-shaped vomit bowl, a roll of micropore tape, the tub of Hydromol. Nothing seems out of place.

She walks over to the window and looks down, half-expecting to see that girl pushing him towards the main road in a wheelchair, but there's no one around except a fat woman in a red duffel coat letting her Labrador relieve itself next to the sign saying *No Dogs*.

She is about to turn away from the window when she sees, on the narrow sill, a grasshopper, the length of her little finger, the compartments of its body so brightly green they could be plastic. It has little bronze beads for eyes and antennae like dress pins. She doesn't like insects, even ladybirds, the way their backs spring open like lockets and they take off without warning. But for reasons she doesn't understand this little creature seems entirely benign.

She can see it faintly quivering as if it were an impatient cat waiting at the garden door. She twists the white handle and swings the window open. The grasshopper sits for a couple of seconds, then springs over the frame and is gone.

ST. BRIDES BAY

She was sitting on a wooden bench in the darkening garden of a bed-and-breakfast on the edge of Solva, under a tartan rug purloined from an airing cupboard that was almost certainly meant to be locked. She was smoking for the first time in twenty-five years and drinking whisky of all things. Golden Virginia, green Rizlas and a quarter-bottle of Glenfiddich impulse-bought from the Nisa Local on the walk back from her daughter's wedding reception. She'd forgotten the physical pleasure of rolling a cigarette, her hands remembering after all this time, the stripy watermark in the paper, the shine of the gummed strip. Tales of trawlermen making them with one hand in the pocket of an oilskin as the boat pitched in the Long Forties. There was a slice of sea between the roofs and, sitting in it, the low silhouette of Skomer. She took a deep drag. Formaldehyde, ammonia, cyanide, arsenic . . . It tasted fabulous. The sun was bleeding into the horizon and a single light shone on the water, far out. She felt a little unmoored.

Mullions. Proprietors Roger and Barbara Hicks. She'd only met the small, cardiganed husband. Bags of lavender in the wardrobe and hand-knitted cosies in the shape of Spanish dancers whose skirts hid the spare toilet roll. Shades of her grandmother's house. Sugar tongs and samplers. She was going to feel rough in the morning.

They made time run downhill, that was always the appeal of cigarettes. Take your feet off the pedals and coast for five minutes.

Two gulls drifted over the garden, high up, catching the last of the daylight, bright peach-coloured W's against the blue, briefly stationary until they tilted their wings to grip the breeze and were carried inland.

Mother of the Bride. It sounded like the title of a horror film.

The light far out. It was an oil tanker, perhaps, or a container ship. Two hundred thousand tonnes at anchor on the black water. A great bank of luminous screens and a bearded captain underlit. They transported three-quarters of everything we used, apparently. Press your ear to the ironing board and you could hear the fading echo of muezzins on the Bosphorus.

Nikki had married another woman. It seemed both astonishing and utterly ordinary. In a church, to boot. Candles and gilt, dead saints and wood polish. Though they had to travel three hundred and fifty miles to find a place that would do it. God bless the Nonconformists.

You never got the future you expected. She'd fought for nuclear disarmament and the overthrow of American-backed dictators in Central America. Now it was same-sex marriage and fascism resurgent on the far side of the Atlantic. Was that perhaps the source of this deep churning? *It doesn't come wearing jackboots. It comes promising gifts for the poor.* The fear that it was ending, this brief liberal summer. The old cruelty reasserting itself.

Do you, Samantha Jane Nixon, take this woman, Nicola Foster Hayle, to be your lawfully wedded wife? Sonorous am-dram voice the man had. Sam shortening their names in the responses. Obstreperous woman. Which was to be applauded, of course.

The gulls, the light, the almost-tears. Was it happening again?

She had looked up at the stained glass and wondered what it must have been like in the seventeenth century, to come in here on a winter morning having seen no images all week apart from the odd woodblock print on a ballad sheet, then witness the low sun blaze through the marriage at Cana, the empty tomb, Jonah and the whale. How could you not then believe in the existence of some better place? Great beams of multicoloured light leaning across the nave like straightened rainbows.

Nikki had been led down the aisle by her father. It was the first time she had been in Philip's presence in three years and he still made her feel small. The formality against which her unspoken animosity seemed petty. That top-to-toe scan meaning, *What are you wearing, Carol?* A speech of which she heard only the presumption that the room belonged to him and the easy laughter of people who felt comfortable in his hands. She watched him hugging Nikki and didn't know which possibility was worse, that it was a performance or that it was genuine.

A long red carpet had been laid diagonally across the field between the church and the hotel garden, a scarlet bridge over green water, leading to a marquee where everything was white except for the floral arrangements in the centre of the eleven circular tables, lilies on this table, roses on that table, carnations on a third. Waiters hovered and darted below a ceiling thick with fairy lights. Duck and ham-hock terrine with damson chutney. Corn-fed chicken breast with wild mushroom and thyme risotto. Almond and pear tart with brandy cream.

Joe, Nikki's older brother, had come from Melbourne, minus Tracey who was in her third trimester after two miscarriages. She'd talked to him briefly about lab work but he'd only landed that morning and he was scratchy and jet-lagged. Sam's brother, Ray, of whom she'd heard hair-raising stories, was sporting a fauxhican and a tattooed cobra which peered over his shirt collar like a reclusive pet. The girl cousins were fascinated, begging him to remove his shirt and show them the creature in its entirety, then shrieking with glee when he complied. Her own sister, Karen, had expanded even further, becoming so like their mother that on several occasions she scanned the room and was briefly convinced that she was in trouble for some as-yet-unexplained reason. Toya, Nikki's friend from college, had gone from crutches to an electric wheelchair in less than a year.

She'd been seated beside Sam's father at the top table. He'd lost a hand in a firefight in Umm Qasr and now ran a boarding kennels outside Gloucester with Sam's mother. They'd met once before for a couple of prickly hours the previous Easter. His face froze while unseen cogs turned for a whole second before he reacted to anything—a joke, a question, a casual remark. She never did work out whether it was a tactic or some kind of mental defect. Towards the end of the second prickly hour, however, they had stumbled serendipitously on shared memories of childhood holidays in poorly insulated caravans on the north Norfolk coast. Crabbing with orange twine and butchers' fatty offcuts, bathtub canoes and seal trips to Blakeney Point. Suddenly they were members of their own little Freemasonry.

There was an exuberant jazz/disco band called the Daisy Chain. There was a large white cake in the shape of the Sydney Opera House. There was Sam's grandmother, twinkling and shameless at ninety-two, using the phrase "my lovers." Men round her like bees, even now.

Nikki and Sam wore identical sleeveless white dresses, lace over the shoulders, satin panels on the bust, stomach and hips, then lace again below the knee. They each carried a bouquet of white roses. Sam was big but beautiful. Thick blonde hair. Femme. Which was doubtless a word one didn't say these days. Not a million miles from the way her friend Lucy looked all those years ago, if you swapped the dress for stone-washed OshKosh dungarees and removed the make-up. Something uncomfortable about that thought.

The light far out. It was rising and growing brighter. It had to be a star. Amazing to think they were up there all the time, invisible in sunlight. Which was doubtless a metaphor for something, though she couldn't say precisely what.

Nikki was not the easiest of teenagers . . . She had dried up in the middle of her speech, a sudden blankness, heart drumming. Who were all these people? Nikki leant over and squeezed her hand. Palpable unease in the marquee. Then she heard birds singing outside and was terrified that they were singing only in her head. A chasm yawned briefly. But everyone was laughing, as if she had planned this in advance and the birds had fluffed their cue. The words came flowing back.

Ryeland Road. The Women's Republic of. That was the last time she'd smoked a rollie. Carob cake and joss sticks, "Total Eclipse of the Heart" and a pink-and-blue Guatemalan throw covering the stained sofa with the sticking-out spring at the far end. Twenty-four, a baby, pretty much. They thought they could change the world. Upper Heyford. The South African Embassy. Facing off against the police in Wapping. Lucy's mum being hit in the head by a brick thrown by a cack-handed anarchist. Six hours in casualty. Playing snap with a policeman who'd broken two fingers in the door of his own van. *Like Christmas in the trenches.* What did happen to the separatist lesbians? she wondered. You never heard about them these days. Perhaps they roamed free over some sapphic Serengeti set aside in perpetuity by a mannish Norfolk baroness. *And that night they were not parted.*

Her own mother was conveniently deceased. That was one blessing. *If women didn't go out to work there wouldn't be any unemployment.* A life spent polishing the boot that stood on her own neck. Christ alone knew what she would have made of today. That constant bitterness. Watching your daughter enjoy the freedoms you had denied yourself in defence of principles which had become antique. Unwilling to admit that the key to the shackles had lain in the bottom of your pocket all along.

You don't want to get above yourself, young lady. Though getting above yourself was surely the whole point of education.

Would they become pariahs when the pendulum swung back, Nikki and Sam? A squirm of panic on their behalf. Though it was never technically illegal, was it? Only counted if a cock was inserted somewhere. *Women do not do such things*. An apocryphal story, no doubt. But excluded from wills, barred from hospital bedsides, children taken away . . . The atmosphere of disgust. How could you breathe it every day without being poisoned?

The tenderness of the kiss after the vows. The weight on her chest when she remembered.

Where was Lucy now? she wondered.

Christ. It just poured through, didn't it? This slippery thing we called the mind. Words and pictures gathering and wheeling like murmurations of starlings. No centre, no purpose, just shapes against the dusk.

She had believed, once upon a time, that it would all become clear, that she would finally reach a point on the gravelled strand where she could turn and see it whole. Though why should anyone expect answers? The insoluble yearning was what drove us. Or this would all be grassland and wild horses and sea-wind.

Shitting shit. She'd burnt her finger. She flicked the butt out onto the lawn where it died swiftly in the dark of the grass.

Four dances in, Nikki had wandered over and sat in the adjacent chair. The Daisy Chain were playing a cover of Chic's "Good Times." Balls of scrunched gold paper from the mint chocolates which had come with the coffee lay scattered over the tabletop. The faint smell of cigar smoke from beyond the canvas. Her sister and her brother-in-law were dancing enthusiastically and it was not pretty.

Nikki put an arm around her. She had indeed been a difficult teenager, determined to be taught nothing by other people and to learn it all for herself, from drugs to algebra. Backpacking across Europe, four trips to A&E. *You OK, Mum?*

She squeezed her daughter's hand. *I'm so happy for you.*

She and Philip had been married for nineteen years. He had accepted her completely in a way that no one else had done. It took a long time to realise that his acceptance was, in truth, a lack of interest. And an even longer time to realise that this was precisely what she had been looking for. If only it had crashed and burnt a little more dramatically, then she could have consoled herself with the knowledge that she had possessed something worth the effort it had required. Wife number two, whom she was seeing in the flesh for the first time, was younger and thinner and less qualified, which was simultaneously satisfying and dispiriting. She had a name, of course, as Nikki pointed out repeatedly. They lived in a four-bedroom house in Clifton which she had looked at on Google Street View perhaps more times than was healthy.

She rolled a second cigarette, running her finger along its length to seal the wet glue, then striking a match. The surprise of her lit hands in the dark, like a tiny Caravaggio. The burning paper flared and settled. She shook the flame out, slotted the dead match back into the box, dropped it in the valley of her lap and took a sip of whisky.

She should be thankful. She owned her own flat. No mortgage, two bedrooms, an allotment. She knew married friends who had been lonely every day for the last ten years.

But how did men do it? At home, at work. They just slipped past. Outside lane, foot down. Greater confidence, less concern for collateral damage, the assumption that they deserved more, the willingness to fight for it. Only last month Steven Lacey had been offered a chair at UCL. Shahid Nawaz was being courted by Berkeley. Twenty-eight sodding years old. Equality wasn't enough. You'd already learnt a long way back to think of yourself as second class.

She'd been wrong about the light. It couldn't be a star, because there were no other stars visible. It had now risen past the Plimsoll line of the TV aerial on the neighbouring chimney. Too static to be a helicopter, too silent. She pictured an alien ship as big as St. Brides Bay, completely invisible till they turned off the cloaking device and it filled the sky. *People of Earth . . .*

Those months that she and Lucy . . . It was a kind of Eden. The floorboards they had painted with a tin of eggshell blue from a skip on the corner, those cheap curtains blowing gently in and out with the summer air. There was a third box, wasn't there, which was not quite forgetting but not quite remembering either. The Rosa Luxemburg poster, ice-cream vans, Jimmy Cliff and Peter Tosh thumping from the squat on the far side of the Tube line.

It was the planet Venus. How had she not noticed? The Evening Star. So strange that they were really up there, not just pictures in books. Mars, Saturn, Mercury. Actual worlds.

She slid her iPhone out of her jacket pocket.

Why had she never tried to track Lucy down? Watching those video clips of Deb Oliver playing bit parts in *Casualty* and *Coronation Street*. Cassie's triplet blog. The *Schadenfreude* of Mr. Carpenter's public fall from grace. But Lucy . . . ? What was she scared of finding out?

She turned the phone on and dimmed the screen. Two hundred and nine unanswered emails plus a text from Joe insisting that she come to the hotel for a *proper breakfast* in the morning. She clicked onto the home screen, that calming photo of the Sound of Sleat she had taken seven years ago from the top of Ben Aslak.

Pandora's Box. She tried to remember the story. Was it the good things which escaped and were lost? Or was it the evil things which got out and caused havoc? A woman refused to do what she was told and was punished for it. That was the real message, of course.

She popped Safari up. Amazing to think that you could draw

down a billion facts from the sky using a machine which sat in the palm of your hand. She remembered hiding under a blanket in that godforsaken caravan in Cromer listening to Radio Luxembourg with Karen. "Telegram Sam" and "Leader of the Pack." The crackle between the stations. Who heard it these days? Some lonely domes hunkering out on the moors.

She typed *Lucy Millen* into Google Images. Too young . . . too young . . . a glamour model in black lingerie . . . a cross-country runner . . . a brown oil painting of a dowdy Lucy Millen who died in 1885 . . . a drunk and dishevelled arrest photo from Knoxville, Tennessee . . . the runner again . . . a teenage Lucy Millen doing a duck face on Instagram . . . the runner . . . the runner . . .

She added *Ross-on-Wye*, where Lucy had grown up, where her parents and two brothers had lived. And there it was, five links down. A story in the *Ross Gazette*. Sweet Christ. She'd been killed in a road accident only two years ago. *Tomasz Hempel (36) of Halliday Road, Gloucester . . . blood alcohol level . . . Weston under Penyard . . .* The elderly VW Polo had veered across the centre line in the small hours of a January morning. It had taken firemen nearly an hour to free her from the wreckage. She had died at the scene. A sudden vision of it. Shattered glass like snow under the glare of arc lights, cannulas and fentanyl, steel squeaking in the jaws of a bolt cutter.

She waited for sadness to overwhelm her, but it didn't come. Instead it was relief which she felt, as if she had walked away from that fatal accident unscathed.

She scrolled down. There was a blurry photo of flowers propped against a hedge in cones of cellophane. There was a bouquet in the shape of a love heart and a bouquet in the shape of an Airedale terrier. There were handwritten notes in sandwich bags to protect them from the rain. There were tea candles in jam jars. She scrolled further down. There was a head shot, badly screen-grabbed from a website, of a woman with a snub nose and thick black hair. A different Lucy Millen altogether.

It wasn't her Lucy who was dead.

She sat back, a little giddy. The world lurched to one side and slowly righted itself.

Movement overhead. She looked up and waited. There it was again . . . and again . . . Bats were slicing through the air above the garden. Pipistrelle or long-eared, probably. The air full of clicks too high for human ears.

She turned back to the phone. It felt reckless. The way you might break something fragile by rummaging in an old trunk. But she couldn't stop herself. A brightly coloured picture. *Click*. Another brightly coloured picture. *Click*. The magpie in us.

Why Ross? Why not do Lucy the honour of assuming she'd escaped? Why not do her the honour of assuming she'd done precisely what she'd set out to do? *"Lucy Millen" Law*.

She was the top hit, a barrister for Lloyd-Franklin Chambers, specialising in immigration and human rights. She'd worked on domestic-slavery cases, on deportation cases, on cases where defendants with serious mental illnesses had been unlawfully detained in mainstream prisons. In her official photograph she was wearing a black waistcoat over a white shirt which managed to look both casual and severe at the same time. Cropped grey hair, head still tipped slightly back to give the impression that you were looking up at a woman of five foot ten, not down at a woman of five foot four. No smile. *We waste our energy putting other people at ease*. Only in that room with the eggshell-blue floor had the guard come down.

She felt a surge of relief, as if she had personally pulled her friend from the wreckage on that night road. Pride, too, that Lucy was still fighting the good fight. Then something less comfortable. Envy? Self-pity? Because what if the flaw lay not just in society, but deep in her own bones? What if the world had changed again and she had been left behind, just as her mother had been left behind, and she had not seen this happening?

It came back suddenly, the image which visited her in nightmares. She was stuck on a runaway wagon rolling on steel rails down a narrow granite tunnel into the bowels of the earth, past the bone pits and the dead cities, into the growing heat, missing turning after turning, the wagon getting faster and harder to control as gravity tightened its grip.

Her finger hovered over the screen. Did Lucy have a partner? Did she have children? The questions felt dangerous. Thunder in the hills. The crunch and crackle of something shifting its weight in the undergrowth.

Stop.

She switched the phone off and laid it very gently, face down, on the tartan rug as if it were the skeleton of a tiny bird. She closed her eyes and took a long, slow breath. *May I be safe and free from suffering* . . . She dropped a pebble down a deep, imaginary well, then waited for the faint splash and that flash of sunlight on the spreading ripples. *May I be as happy and healthy as it is possible for me to be* . . . She dropped another stone down the well. *May I have ease of being* . . . She dropped a third stone.

She waited, then opened her eyes. The stars were finally out. Cassiopeia, Orion . . . That was pretty much her limit. She remembered walking onto the balcony of that hotel in Wānaka, the shock of looking up to find that someone had rearranged the constellations.

Scale. It was the one thing that had never lost its ability to unnerve and amaze her. The worlds we contained and the worlds that contained us. The Sloan Great Wall, the Eridanus Supervoid. Three million galaxies hidden behind your outstretched thumb. And sixty million cells inside that same thumb, every one a frenzy of looms and trolleys and pumps. A million miles of DNA.

The temperature was falling and she could feel the air growing rapidly damper. She had begun to shiver. She bundled the tobacco, the papers and the lighter in the rug. She drained the tumbler and slipped it into a jacket pocket, the bottle into the other. There was a portable convector heater at the back of the cupboard in her room. She could put that on and stand over it for ten minutes. She got to her feet. Nikki and Sam would be in bed in that cottage in Little Haven by now. In the morning, with luck, they would throw back the curtains on that stupendous view and the blue sky the Met Office had promised.

This too was an actual world. You had to tell yourself that every day. With a breathable atmosphere and butterflies and thunderheads and yew trees so old that Roman soldiers had rested in their shade.

She would get up at eight and head down to the hotel for breakfast with Joe. She would order scrambled eggs on toast and a strong black coffee. They would talk about Tracey, they would talk about the baby, her first granddaughter. She held the rug to her chest and made her way back towards the lights of the house.

NOTES AND ACKNOWLEDGEMENTS

"The Mother's Story" is a reworking of the myth of Pasiphaë and her son Asterion, otherwise known as the Minotaur.

"The Bunker" was written for *Eight Ghosts: The English Heritage Book of New Ghost Stories*, published by September Publishing in 2017, each story being inspired by a particular English Heritage property. "The Bunker" was inspired by a visit to York Cold War Bunker.

"D.O.G.Z." was first published in the second issue of *INQUE* in 2023.

"The Wilderness" was inspired by the H. G. Wells novel *The Island of Dr. Moreau*. *The Stars My Destination*, from which a line is quoted on page 156, is by Alfred Bester.

"The Temptation of St. Anthony" is very loosely based on the life of St. Anthony the Great, otherwise known as Anthony of the Desert or Anthony the Anchorite. Most of what we know about him comes from the *Life of Anthony* written by Athanasius of Alexandria *c.*360 CE. This story was first published in *Granta 152: Still Life* in 2020.

"The Quiet Limit of the World" is a reworking of the Greek myth of Tithonus in which Eos, the goddess of dawn, falls in love with a mortal man and asks her father, Zeus, to grant him eternal life while forgetting to ask for eternal youth as well. The title is a phrase borrowed from Tennyson's poem "Tithonus."

"St. Brides Bay" was written to accompany Virginia Woolf's short story "The Mark on the Wall" on the centenary of its first publication, in 2017 in the Hogarth Press's *Two Stories*.

My biggest thanks go to my GP, Dr. Andrew Schuman, and Mr. Shakil Farid and the rest of the team at the Oxford Heart Centre at the John Radcliffe Hospital for the triple heart bypass without which I would not have been alive to write the later stories in this collection or to edit those already written.

Thanks beyond measure to Sos Eltis, the love of my life, my best friend and my sternest editor.

Many thanks to Clare Alexander, agent and unshakeable rock over more than twenty years.

Huge gratitude, too, to my editors Clara Farmer and Bill Thomas and the rest of the teams at Chatto & Windus, Vintage and Doubleday respectively. Thanks, too, to the eagle eyes of my copy-editor Mary Chamberlain.

These stories were written over such a long period that I have doubtless forgotten many of the friends, old and new, and writers, dead and alive, who have contributed in numerous ways, big and small, concrete and intangible, to them, but I can't sign off without saying thank you to Common Ground café/workspace in Oxford, where this book was finished and the beginnings of the next have already been written.

ABOUT THE AUTHOR

Mark Haddon is the author of the novels *The Porpoise*, *The Red House* and *A Spot of Bother*, as well as the short-story collection *The Pier Falls*. His novel *The Curious Incident of the Dog in the Night-Time* won the Whitbread Book of the Year Award and the Los Angeles Times Book Prize for First Fiction and is the basis for the Tony Award–winning play of the same title. He is the author of a collection of poetry, *The Talking Horse and the Sad Girl and the Village Under the Sea;* has written and illustrated numerous children's books; and has won awards for both his radio dramas and his television screenplays. He teaches creative writing for the Arvon Foundation and lives in Oxford, England.